AMERICAN VISA

a novel by
Juan de Recacoechea

translated by Adrian Althoff
with an afterword by Ilan Stavans

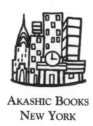

AKASHIC BOOKS
NEW YORK

This is a work of fiction. All names, characters, places, and incidents are the product of the author's imagination. Any resemblance to real events or persons, living or dead, is entirely coincidental.

Published by Akashic Books
©1994, 2007 by Juan de Recacoechea
English translation ©2007 Adrian Althoff
Originally published in Spanish under the same title in 1994 by Librería-Editorial Los Amigos del Libro, Cochabamba-La Paz, Bolivia.

Bolivia map by Sohrab Habibion

ISBN-13: 978-1-933354-20-0
ISBN-10: 1-933354-20-8
Library of Congress Control Number: 2006936532

First printing
Printed in Canada

Akashic Books
PO Box 1456
New York, NY 10009
info@akashicbooks.com
www.akashicbooks.com

For my wife Rosario and my daughter Paola.
In memory of Don Antonio Alborta.

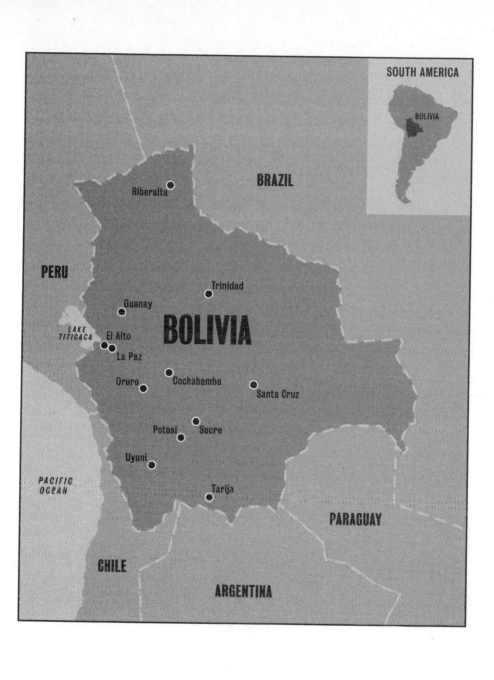

SOUTH AMERICA

BOLIVIA

BRAZIL

PERU

Riberalta

Trinidad

Guanay

BOLIVIA

LAKE
TITICACA

El Alto

La Paz

Oruro

Cochabamba

Santa Cruz

Potosí

Sucre

Uyuni

PACIFIC
OCEAN

Tarija

PARAGUAY

CHILE

ARGENTINA

Part One

Chapter 1

The taxi ground to a halt. The stocky driver swiveled his beefy head around and, struggling to contain his fury, exclaimed, "We can't go this way!"

"What's going on?" I asked.

"Can't you hear the band? They're dancing right over there, practicing for the Great Power of Jesus parade. Those pricks are blocking traffic!"

The dense and tedious cadence of a llama herder's dance sounded off in the distance. Flushed from the impotence of being stuck in traffic, the taxi driver's face inflated like a comic-strip frog. The clamor of horns was intense, unbearable. The driver stretched his arm across the back of the passenger seat, fixed his frustrated gaze on a distant point, and waited.

"Where are we?"

"Plaza Eguino. You'll have to get out here."

The man was right; we were tied up in a knot of cars and buses.

"How much do I owe?"

"It'll be ten pesos." He spoke without blinking, looking me in the eyes.

"For twelve pesos I can get to Oruro."

The taxi driver smiled and blinked nervously several times. He seemed to be running out of patience. "We've stopped at all the hotels on Muñecas Street and Manco Kapac. We've been driving in circles for half an hour."

"That's not my fault," I pointed out. "The hotels are full."

"That's just the way it is."

"Let's make it seven. That way we're even."

The taxi driver remained motionless, an Andean monolith.

I took out ten pesos and placed them in his sweaty palm.

"If you go down Illampu Street, you might find a room," he said.

The driver opened the door, lowered my suitcase from the luggage rack, and placed it on the sidewalk beside a young woman selling lemons dressed in the traditional clothing of Potosí: a stiff cloth hat in the shape of an inverted bowl, a homespun thick brown skirt, and, covering her upper body, several layers of dark, multicolored blankets. I sat on top of the knee-high adobe and stucco wall that encloses Plaza Eguino. Wind whipped down from the Andean plateau, stirring up swirling clouds of dust on the rugged mountainsides that hug the city of La Paz. The girl from Potosí looked at me askance, took four lemons from their place in the tiny pyramid she had constructed on one of her blankets laid out on the pavement, and showed them to me without saying a word. I declined her offer with a slight head motion. A boy no more than ten years old and skinny as an Ethiopian approached stealthily, shifting hesitantly. I thought he was after my suitcase, so I stuffed it awkwardly between my legs. The boy looked like a rogue. The wind mussed his thick mop of hair.

He stopped two steps away and eyed me with that elusive scan typical of the Aymaras.

"I don't have any money. You're wasting your time."

"I'll carry the bag for you," he proposed.

"Do you know a cheap hotel around here?"

He motioned with his index finger toward a jumble of alleys and dilapidated hovels.

"How much will it be?"

"Two pesos."

His Oriental-looking face had been burnt brown by the high-altitude sun. His eyes were emotionless, the eyes of a survivor.

The boy heaved my suitcase up on top of the wall, then onto his shoulder. I followed him down narrow, cobblestoned sidewalks jammed with people. It was early evening and the temperature was misleadingly pleasant. During the winter in La Paz, the air is lukewarm toward the end of the afternoon, when the sun flees beyond the mountains to the west, only to freeze abruptly as soon as the shadows arrive. It was becoming difficult to wind through the endless rows of street vendors hawking their merchandise. An appetizing odor of burnt pork fat filled the air, but it wasn't the time for such an indulgence. I needed to find a cheap room as soon as possible in a city that I struggled to recognize; half a million hungry peasants had changed its face. These immigrants from the sterile Andean plateau had taken over La Paz's higher-elevation neighborhoods, like ants swarming over a beehive. A wild rustling accompanied their movements. This gray, unruly mass transformed the entire city into a gigantic marketplace.

On Illampu, a cobblestoned artery flanked by party specialty shops and pork rind sellers, papier mâché dolls hung, fragile and festive, above old front doors of carved wood. To keep pace with the boy, I had to jog and sidestep the voluminous half-breed women seated like tired octopuses on the edges of the sidewalks. The kid stopped at the corner of Graneros, a steep colonial corridor that winds like an alleyway in an Algerian casbah, cobblestoned and slippery, climbing amid colorful garments hung out to dry. The competing smells of old clothing, fried pork rind, and urine were enough to make anyone nauseous, even someone accustomed like me to the fetid effluence of Bolivia's cities.

"There's a hotel over there," the boy said.

Twenty steps away, up Graneros Street, I made out a yellow, weather-beaten sign illuminated by a dying light bulb.

"Hotel California," the little rascal exclaimed.

I paid him the two pesos and picked up my suitcase. After pushing through a swinging door, I found myself inside a chilly and spacious lobby. Various bored-looking guests sat watching a television news program. I turned to the reception desk, which consisted of a kind of wood pulpit bracketed on both sides by a waist-high handrail. A dry, lean man with white skin dotted by an enormous number of tiny freckles stopped doodling in an accounting ledger and directed his beady blue eyes at me without the least bit of deference. He wore glasses and his eyebrows, thick and bristly, looked like sulfur-colored brooms. His reddish hair and mannered bearing gave him the look of a decadent descendant of Celts. He was wearing a simple cherry-colored wool sweater and jeans. He managed, barely, to give a hint of a smile like that of a low-paid public employee.

"I need a room for one week," I said.

The man breathed in the lobby's heavy air, as if to pronounce a sentence. He adjusted his glasses with studied affectation and looked me over from head to toe. "We've got three kinds of rooms: facing the street at ten pesos, the first patio at eight pesos, and the second patio at five pesos."

"I'll take one in the second patio," I hastened to say.

"I'm the manager. My name's Robert," he stated with an unpleasant little smile. His pupils grew as calm as two blue marbles. "Only one person?"

I shot a furtive glance over my left shoulder. I was alone, so alone that I felt like crying.

"It costs five pesos per day," Robert said, "not including taxes."

"I don't need a receipt."

"You'll have to pay for the seven nights up front. It's the rule."

I counted out thirty-five pesos and handed it to him.

"And you'll need a valid ID." He laid his slippery conjurer's fingers on the edge of the desk and seized the document.

"A week from now I'm traveling to the United States," I offered. "I've come to La Paz to get my tourist visa."

The redhead arched his eyebrows. The corners of his mouth got longer and a condescending sneer appeared. He looked up, his gaze displaying incredulity. "Your ID says that you're a teacher." He looked at me as if he had read "astronaut."

"I was. Now I'm a businessman," I clarified.

"Now we're all businessmen. For us Latin Americans, the black market has become the only way out . . ." He let loose a wicked little laugh. As he worked on copying my personal information, I looked around at the regulars in the lobby: the majority were young women with ample breasts and oversized derrières trapped in bright-colored jeans. They were unmistakably hostesses or cheap whores, of the type that spend half their lives saving a few pesos to support their families living in remote tropical villages.

One of them stopped flipping through a fashion magazine. Her hot gaze settled on me for an instant. Solidly built, she possessed a certain primitive sensuality; her cinnamon skin radiated seductive and sun-toasted fragrances. I tilted my head like an altar boy and she smiled.

In response to this, the manager abruptly struck a small nickel-plated bell on his desk. The shrill jingling ripped through the air and returned with a shy echo from the thick walls of the big, ancient house. At that moment—I don't know from where—the bellboy appeared, a youth about fifteen years old with his hair combed stiffly, looking like he had just received an electric shock. His breath smelled like the neighborhood. His round face, covered with pimples, resembled a beat-up rag ball. The manager returned my ID and ordered: "Show the gentleman to room forty-five."

Immediately, we submerged ourselves in a labyrinth of passageways and staircases. Before long, we passed by a confused tourist apparently lost in that avalanche of tunnels, which seemed not to lead anywhere. The bellboy panted as if he were running a marathon, grumbling and thinking out loud, muttering curses. Eventually, we found a spiral staircase that led us to the second patio. I realized that the hotel was nothing but an old remodeled estate, probably constructed at the beginning of the twentieth century, a time in which the landowners of La Paz were masters and gentlemen from the Andean plateau, from the narrow warm valleys, and from the subtropical forests. It was their custom to build enormous mansions in the newly formed city to receive the frequent mule trains carrying potatoes, cereals, fruit, and coffee. At the center of the patio a half-dozen withered trees swayed, rocked to sleep by the nocturnal breeze in what was once a garden. This far corner of the hotel consisted of a single floor, its slovenly appearance suggesting that it was intended for guests of low status.

The bellboy opened the door to room forty-five and placed my suitcase beside the bed. I had resolved to administer my meager budget with Swiss meticulousness, which is why I only gave the kid a fifty-cent tip. He stroked the coin, flipped it in the air, caught it, and observed me with visible resignation. Once he realized that I wouldn't budge, he left without closing the door. My sad lodgings didn't resemble anything like a guest room; they were more like a cell for a Trappist monk. Beside the bed, I noticed a wardrobe intended for someone the size of a dwarf, a wooden crate painted blue that was supposed to pass for a night table, a rickety chair that at the least contact emitted a pitiful groan, a frameless mirror, and an ancient-looking chest of drawers. The floor was ice cold and made of brick. The naked lightbulb hung tenuously from its socket, oscillating to the beat of sharp wind gusts slipping under the dilapidated door.

I pulled back the linen curtain. Menacing iron bars rose up behind the glass. The small window faced a narrow alleyway in which a homeless dog, emaciated and despondent, timidly sniffed a trash can. I went out to the patio to look for the bathroom and found it in the back, next to the washing machine: a cement toilet, a chipped sink, a shower from which trickled apathetic drops of freezing water. In one of the corners lay a plastic bucket that apparently served to flush the toilet. I returned to my room. Confused flies and moths fluttered around the dim bulb. I emptied my suitcase; I owned less clothing now than when I joined the military as a buck. After hanging my single pair of pants on the clothing rod in the wardrobe, I arranged my three shirts next to my extra change of underwear on a shelf below and placed my dress shoes at the foot of the folding bed. I picked up my gray English cashmere suit—the one I would wear for my visit to the imperial consulate—as if it were a glass doll, looking it over carefully for any compromising stain. Upon seeing that it shined impeccably, I placed it on the back of the chair. I felt the bed. Only one homemade blanket, mended like an old lady's underpants, and a pillow as hard as a rock, meant for a poor man to sleep on. A couple of nights in these conditions and I'd be ready to catch pneumonia.

I went out to the patio again, intent on demanding an extra blanket from the manager. I noticed, then, the presence of a hunched-over old man who seemed to be returning from the bathroom, a red jacket with blue stripes draped over his back. He was wearing corduroy pants of a dull, undefined color, bulky mountain-climbing shoes, and, on top of his head, a brimmed wool hat, a relic of better times. He walked painfully, supported by a strange cane resembling that of a witch in *Macbeth*. He looked up and inhaled three times; each time he did so, an asthmatic whistle heaved up from his chest, accompanied by an unsettling rattle.

"Good evening," I said in greeting.

The old man adjusted his glasses and his gray-clouded eyes studied me with malicious irony.

"Above all, a cold evening," he replied.

"I'm in room forty-five," I said. "I just arrived. Do you think I'll be able to get an extra blanket?"

He ran his fingers through his magnificent Prussian moustache, gray-haired but still martial. "I tried to get the same thing three years ago," he said, "and I'm still waiting. The doorman is as stubborn as a Scotsman, but perhaps with a few pesos . . ."

"It's colder in my room than it is out here," I commented.

"The owner couldn't care less about that. We in the second patio don't enjoy prerogatives. They tolerate us, but they don't let us complain." He put his hand on his chest and smiled. "I'm an asthmatic and every trip to the bathroom exhausts me. That's what I get for making a pittance of a salary. How much time do you, sir, plan to stay in this Ritz of the upper barrios?"

"Until I get my American visa. I'm going to visit my son who lives in Florida."

The old man smoothed out the few hairs he still had on his head and, with trembling fingers, scratched his scalp with a slow and exasperated motion. With each breath, he seemed to be gasping for air. "So you're only at this resort for a few days? What blessed luck. I, unfortunately, didn't have any children. Otherwise, I wouldn't be in these parts. What's your name?"

"Mario Alvarez."

"Is your family from La Paz?"

"We used to live in Oruro, but I was born in Uyuni."

I noticed a sudden expression of disenchantment cross his face. "I was in Uyuni forty years ago," he commented. "In those days it was a progressive little place, but now, as far as I know, it's turned into a ghost town."

"The only thing that moves out there is the wind."

"One of those useless doctors at the public hospital advised me to go to Uyuni or to Río Mulatos to live, because of my asthma, which is constantly worsening. He told me the higher you get, the drier it gets, and the drier the better. But who the hell would I talk to in Río Mulatos? Better to die of asthma than of boredom. For all their defects, these accommodations are a cure for my solitude. Here we have whores and vermin, but it's better than deafening silence."

"How long have you lived here?"

"Three years. An extraordinary feat, when you consider all the viruses floating around, not to mention the fact that I'm always strapped for cash. Of course, we in the second patio are allowed to pay on a monthly basis. This is a pious act on the owner's part. He's a diabetic gentleman who lives cooped up on the first floor of the hotel in the company of his wife, a terrible woman who brought him here from Potosí. She's a nurse and takes care of him the entire goddamn day. Some say it's for his own good, but I see him deteriorating. Rumor has it that she wants to send him to the other world as soon as possible and take his fortune. The man's a millionaire. Besides this dumpy little hotel, he owns three or four houses scattered throughout Miraflores, not to mention a pair of apartments in Buenos Aires, Argentina. Imagine that! He prefers living in this run-down Rosario neighborhood in La Paz to the Queen of the River Plate. Who could ever understand our poor rich people? The nurse, the manager, and that rich guy make a sensational trio."

"I've only met the manager. Where did he get his reddish hair?"

"His father was a Scottish engineer who got hired by the Bolivian Mining Company as an economic advisor during the first Paz Estenssoro government. He stayed a few years, enough to make a killing, and then he left. Nothing else was heard of him. In the meantime, he had impregnated a poor, naïve cashier at the Central Bank. He'd led her to believe that they'd get married and live a grand life in the bleak city of Edinburgh. The manager is the kid who was born from this exotic union. He speaks the queen's English and botches Spanish like a peasant. He cordially hates all of us in the second patio. He hates me for being broke, he hates the trans-vestite from room forty-two for being who he is, he hates the wine vendor for not wanting to slip him a single bottle of Chilean merlot, and he hates the ex-goalie for Chaco because he occasionally sleeps with one of the girls from the Tropicana cabaret. He can't stand competition . . ."

The old man extended his smooth, limp hand to me.

"My last name's Alcorta, my first name Antonio. My good friends call me Parrot for my magnificent Cervantine nose."

"What time do you have?"

"It's 9:10, a terrible time for me. I have to look for my damned

Tedral. It's a pill for asthma. During the day I forget to buy it and at night I have to go out and look for a pharmacy nearby."

"If you'd like, I'll go buy it for you."

"I appreciate your kindness. The people from Oruro are known for their generosity. However, after a long trip I don't advise you to walk up and down La Paz's steep streets. You could catch emphysema and fall into the hands of the doctors at the public hospital, which is like landing in the arms of Mengele, the famous Nazi doctor at Auschwitz."

"I wouldn't be surprised if Mengele's an advisor to the Interior Ministry."

"I hear he's been seen around here holding hands with Klaus Barbie, the butcher of Lyon," he added.

I liked Don Antonio. He was a person without visible frustrations. His appearance revealed that his age was catching up with him and he was going through hell, but I could also tell that he was weathering the hard times with a certain grace. Heavy breathing aside, he seemed in good shape. His pinkish skin exhibited the vitality of a man twenty years younger. I excused myself and, as was to be expected, got lost for a good while amidst the tangle of passageways. Only some lunatic architect could have designed them.

In the lobby, the manager was sprawled across a velvety armchair, playing a game of chess with a bald man whose face was the spitting image of Groucho Marx. One of those Venezuelan soap operas was on TV showing pretty women and people screaming their heads off at each other. The spellbound audience didn't miss a thing.

"Could I have an extra blanket?" I asked humbly.

The manager looked up. He tilted his jaw to the side like a camel. "Coming from Oruro, I'd have thought this would be like spring."

"In Oruro I don't sleep alone."

"I'm sorry, but we don't have any extra blankets."

"I'll give you two pesos if you can give me one blanket."

The redhead stood up parsimoniously, smiled, and put his hand on my shoulder. "We'll see if I have any left."

He twisted a door handle and disappeared behind the Chinese folding screen separating the two offices. He returned awhile later carrying a black blanket with yellow trim that smelled awful.

"It's all I could find back there," he explained. He put it in my hands and added, "It'll be two pesos per day."

"That's absurd," I protested. "For four pesos I can buy myself a new one."

"It's up to you, Señor Alvarez." He smiled like a villain out of a 1950s movie.

"I'll return it tomorrow," I said.

I went back to my room and faced the mirror. Pale and haggard, looking like a shipwrecked man who had just been rescued, I would surely be denied the visa. I urgently needed a shave and a good haircut. I nervously rubbed my chin and felt yet again that old unease and lack of self-confidence. In an attempt to cheer myself up, I downed some cheap *pisco** from an exotic-looking little bottle that I kept in my jacket for emergencies. I undressed, put on a pair of wool pajamas like those worn by gold miners in the Klondike, and turned off the light. The problem was that I couldn't turn off the noise. In that neighborhood, night and quiet didn't seem to go together; for hundreds of thousands of Aymaras it was the start of a work day. Around midnight, the noise outside became almost unbearable. It sounded as if a horde of bees was rustling inside my eardrums. I heard Don Antonio's monoto-

A sweet liquor made from grapes, produced primarily in Peru and Chile.

nous little cough. At 1 in the morning, finally, silence. After a few moments of complete darkness, the ocean appeared. It was a sign that everything was in order. I slept.

Chapter 2

I was violently awoken by the sound of ringing bells. I cursed that medieval custom of calling the faithful to mass; priests can't care less about anyone else's sleep. From the bright maroon glare, I saw that it was sunrise. The bells of the parish church seemed to be tolling right in the back of my neck. It felt like the legendary Charles Atlas was pounding a gong deep in my brain.

I went out to the patio in my pajamas and didn't see a single guest. Either they were deaf or had gotten used to the bell ringer's outrageous sadism. I donned my street clothes under the sheets and covered my ears with wads of toilet paper, but it was impossible to go back to sleep. Tired and in a bad mood, I lit a cigarette, and then the saying of a drinking buddy from Oruro popped into my head: *The Yankees read your face. If you look nervous, you're finished.*

The bell ringer's torture suddenly ceased. I put out the cigarette and tried to fall asleep again, but I only got halfway there. After dozing a little I rose with the lethargy of a military sentry. I waited a bit and then headed for the shower. The bathroom was freezing and a stream of frosty water flowed from the showerhead.

As a little kid, whenever I had to pass a seemingly impossible test, I used to think about the Cossacks on the Russian steppes and would then forge ahead fearlessly. Back then anything was possible; all I had to do was close my eyes. Nowadays, wearing coal miners' goggles wouldn't be enough. Reality no longer disappeared, even with anesthesia. I stepped into the shower. I didn't have the hard skin of the cruel Cossacks, so I let out a shriek, and hurriedly rubbed soap over my body. Afterwards, I got dressed in my best clothes. I was wearing the new Prince of Wales suit that I'd had custom-made to impress the feared American consul.

I longed for a razor specialist for my shave. I wanted the complexion of a Dutch baby and a haircut just like a model in the magazine *Hola*: a half-naked Spaniard with his hair slicked back, matador-style. I opened up a tiny bottle of cologne and treated myself to deft dabs on the lobes of each ear. I repeated this operation various times in front of the mirror. I saw the smile of a castrated evangelist on his way to heaven, of an innocent armadillo who wouldn't leave Oruro, Bolivia's famed folklore capital, for anything. In one of my jacket pockets, I was carrying an ID card proving I was a founder of the *Diablada Auténtica* dance group. "A couple of weeks will be enough," I repeated out loud, firmly but humbly. "I'll miss my country. My son made it over there, but I'm a different kettle of fish, Señor Consul."

I held out the statement from my bank in Oruro. According to the figures, I had a sum of five thousand pesos, a tidy fortune. The Americans wouldn't know that for two months I'd begged some friends to make deposits into my meager bank account, then sent them each checks in return. According to the experts, the bank account was of considerable importance. A notary famous for his skills as a forger had also written me up a convincing contract of sale on a house in downtown Oruro. That blessed document had me down as the owner of a three-story mansion valued at seventy thousand dollars, properly registered in City Hall records. With this pair of parchments, a no from the gringos was unlikely. I left with a renewed confidence.

Silence reigned in the hotel. In the lobby, the redhead was reading a newspaper and drinking a cup of tea. Two backpackers who looked like Vikings pored over a map of Bolivia, while an elderly lady with a tortured face, her torso covered by a horrible yellow robe, studied them suspiciously.

The manager stopped reading the newspaper, looked up at me, and asked, "How did you sleep?"

"You should know. I'm two steps from the bell tower."

"It's a matter of getting used to it."

"You ought to speak with that guy. The bells shouldn't be rung as if we'd won the World Cup," I complained.

"Give him a few pesos and you won't hear a peep tomorrow."

"It would be better if you could give me another room," I said.

"The hotel is full. Sorry . . ."

The Rosario neighborhood, the liveliest section of the city, exhibited at this early hour, 8:30, a discreet, almost nostalgic face. The pealing of the bells faded to a faint, imploring ringing. Since the street vendors had not yet descended from the bedroom city of El Alto, traffic flowed smoothly on the famous Illampu. A few faithful Catholics, the kind who don't miss a single mass for anything in the world, entered the church in whose doorway a diminutive priest stood rubbing his hands together to keep warm, while contemplating the blue sky through which a few tiny white clouds passed unhurriedly.

I looked for an open café and found a spacious, simple, and clean place called El Lobo at the corner of Santa Cruz and Illampu. I sat down and called for the waiter, a half-asleep guy who handed me a menu written in Spanish, English, and another language I didn't know.

"What language is this?" I asked.

"Hebrew," he answered.

"A Jewish café on Illampu Street?"

"Restaurant," he clarified.

I opted for the American breakfast of eggs, ham, toast, and coffee. The price was prohibitive, but my face needed to shine, healthy and alert for the American consul. After taking my order, the waiter left for the kitchen. I glanced around at my surroundings: pencil drawings of Andean peasants, rugged landscapes of bluish mountains, the usual naked children running around huts of mud and straw. Three maps of Israel were tacked to the wall in the back. The red-varnished wood tables were adorned with flowery tablecloths. A three-foot-tall vase stood on top of each table and held a velvet rose bearing Bolivia's national colors: blood-red, gold, and forest green. For the neighborhood, it wasn't bad.

While I waited for breakfast, the place filled up with tourists. A line of boisterous youngsters entered. I guessed that they were Jews; the tonality of their language evoked millenarian lands. They were of all colors and types. From the dark Yemeni to the blond Teutonic, they exhibited all of the Levant expressions. The boys had that somnolent and sensual Mediterranean bearing; the girls were attractive, with enormous anxious eyes, breasts that burst out of their cotton T-shirts, and conspicuous, undulating buttocks. From the way they were dressed, you would've thought there was a beach right around the corner. They shouted to one another, laughing as young people without inhibitions tend to do. A man with white curly hair and the look of a Jewish native of La Paz welcomed them in broken English. He started to order the waiters around, so I figured he owned the place. The waiter who had taken my order brought my ample American breakfast and placed it on the table.

"I've never seen so many Jews together before," I commented to the waiter.

"They've come from Cuzco and they're going to Chile."

"Do they have money?"

"It's cheap for them. They don't spend much and they're organized."

"The Jewish chicks aren't bad."

"They stick to their own kind; they don't give us locals a chance. If you want more coffee, just let me know. Refills are half-off."

Accustomed as I was to tiny, poor, proletarian meals in the last forty years of my existence in Oruro, I had indigestion before even tasting the food in front of me. Third World poverty had weakened my stomach. Any sort of excess brought sharp pain to my intestines, opening up a Pandora's box of gases accompanied by aquatic noises, as if a tiny diver were scouring the insides of my guts. I attacked the feast prudently, waiting for a sharp remark from my abdomen at any moment, but as I ingested the food, a certain optimism and juvenile excitement came over me. The man who seemed to be the owner passed between the tables, smiling and joking. Upon arriving at mine, he looked at me as if I were a well-dressed aborigine who had never had a breakfast like this, even in my wildest dreams.

"It was a good idea to open a restaurant in the neighborhood," I said.

"The Jewish kids are fascinated with our culture. They're crazy about colorful blankets, ponchos, *quenas* . . ."

"They're far from home."

"Jews are travelers. Sometimes they're forced to travel without being consulted," he said derisively, "like in the last World War."

"These people here look different than the Jews of the last World War."

"They're healthy and they have a different mentality. Besides, they don't let themselves get abused anymore."

"I wish *we* were that way! Everybody abuses us."

The man smiled. I was on shaky ground.

I had a tough time finishing off that Bunyanesque breakfast. I felt like a recently freed inmate who'd been invited to a hundred-dollar banquet. I lit a cigarette and observed the scattered Jewish tourists. A bus waited outside to take them to Titicaca, the highest navigable lake in the world. Our national consolation is possessing the highest everything, whether it's the world's highest stadium, highest velodrome, or highest anything else. It's compensation for our frustrations.

A Jew with a face like Jesus who was wearing an orange turtleneck sweater bid farewell to everyone in the restaurant with a celestial glance. Walking hand in hand with him was a freckle-faced female compatriot of mine as tall as his shoulder, who carried in her other hand a book by Borges. The Jewish youngsters didn't leave a crumb on their plates. The restaurant emptied.

The owner shouted, "Twenty-five breakfasts! Everything's paid."

The owner's wife, who worked the cash register, stuck her head out through the window facing the kitchen. "Did they leave?" she asked.

"They've cleared out," one of the waiters assured her.

The dawn cold gave way to a mild start to the morning. Through the restaurant windows, the sun now showed a languid and earth-colored city. There was hardly any clattering on Santa Cruz Street, but half-breed women, wrapped in blankets and traditional Andean flowing skirts, were setting up their stands and canopies to sell absurd alcoholic concoctions that poison the miserable plebes of La Paz's upper barrios on a daily basis.

Moments later, the young dark-haired woman I had seen the previous night in the Hotel California entered the café. I recognized her slanted eyes and indolent demeanor, typical of women from Bolivia's eastern lowlands. She walked spiritlessly, her fat rump swaying from side to side, and yet her robust legs gracefully supported her stunning, hefty body. Her breasts, pointing directly at me, seemed to ask to be caressed fervently. Without thinking twice I walked over to her table and uttered, with the voice of someone who'd been out all night, "Can I sit down?"

"Of course."

She yawned unabashedly and asked me for a cigarette. After inhaling an impressive quantity of smoke, she shot it out through her nose like a raging dragon.

"Did you just get up?" she asked.

"Who could sleep through those bells?"

She still had on makeup from the night before. Bluish shadows surrounded her eyelids, her cheeks were illuminated with blush, her eyebrows were accentuated, and her eyelashes sticky-looking. Her lips, fleshy like an Asian woman's, rounded out her veneer of a nocturnal zombie.

"I just got off work. I still smell like perfume." She smiled tiredly. The whiteness of her immaculate teeth contrasted with her cinnamon skin that smelled of the countryside. She removed her leather jacket and put it over her chair. She clearly wanted to show me her bust, even if it meant ripping her cheap, low-cut blouse. The waiter reappeared and served her coffee as black as tar.

"You know, today's a big day for me. I'm going to the American consulate to apply for a tourist visa."

"You're going on vacation?"

"My son lives in Florida. He sent me a ticket three months ago."

"What does your son do up there?"

"A little bit of everything, I think. He studies Business Administration in his free time."

After each sip of coffee, she would look up and instinctively open her mouth halfway. There was an intention behind every one of her gestures. She wasn't my type. I'd never liked strong women. My ex-wife was skinny, so skinny that sometimes when I made love to her, I would lose her. I used to love to embrace her and leave her breathless, dominating her with my body, feeling her defenseless, incapable of looking straight at me. I remembered her silhouette: always fragile, always quivering from anxiety or from cold, and delineated by the oppressive sun of the Andean plateau. Antonia was thin and trod lightly over that godforsaken land. Her spirit was a reflection of her body: hesitant, intimidated, until one fine day she decided to fly away and leave me grounded, just like that. I heard later that she'd found her soul mate. It's always the same old story.

"What's your name?" I asked.

"Blanca."

Blanca, in contrast, was a luxurious product of the Amazonian savannah. She transmitted that sensual magic of brown-skinned women from Bolivia's lowlands.

"You want to stay in the U.S.A. for good," she suggested, "or am I wrong?"

"No, I don't."

"Then why are you so nervous?"

"I didn't sleep at all. If I don't get a good night's sleep, I'm a mess the next day."

"You're all dressed up," she pointed out, laughing, "but your long hair and beard don't go with your outfit."

"I'm going to fix that right now. My godfather's a barber."

"I don't understand why people dream of going to America, since you get screwed over there just the same when you don't have money. A friend of mine just came back from New York; she'd been working on an assembly line in a plastic toy factory. She aged at least ten years. She says in that country everybody's afraid and goes around alone and nobody hangs out with anybody else. Now she's back working in a cabaret here on El Prado, so she's okay again."

She observed me sardonically, sipping coffee from a little spoon.

"I don't have anything to do here," I said. "If I were a woman I'd go out and dance, but I was born the wrong sex."

Her gaze, still shrouded in the previous night's squalor, seemed to caress me. "Maybe it's because of your age. How old are you?"

"Pushing forty."

"Just like my father, but he spends his life passed out in a hammock and barely moves. His liver is as flat as a pancake. What with all that *aguardiente* he drinks, he's not much use anymore. I bust my ass and then some to send my family a few pesos each month."

"Everyone does what they can with what God gave them."

"I come here for breakfast every day," she said. "At least here you know what you're eating."

"Just now there were a bunch of Jews in here."

"I thought they were German or English." With her elbows propped up on the edge of the table, Blanca rested her chin on her clasped hands. Her fatigue made her look even sexier.

"And you, where do you work?"

"At a cantina in Villa Fátima."

"Are you any good?"

"Ha! The men around here like women from the tropics. For them it's like taking a hot shower." Changing the subject, she teased, "They sent you to the second patio."

"There're no secrets in that damned hotel of ours," I said.

She reached out and caressed the back of my hand with her thumb, fat like a paunchy worm. "Everyone knows everybody else's business. The manager sleeps with the girls who don't pay on time. He tells them everything, like a nosy old maid. Be careful with that one; he's white, but he has a black soul. Redheads are wicked like snakes. Luckily, I've never been short of money. That's why he despises me."

She knocked lightly on the wooden table and called for the waiter. The guy strutted toward us like a runway model.

"Another coffee?" he asked.

"With a drop of milk," Blanca requested.

"How can you sleep after drinking so much coffee?"

She shrugged and pressed a cigarette between her lips. "I'm used to it. I hardly feel the pillow. I sleep like a rock. Not even the bell from that lunatic at the church manages to wake me. I get up at 2:00 and eat lunch here, then go back for an afternoon nap till 6:00. If I didn't stick to that schedule, I'd get burnt out in a week. Where I work, we all have to drink a lot. Most of the clients go there to get wasted."

She smiled despondently. The waiter left a second cup of coffee with a drop of milk.

"You look anxious. Is that visa important?"

"Time's running out for me. If I don't travel now, I never will."

Blanca picked up her glass and fixed her gaze on an invisible point behind me. She looked as aloof as a daydreaming adolescent.

"You've never wanted to travel?"

"What would I do in another country? I'd rather try to get by here."

"You're as fatalistic as the Arabs."

"You know what I really want? To save a few pesos and set up a gro-cery store in Riberalta, where I was born. If I can, I'll get married, and if not, I'll go it alone. Either way, I'll be okay. I would like to have a boy, though. I already have a little girl who lives with my parents."

She put out her cigarette and then stroked her muscular hustler's arms delicately as they took in the sun. "And if they deny you the visa?"

"Don't talk like that. You'll jinx it."

She left ten pesos on the table and said, "I'll be in the hotel. If they give you the visa, we'll go out for some beers."

Chapter 3

Outside, the wind was whipping up tiny clouds of dust on the edges of the sidewalks. It tugged powerfully on the tents set up by the street vendors. In a seemingly endless line, half-breed women were preparing to spend the day selling every sort of trinket imaginable and struggling to keep their butts warm on the frosty asphalt. I bought a wooden charm from a scraggly old lady. She told me it was from Chiquitanía, and that it would bring me good luck. It was a miniature bull made of palm wood, but it had only three legs and one horn.

"A demon ate one of the legs and a horn when the bull conquered it," she said proudly.

I started down Santa Cruz Street. It was one of those mornings that make you forget that life is hard and then you just die. When I arrived at Plaza San Francisco, a fortune-teller approached me and waved a hand of playing cards right in front of my nose.

"Take one. These Tarot cards don't lie. One peso to try your luck," he said.

It didn't seem prudent to size up my luck after buying a charm, so I continued straight ahead. I felt sure I'd be able to find my way from Plaza San Francisco to my godfather Ambrosio's barbershop, which I hadn't seen in years. My haircut was boxlike. If the American consul were to see my long hair, the conversation would be over before it had even started. A visitor's external appearance matters a lot to those yuppie gringos. I'd seen it a hundred times on television. The ones who belong to "the establishment" are immaculately dressed and the rest look third-rate.

I strolled through El Prado. It had been ten years since I was last in La Paz. The city had grown enormously, vertically more than anything. The newly erected skyscrapers downtown didn't compare to those of Dallas or Houston, but they impressed migrants from rural provinces who let themselves get duped by mirages. As in nearly all Latin American capitals, in La Paz "progress" is enshrined in framed cement blocks that give a false sense of prosperity. It's when you start snooping around the place that you smell the misery and underdevelopment.

I vaguely remembered that my godfather's business was in San Pedro. I asked the first traffic cop I spotted on Riobamba Street for directions. With his nearly unintelligible mumbo jumbo, the officer led me to understand that I should go up to Plaza Sucre and ask someone there, which I did. Once in the plaza, I approached a shoeshine boy. With the use of universal hand signals, he showed me the way to go. It didn't take me much longer to find it. The Oruro Feeling hair salon was built into the first floor of an old tenement. It faced the street and received the morning sun head-on. I pushed open the Wild West–style swinging door and found myself inside a tidy, traditional waiting room.

Three poor-man's barbers, each wearing a white work coat, received me with Chaplinesque bows. One of them beckoned to me and said, "Over here, señor."

I recognized my godfather; he was the oldest and thinnest one. He came close and I thought he was going to embrace me. Instead, he hurriedly removed my jacket and, without losing for a moment his tip-seeking smile, asked, "Hair and beard?"

I nodded. He led me by the arm to a majestic chair reminiscent of

the Al Capone era. His cold hands brushed my head with a certain del-
icacy. He didn't recognize me.

"It's been at least three months since you last went to the barber,"
he commented.

"Sometimes I cut it myself," I said.

"No wonder. I bet they sold you one of those plastic gadgets with a
shaving blade."

"Can you tell?"

"You look like one of those Amazon Indians the missionaries try to
convert by force."

My godfather settled me in as if he were about to execute me in
an electric chair. He studied my head from every angle and concluded:
"We'll make you look like new." Before I could open my mouth, he
lifted me out of the armchair and dragged me over to a seat beside an
enormous tub. They had an electric device that released hot water
when the faucet was turned on. I suffered two rounds of shampoo
with boiling water. Once back in the armchair, my godfather grabbed
an enormous comb and parted my hair in two. As he was about to
cover me with a white sheet, I asked him, "Aren't you Don Ambrosio
Aguilera?"

That beard-shaver seemed to think I was some loan shark in dis-
guise. He didn't dare answer yes or no. He smiled with the innocence
of Saint Francis of Assisi.

"I'm your godson, Mario Alvarez," I explained. His expression didn't
change; the old man pretended not to hear. "The son of your friend
Jacinto Alvarez, from Uyuni."

He spun the seat around and I noticed that his breath smelled of
beer. He looked at me through a gigantic imaginary microscope. "It
can't be; you look much older."

"I just turned forty. My father would have been sixty-five. He was born in February and you were born in June."

He pressed his palms together and gave me a moist, foaming kiss on my forehead. "I met you when you let out your first cry. Where have you been?"

"Oruro."

"You don't look so bad."

"Over there, it's so cold your body gets preserved like a mummy. The last time you saw me was back at the Oruro carnival in '82. You had a heart attack while dancing the *kullawada*. You couldn't believe it was happening. You looked around at your friends and laughed incredulously."

"You've got quite a memory. Even I had forgotten that heart attack. You look a little bit like your father. Your nose is exactly the same. How many years ago did he die?"

"Six—he died in '87."

"Hmm . . . looking at you, I see him too, the same expression of pent-up anger. Are you married?"

"She went to Argentina to try to find herself."

He opened his mouth like a fish out of water, then arched his eyebrows. "And she found herself?"

"She found an Argentine guy who fixed the problem for her."

The two other barbers found it just as funny as my godfather did.

"She's still in Argentina, in Mendoza. The guy opened up a restaurant on the highway to Chile."

They all laughed in unison. Don Ambrosio let out a guffaw that ended in a fit of violent coughing. He doubled over as if someone had dealt him a crushing blow to the stomach. He stomped on the floor several times, kicking up clouds of dust. One of his helpers, a fat man with a bloated belly, slapped his back several times. The old man flung the door open and launched a gob of spit onto the street without bothering to check if anybody was passing by.

"What do you do?" he asked, still visibly entertained.

"Everything and nothing in particular. I'm a teacher, but what I really did back in Oruro was sell contraband from Chile."

"We've become Chile's Persian market." He didn't stop looking at me, as if he had before him one of those abstract paintings that, you can't tell for sure, might be turned upside down.

"Are you going to leave me like this with wet hair? I'll catch a cold."

He started to cut my hair with a razor. His hand wasn't very steady. Each time he passed close to one of my ears, a chill ran down my spine.

"Before he died, my father told me that if I ever needed anything, I should come to see you," I said.

Don Ambrosio turned slightly pale and held his breath. He was certain that he was going to be hit up for money.

"I need a haircut just like the one in the photo." I pointed to my chosen model in the magazine.

"This guy has wavy hair, but yours is straight like an Indian's," Don Ambrosio said.

"So what?"

"You don't have the head for that haircut," one of the barbers remarked. "That guy's head is square-shaped and yours is like a rugby ball."

"Besides, godson," Don Ambrosio said, "this guy looks like a fruit. Why would you want to look like him?"

"I have to go to the American consulate to apply for a visa."

"Ahhh!" all three exclaimed at once.

"I'd go for a crew cut," the pot-bellied man suggested, "with the part down the middle, but not like a tango dancer's—disguised, without making it obvious."

"I like the haircut in the picture," I stressed.

"If you want it, there's no fighting it," my godfather said. "I'll leave you looking just like him. Of course, this guy in the picture is twenty years younger than you and he's tanned like a swimsuit model, while you, godson, look like you've just spent the night on the train from Chile."

"The beard too," I said seriously, "but not the moustache."

"Now I see what's going on with you," Don Ambrosio said. "Those damned gringos have got you scared."

"It's not easy to get a visa. You have to go there looking sharp," I declared.

"Elegant suit, shiny hair," chimed in one of the other barbers, who looked slightly bigger than a dwarf.

My godfather continued with the razor, now and then comparing my head with the picture and turning it from side to side.

"What did you teach?"

"English."

"The teachers here are just as screwed as the miners."

"In a serious country, it's an honor to be a teacher."

"Honor doesn't mean anything here anymore. What matters is money. It doesn't matter if you earn it selling cocaine or renting out your rear end. The issue is getting a piece of the pie."

"This was once a country of decent people."

"The new money isn't clean, that's for sure. Is that why you're going?"

"I'm leaving because I'm washed up and I want to see my son and raise him so that he doesn't end up looking like me."

"Your father, he was a great man," Don Ambrosio said. "A poor but impeccable man. He didn't owe a cent to anybody and never refused to do a favor. You don't find people like that around here anymore."

I was starting to look more and more like Humphrey Bogart from *The Treasure of the Sierra Madre*. Don Ambrosio was removing locks of my hair furiously, like a sheep shearer.

"My father used to say you were the best basketball coach that Bolivian Railway ever had," I said.

Don Ambrosio stopped cutting my hair. He smiled, obviously pleased. "Those were good times. Oruro was once a promising city: theater, good cafés, excellent brothels, and Slavs everywhere. The brothels were lounges with pianos, and the hookers used to wear long dresses. The money flowed back then. British pounds!"

The haircut I saw taking shape didn't bear the least resemblance to the one in the Spanish magazine. He gave me the same haircut all the half-breeds usually get, with a tacky part down the middle. It was actually more of a path than a part. The sides of my poor head resembled coca crops planted on a hillside.

"After the shave, you'll look like that Argentine singer Carlos Gardel," Don Ambrosio said.

The shave felt like Turkish torture, not so much for my godfather's trembling hand, as for how dull the blade was. With each stroke, I felt my skin peel. All the scraping had left my chin the color of a carrot.

Even so, the face I saw in the mirror after that hazardous haircut looked ten years younger.

"How do you like it, godson? The visa's in the bag. Scent!" he shouted. "The kind we spray on the tourists."

The short, fat helper shot me with a squirt of German cologne made between the First and Second World Wars. I smelled like a cheap whore from a half-block away.

"How much do I owe you?"

"Not a cent. It was a pleasure. I did it in memory of your holy father."

"Sensational!" declared the pot-bellied man, "When the boss puts his mind to it, no hand in the neighborhood is better."

"You're missing something," Don Ambrosio said. "Something . . . something . . . The gringos don't like handsome Latin men, they think they're going to screw all the blond women. They want them drowsy-looking. I've got the solution."

He pushed open the front door again and spat without looking for the second time.

"The eyeglasses," he said. "With these, it's a done deal, godson."

He opened the drawer of one of the sideboards and proudly displayed a pair of round lenses with metal rims that exuded somnolence. He turned the armchair around and put them on me. I looked like a mountain-sick James Joyce.

"These glasses, my dear godson, have quite a history. I got them from a German man who used to come to me for his haircuts in the '50s. Back then, I rented a place on Comercio Street. The owner, a real bitch, kicked me out so she could open up a shoe store. This German guy was a wreck when he escaped from his country. Being a Nazi and all, the authorities wanted to jail him. He came over here with a few pieces of jewelry that he'd undoubtedly robbed from some Jews and set up a cake shop. He told me that in Berlin he'd worked in theater and he'd sometimes worn these glasses for fun. They're not prescription, just plain old glass. They go with your hair; they give you a serious look. What profession did you put down in your passport?"

"Businessman."

"Not bad. If you had put down teacher, they would send you home right away. The gringos know what our poor educators earn."

"I've got everything I need."

"They pay attention to everything, and it's even worse now, what with the cocaine and all. They imagine that every one of us is carrying at least a hundred grams." He looked at me, grinning. "Talk to them in English," he advised. "That flatters them."

"I know the bit I'm going to tell them by heart."

"Before you leave, stop by if you need anything else; I'm not talking about money, because I'm broke. Cutting hair doesn't pay what it used to. Those damned peasants have moved here from their villages and set up hundreds of barber shops."

He walked me over to a special mirror that looked like something straight out of a royal court. It was an almost magical mirror, one that retouched images. I looked more like a pharmaceutical salesman than I did Carlos Gardel.

"Good luck," he said. "You want a beer?"

"Better not. If I start with one, I won't stop until two dozen."

"What do you plan to do in North America?"

"Anything."

"My little boy, Raúl, is in Chicago. He knows a lot of people. Earns eight dollars an hour selling telephone books."

"A fortune!" I exclaimed.

"You've gotta have experience to work there."

I looked at my godfather for the last time. He resembled a withered scarecrow: bony, yellow, with a bitter face and the unmistakable veneer of a hardened drinker. I shook his hand, left the shop, and hailed a taxi at Plaza Sucre. The driver was already taking a few passengers to the

Finance Ministry and said he would leave me close to the consulate at the corner of Ayacucho and Potosí.

I arrived just before 10 in the morning, a chic time to see the gringos. I found the consulate in a run-down building. The line of visa applicants was gathering on the steps leading to the second floor and a pair of city policemen were busy cramming all the people together. Everybody seemed on edge; at least thirty people were pushing and shoving each other. A few were protesting the slowness of the line and others were waiting silently like obedient lambs.

I've always been good at tricking dumb people. I went up to the entrance with the pretext that I was carrying official correspondence. Once face-to-face with the policeman guarding the access to that sacrosanct consular delegation, I slipped him five pesos with the agility of a pickpocket. The policeman was confused and embarrassed, but he looked at me proudly and then indicated with a laconic head gesture that I should proceed. Next up was a second policeman who was seated behind a little table beside a rectangular wooden arch that served to detect metal objects: guns, knives, etc. The guy asked me the reason for my visit. I answered that I had come to apply for a tourist visa. He stared at me without batting an eyelid, holding the stolid expression of a Gurkha sentinel.

"Go ahead," he said, indicating the metal detector.

I passed below that investigator of bad intentions without sounding off any alarm. Immediately, I went up to an American Marine wearing a spotless uniform who was asking for IDs from behind a glass window.

I handed him my ID. My pulse deviated from its normal rate and started to gallop nervously. The Marine, a handsome young man, shot me an emotionless glance with his deep-set blue eyes.

"Take a number and wait your turn," he said in correct Spanish. My pulse raced like an astronaut's; it must have been about a hundred beats per minute. I discovered a vast carpeted waiting room, in which there were various rows of armchairs. All of the seats were filled and a number of people were standing. I obtained a number from a ticket machine: thirty-eight. I found a space to stand at the back of the waiting room near the windows through which the warm morning sun penetrated.

The visitors exchanged notes quietly, as if in a convent. The murmurs were an unmistakable sign that they were wetting their pants out of fear, and with reason. The three interviewers, two men and one woman, protected behind a wide desk, announced the numbers. They were at number fourteen. The two men were clearly American and the woman, young and attractive, looked Bolivian. I studied them thoroughly, as my fate was now in their hands. The one in the middle, who looked like the boss, was a well-built guy weighing about 220 pounds with a bull's neck and the thick head of an American football player. His round and tough-looking face was the prototype of the uncouth, kindhearted American. He was dressed appropriately, with a tweed jacket, white shirt, and bow tie. Everything about him gave off the impression of clinical asepsis. He didn't smile easily and maintained a certain distance as he conversed with the interviewees. He looked over the documents they gave him without much conviction and, depending on the case, either returned them or put them into a pile on a nearby desk. The second man was a non-Hispanic black, of pure African stock. Standing about 6'3", he had the body of an athlete. His shirtsleeves left exposed his long, wiry arms, which he waved around parsimoniously. His enormous hands shuffled through applicants' papers like two massive crabs. He appeared to be a "shut up and obey" kind of official. Without being very friendly, his demeanor was polite. He had the face

of a middle-class educated black man, eager to make a career as a public servant. He didn't speak much Spanish and whenever he couldn't
think of the right word, he'd say it in English. I decided it would be better to talk to him than the burly white guy, who seemed shrewd and
tricky. The woman, who looked slight and fragile, initially seemed the
most reasonable, but as the minutes passed I noticed her inflexibility
with the people she interrogated. In short, the most prudent strategy
was to try to come across the black man and then to ingratiate myself
with a little gab and some lies.

I endured the languid passing of time. Half an hour later they
called number twenty-five and I was finally able to sit down in the
back. My pulse was still off-kilter and I felt increasingly apprehensive.
I began to notice intermittent wails coming from the other side of the
room. Applicants for visas who didn't have their papers in order were
sent to a confessional booth, where they tried to explain everything to
the consul himself, who had the final say in the matter. About one in
every three people was sent over to chat with the big boss. If he had
any doubts about you, *ciao*—you were out on the streets. The consul
wasn't physically impressive—he was chubby, seemed good-natured,
and laughed often—however, upon finding the slightest defect in
someone's papers, he became as rough and stubborn as a mule. He listened to my fellow countrymen's whimpering with the smug smile of a
friendly policeman, but later, with the severity of a public prosecutor,
he denied them tickets to paradise.

I was seated beside a woman in her twenties who was accompanied
by her father. The girl was a bundle of nerves. She continually rubbed her
hands together, wiped her nose as if she had a severe cold, and took her
glasses off and put them back on every three seconds. Her father, a man
in his fifties, was trying in vain to calm her. It was useless. The girl, star-

ing straight ahead as if surveying a scaffold, seemed not to hear anything.

Her father said to her, "With the shares from the beer company, there won't be any problems. It's a lot of money and I have twenty thousand dollars right here with me. Don't be ridiculous. Besides, we have the deeds to our houses here with us. Calm down, you're even starting to make me nervous."

The girl's mouth was dry and she was on the verge of crying. The Americans were strict when it came to your assets: proof of properties, current tax records, and checking accounts. I had everything I needed, but my documents were all forged. My only hope was that the consular officials would fall for the fraud. It wasn't impossible, I just needed the luck of a gypsy.

At 11:30 on that fateful morning, a suffocating heat prevailed. So many people and so much anxiety seemed to raise the temperature. The three consular employees drank coffee, chatted, and paced around, sweating, seeming ever less friendly. With the hours' passing, they began to look embittered and tired.

"Thirty-one," announced the female interviewer.

The young woman at my side stood up and hesitantly lugged her pile of deeds and documents that would have sufficed to liberate a Jew from the hands of the SS. She stopped before the big-headed man with the tweed jacket and handed him her papers, then turned around to look at her father for encouragement. Her father smiled at her. The girl and the guy in tweed conversed for a few minutes, with the former responding timidly to the latter's interrogations. The torture didn't last long; the executioner seemed to be sick of interviewing. He had decided to shorten the questioning. The girl left gracefully and returned to her seat, looking satisfied. Her father happily kissed her on the cheek and asked, "What did he tell you?"

"He told me to come back in three days; they're going to verify everything."

"Did you show him the shares from the beer company?"

"Yeah, that impressed him. I don't think there'll be any problems. He tried to confuse me, but I didn't let him."

The color had returned to the girl's face. She said goodbye to me with a hint of a smile.

Verify the documents, I thought. *What the hell is that about?* Trembling, I moved forward to the first row and settled into an empty armchair. That bit about the verifications was like a knife through my heart. *If they try to verify them, I'm screwed.*

Number thirty-five stepped up. He was assigned to Magic Johnson's kid brother, who was sweating a river, as though he were in a Turkish bath. On my right side, a modestly elegant woman, discreetly perfumed, waited stiffly while reading a magazine. From time to time she raised her head and looked around disdainfully at her surroundings.

"Excuse me, señora, but I couldn't hear," I said. "The documents— don't they check them?"

She replied in a hoarse, mannish voice, "It's necessary. A lot of people forge them. Imagine all the people who want to leave the country and how easy it is to falsify documents. Everything and everybody is corrupt these days. Years of political chaos have led to our ruin, to a moral catastrophe. Don't you agree?"

"Of course," I hastened to answer.

"Is this your first time applying for a visa?"

"Yes. I'm going to visit my son."

"The first time is somewhat difficult. They have the idea stuck in their heads that all the people who travel as tourists are going to stay on to work."

"I would never do that," I said. "I'm old. Besides, I love my country."

She looked at me as if I'd uttered an insult. "You're lucky!" she said sarcastically. "I can't live in Bolivia. I can't get used to it. It's swarming with Indians! Aren't you scared of them?"

"I've never thought of it."

"Bolivia has the highest birthrate in Latin America. In five years, the Indians will be living in places like Calacoto—in *our* neighborhoods."

"For you, then, it's a good thing they won't make it to . . ."

"Chicago, Illinois. I live there with my husband, who's a doctor. I'm from Cochabamba."

"Cochabamba's a nice place, but overpopulated," I said.

"That's because of the land reform. Now the crooks who grow coca own the land. What irony, those so-called revolutionaries . . . And you, do you have everything together?"

"Together?"

"In order?"

"I have the deed to my house and a copy of my bank statement."

"They look closely at those things," the doña said. "I think they even hire detectives to do background checks at City Hall and the banks. The gringos don't sleep."

"Detectives? That's got to be an exaggeration." My heart stopped beating for an instant. I coughed and rubbed my chest, the source of my body's lifeblood.

"Is something wrong?"

"The ups and downs in this city; Oruro is flat."

The black man with praying mantis arms called out, "Thirty-six." A nun with a rosary and a Bible stepped forward. The black man greeted her with a smile that revealed his white shiny teeth.

"What number do you have?" I asked.

"Forty-four. I hope they make it to me. I want to take a flight the day after tomorrow. My issue is a simple passport renewal. I'm a U.S. resident, but I still keep my Bolivian passport, even after fifteen years in the U.S. How about that?"

"Congratulations. You're brave."

"It's a kind of insurance to be a resident. I can enter and leave the States legally, whenever I want."

"Thirty-seven," the young woman announced. This was the worst thing that could have happened to me. The brawny man was going to interview me. I was sure to have a rough go of it. His facial expressions were sinister. He was biting his bottom lip, looking for a victim. I was the victim.

I would have sold my soul to the Devil for that visa, but there was no time for ceremony. The burly official was arguing with a young man wearing blue jeans and a loose-fitting jacket. "You should speak with the consul, maybe he'll understand," he said.

"This is my acceptance letter from the university," grumbled the boy. "Why should I see the consul?"

"Step aside. It's a matter for the consul."

In the confessional booth the Imperial Inquisitor waited impassively, like a statue.

"Thirty-eight," the bigheaded man called out.

Nobody stood up! Paralyzed with fear, I couldn't budge, or even think.

"Thirty-eight," he repeated.

My legs started to tremble uncontrollably. An acute stinging sensation in my crotch made me wince. My loins felt like they were on fire. The bigheaded man unceremoniously retired my number and announced thirty-nine.

Fifteen minutes passed before I could feel my legs again. I asked the American Marine for my ID and left the consulate.

I was a coward, a stinking coward. Worst of all, I knew I'd never return to the consulate.

"Detectives!" I stuttered out loud. "Now what?"

I urgently needed a drink, something strong that would hit me immediately. I scoured Potosí Street and found a bar on the first floor of a hotel. The place was tiny, but charming. It was wood-paneled, which gave it an intimate, distinguished appearance. A coffee machine operated by a young boy with affected, womanish mannerisms stood on top of the bar counter. I found a seat beside the window facing the street. A dark-skinned girl who smiled easily, wearing a white blouse and a black skirt, waited to take my order.

"One cognac," I requested.

"French?"

"Better if it's French," I said.

It had been a long time since I'd drunk one. Its price was prohibitive, especially given my current circumstances, but I was a ruined petit bourgeois who longed for the past. My nerves could only be calmed with fancy sedatives. I asked for a pack of cigarettes. It was a silent bar, nearly enveloped in shadows. The customers gave the impression that they were waiting for the go-ahead from some hidden director to begin conversing. The quiet in the bar allowed me to meditate on my situation.

My quest for a visa had become a fiasco. Neither my forged documents nor my bank accounts were of any use. I didn't have the balls to face the interviewers. It was all the fault of that lady who told me that they hire detectives to examine the documents. If that were true, they would surely return the documents to me with a bloody "no" and not allow me to appeal. If they deny you the visa once, they've denied it to you forever. If, on the contrary, the assertion of that Illinois resident was false, then I'd shot myself in the foot like a fool.

As far as I was concerned, things couldn't get any worse. The girl brought me the cognac and I lit a cigarette. Returning to Oruro would be impossible. The Slav I used to work for had hired another guy to sell his merchandise. Finding a new gig for my daily sustenance would be like asking a blind man to catch a fly with two fingers. My buddies since childhood had bidden me farewell with parties that cost a fortune; even the girl I'd been dating, a cashier at a local shoe store, treated me to a glamorous dinner in the hotel beside the bus terminal, followed by an under-the-covers workout till dawn. When I left she shed tears like Mary Magdalene and said she'd write me once a week. I paid off my outstanding debt to my landlady for the use of two rooms and her kitchen. I even went to the cemetery and paid my respects to friends and relatives in the other world. I'd kissed Oruro goodbye forever. Return? Looking like what? A defeated man with his tail stuck between his legs? No way. Either I would travel to the United States or I would commit suicide. I had no other choice. The idea of killing myself was not new to me. In reality, I'd thought it over an infinite number of times ever since Antonia abandoned me and left me alone in the world. I probably would've done it already if it hadn't been for my son, perhaps the only link I had to this earth that has treated me so badly. I wanted to see him grow big and strong like a gringo, without complexes or fears. When he left, he told me he'd never return.

The cognac shook me up a bit, but it didn't calm my nerves. I asked for a second drink and downed it. The bill was enough to cover two lunches. The American visa was costing me like a good whore. The mere idea of a trip to the U.S. had buried that chronic depression that had plagued my entire adult existence, that sense of impotence that made anything I did seem futile. I had come once again to be trapped in a tangle of doubt and indecisiveness. I went out onto the street and rambled from one place to another with no particular destination in mind. The sun shone magnificently and the temperature was mild. If everything had gone well, this would have been a blessed day. But it had gone to hell! My luck was like a coin that I always flipped onto the wrong side. I didn't have any solutions. I couldn't change my karma.

My return trip was a true excursion. I walked up Sagárnaga Street, past the hardware and textile shops. Here, face-to-face, but without flags or weapons, Arab and Jewish merchants look each other in the eyes. They are old leftovers from the waves of migrations that reached Bolivia before the Second World War. Their hardware stores look old and somber. They've never been refurbished, not even with a second coat of paint. Vendors in the middle stretch of the street offer tourists, mostly foreigners, a series of attractions that include ancient silverware, wood carvings modeled after Aymara figures, alpaca sweaters, and ponchos. Medicinal herbs are sold alongside symbols of indigenous witchcraft, such as llama fetuses, which you're supposed to bury for good luck before breaking ground on the construction of a new house. Further up the street, hunched-over porters with bulky bags of merchandise slung over their shoulders weave between barrels containing fruit for sale. Everything is perfectly laid out.

I arrived exhausted at Illampu. The cognac and the steep climb had caused my heart to race, forcing me to slow down. I leaned against a flimsy adobe wall that barely supported a tavern catering to lowlifes and prostitutes. A terrible stench of cheap liquor emanated from inside. A beggar covered in dirty rags sang the official anthem of La

Paz. His face, deformed by the venomous concoctions served in nearby dives, was bruised and covered with scars. I took my time and avoided the fruit barrels propped up on the sidewalks. Thank God Illampu is flat, a rarity in this mountainous metropolis.

In the Hotel California lobby, the manager drowsily played a game of chess with a fat and content-looking guest, who, with his dashing Borsalino felt hat, appeared to be from Beni. He was probably a wealthy rancher, one of those who catches a plane just to count his livestock grazing on the vast haciendas on the eastern plains. Having sold off a percentage of their herd, they return each week with money bursting out of their ears to spend a little winter vacation here in the high Andes. The redhead looked at me playfully, as if he were trying to guess my mood. I picked up the key to my room and delved deeply into that sea of passageways, hoping to stumble upon the second patio. This time, I made it there without getting too dizzy.

Don Antonio, sprawled on a wicker chair, was nodding off as he basked in the sun. His chin rose and fell rhythmically over his jacket collar. Two other sunbathers had joined him: a large, baby-faced man and a girl trapped inside a guy's body. Set against his tacky surroundings, wearing a cabaret-style red robe with tassels at the fringes, the latter was a glowing apparition: scrupulously tended pale-white skin, dark-greenish makeup, and a crown of flashy bleached-blond hair. He greeted me with a tender smile.

Don Antonio woke with a start and let out a groan. "Let me introduce you to Mario Alvarez, a native son of backward Uyuni who lives in backward Oruro."

"Good afternoon," I said.

"Señor Alvarez," he continued, "allow me to introduce two of the Hotel California's most restless and infamous guests: Señor Antelo,

Chaco Oil's famous ex-goalie-turned-shrewd-politician of the MIR*
party, and our erotic jewel, Alfonso or Gardenia, depending on the circumstances. The best wine-and-cheese seller in La Paz also lives here.
He leaves the hotel at 7 in the morning and doesn't come home until
after dinner. Every day he walks the entire city from top to bottom with
Teutonic determination. You'll meet him soon."

The ex-goalie seized my right hand and squeezed it like a damp
cloth.

"Nice to meet you," he said. "I visited Uyuni once back in the '70s,
when my team was on a cross-country tour. We won six-zero. At that
altitude, even the goalies get tired. Lucky for us Uyuni was such a bad
team."

"Antelo is homesick for Santa Cruz," Don Antonio said. "We're
crossing our fingers that the government makes him Director of
Customs there. If he gets the job, we'll thank our lucky stars."

The ex-goalie smiled pleasantly. I vaguely remembered him. The
high balls were his bread and butter, but he couldn't stop a low ball to
save his life. He was so clumsy that one or two forwards used to help him
defend corner kicks. If he didn't like a penalty called against his team, he
would shove the referee in the chest. As far as I knew, he'd never once
stopped a penalty kick. He always seemed to dive the wrong way.

"I'll make it back home one of these days," Antelo said. "If I land
a gig with Customs, I'm taking you all with me."

"Hey, Alvarez, you're looking a little down. What's wrong?" Don
Antonio asked.

"I blew my visit to the American consulate. I didn't have the balls
to go through with the interview. I chickened out."

*The Movimiento de Izquierda Revolucionario (Revolutionary Leftist Movement) was the ruling political
party at the time of the original writing of this book in 1993. It has been one of Bolivia's largest parties since
the 1970s.

"Too bad," Don Antonio murmured, "your papers weren't . . ."

"I heard they hire private detectives to check every last detail. They even stick their noses into bank and City Hall records."

"And now what will you do?" Gardenia asked.

"I have no idea. All I know is I won't go back to Oruro. Anything but that."

"Maybe it was all a false alarm," Antelo remarked. "Just go on back to the consulate."

"I need to leave now. I have a plane ticket and I've got a few pesos put away for my first week in Florida."

"How old are you?" Antelo asked.

"Forty."

"I don't get what the big deal is. It's not easy to find work at your age. In a country as dynamic as America, forty is like seventy here."

"It's all because of our damned and blessed cocaine," Don Antonio said. "They think we're all potential drug traffickers."

"It's our curse and our mainstay," Antelo said.

"Che Guevara called it the atomic bomb of the Third World," Don Antonio added. "No need to worry, Alvarez. If you can get me a hot chocolate from Café Verona, I'll let you in on a secret that I save for only my closest friends."

"The hot chocolate is yours," I affirmed.

"Listen up: A few months ago, a run-of-the-mill tramp claiming to be a hairstylist arrived from Tarija. She said her dream was to open a hair salon for wealthy Latinos in Washington, but that was just a gimmick to reel in richer clients. During the interview she showed the consul her goods and promised him a good time, but being a Quaker and all, the gringo didn't bite. He denied her the visa and the poor thing walked around looking battered, like a lamb awaiting slaughter.

But when I bumped into her a few days later, I'd never seen her so happy. She flashed me her passport bearing the royal stamp from the American consulate, begged me not to rat on her, and then spilled the beans. Some shady travel agency had fixed her visa problems for cash. Supposedly, it was all done legally through their connections at the consulate. So this hairstylist left town and is surely mooching off horny Latinos in the States. She was a real babe, filled out and well-fed. Hadn't read a single book in her life, but she was still smart as hell."

"She probably married a gringo," Gardenia interjected in a voice like Marlene Dietrich's.

"Do you know where that agency is?" I asked.

"In a building behind the Cultural Center. I think it's called Andean Tourism, something like that. Go on, they'll take care of your problem."

"As if the United States were paradise," Gardenia protested.

"I hope you aren't freaked out by gays, Señor Alvarez," Don Antonio jeered.

"To each his own," I replied.

"Good man. People from Oruro are cool," Antelo remarked placidly.

"The people in Oruro are selfless and exploited. Their thankless destiny is to dream about pie-in-the-sky public works projects," Don Antonio said. "In colonial times, the Spaniards ran off with the silver from Oruro's mines to finance their absurd wars in Flanders. During the Republic, the cream of Bolivian society used Oruro's silver and gold to travel and live the good life in Paris. Since the 1952 revolution, union bosses and the fat cat owners have made a killing off the mines."

"But Don Antonio, you were a member of the party that enjoyed the spoils of power for almost thirty years," Antelo said.

"I was an idealist," Don Antonio asserted. "I naïvely believed in the revolutionary program."

"You were a slacker and you blew your money playing cards," Antelo said pointedly. "If you'd saved all the money you raked in from the revolution, you'd be retired in Mexico right now."

"Do you get a pension?" I asked, intrigued.

"I'm a retired diplomat, but I forgot to apply for my pension."

"What do you live on?"

"I live off my friends, which now include you, and from the weekly sale of books from my exquisite library. Every two or three days, Antelo and sometimes Gardenia here sell one of the classics from my collection. That's how I pay the hotel from time to time. I don't eat much, just three lunches a week in a cheap restaurant. But I do eat chocolate cake religiously; without my chocolate, I would be in the cemetery with the rest of my family by now. Gardenia takes me along to his wild orgies every now and then. I never get a piece of the action, but I always eat a lot while I'm there. Also, the salesman slips me a slab of fine cheese each week."

"Which author is getting the axe today?" Gardenia asked.

"Next up is Turgenev, the great nihilist."

When Don Antonio noticed that Antelo had gone back to his room, he announced: "I'll bet you anything he went to dust off the old photographs from his soccer days. He'll want to show them to you, Alvarez, along with his newspaper scrapbook. Tell me something: Do you think an ex-goalie can become a famous politician?"

"He was an awful goalie. Maybe he'll make it as a politician."

"Don't be surprised if he's appointed Customs Director," Gardenia said.

"He's got connections and he's about as righteous as John

Dillinger. He's a solid guy, but you can't expect miracles from him. It would be great news if they sent him to Santa Cruz because he'd land us all sinecures. I'd pray for his soul for the rest of my days," Don Antonio said.

"The poor guy looks like such a freak," Gardenia commented. "He walks with his legs bowed, like he's always looking for a ball in the air." He laughed, covering his mouth with his hand.

Antelo hadn't given me enough time to slip away to my room. He returned just then with a bulging folder tucked under his arm.

"It's that time, Alvarez, my friend. You'll have to swallow the whole story, from his days as a child prodigy to his Olympic lap bidding goodbye to the fans at Siles Stadium. A nightmare," Don Antonio whispered.

Antelo invited me to sit on a patch of grass growing reluctantly in the middle of the shrub-enclosed patio. Don Antonio hadn't exaggerated. I heard about Antelo's long, painful career, from the first time he kicked a soccer ball in a sandy lot of a small town in Santa Cruz, to his last save against a dark-skinned fellow named Gadea, who tried to get tricky and weave with the ball inside the penalty box. His photo collection was staggering. I also had to put up with his running commentary. His voice droned on like that of a congressman reading an endless, rambling speech before his colleagues. He made me drowsy and almost put me to sleep.

"What do you think?" Antelo asked once he had finished.

"Someone ought to write your biography," I said. "The fans would eat up every detail of a story that fascinating."

"See?" he said, turning to Don Antonio. "I'll dictate and you'll write."

"Really, thanks for the invitation," Don Antonio said, "but writing about soccer would be pure torture for me. I would rather be the owner's confessor."

"Confessor?" I asked.

"Once in a while, the owner of this sacrosanct hotel asks me to read him poems by Tamayo, Santos Chocano, and Borges. In Buenos Aires, he took a liking to poetry. He claims to have been a friend of Victoria Ocampo's, but I don't believe it. At each get-together he treats me to a hot chocolate and gives me ten pesos. He has also ordered the manager to go easy on collecting my rent."

"We could make money off my biography," Antelo said.

"We'll get rich working for Customs," Gardenia interjected. "You'd better not forget about us when you make it big."

"I'm not that kind of guy," Antelo protested. "I swear I'll take you to Santa Cruz with me, Gardenia, just so you can carry on your debauchery there."

"The biography I'd like to write is Gardenia's," Don Antonio said. "By day, a naïve-looking kid who passes for an altar boy; by night, an erotic Lolita with fewer inhibitions than Emperor Caligula."

Gardenia tossed his head back, let out a roar, and shot me the glance of a naughty geisha.

"Alvarez, you'll be in for quite a surprise when you see him at night. A Venetian carnival mask couldn't do a better job. The men she tricks don't realize their mistake until it's too late. After knocking back two drinks, our baby Gardenia is more mouthwatering than Tadzio in Thomas Mann's *Death in Venice*. Have you read it?"

"I saw the movie," I said.

"It's beautifully told with a refined German's lean, elegant prose."

"And how would you know Gardenia is *mouthwatering*?" Antelo inquired. "If *you* know, you'd think everyone would."

Don Antonio chuckled. "I might be a salt statue from the waist down, but my imagination is a cyclone."

"Have you ever written a book?" I asked.

"A long time ago, I started a harrowing story about my confinement in the National Stadium in Santiago, Chile, where I was imprisoned by General Pinochet for six months. I never finished it. If only I had some peace and quiet and a typewriter."

"You had one until just recently," Antelo said.

"I sold it at half-price. That's one of my biggest faults. I sell everything that lands in my lap."

"He can't help himself," Gardenia said.

"I admit it's nothing to be proud of," Don Antonio lamented. "It boils down to laziness. I rely only on my talent."

"Talent is not enough. You need to work harder," Antelo said.

"Too late for me," Don Antonio replied. "What I ought to write now is my epitaph."

I glanced at my watch: 3 in the afternoon. I jotted down the address of the travel agency and said goodbye to those characters.

Chapter 4

The taxi dropped me off in front of the Cultural Center. Luckily, a mild breeze was cooling off the dry, sunny afternoon. A line of stores wound like an accordion around the base of the building. I walked hurriedly to the other side of that enormous structure and asked the bellboy for the Andean Tourism Agency.

"Eleventh floor, left-hand side," the doorman indicated with an expression of such disgust that he seemed to be suffering from ulcers.

The eleventh floor was jammed with law firms and notary offices, but I managed to find Andean Tourism at the end of one of the hallways. I was greeted by the unpleasant stare of a secretary who was wearing sunglasses and had her hair done up in an Afro. With a quick, haughty upturn of her nose, she showed me to an ugly plastic chair. Aside from the secretary, nearly everything in that tiny office was made of plastic. A mountain of tourist brochures, tickets, and pencils stood on top of the desk. The lady periodically glanced up at me, distracted. Her expressionless eyes seemed to be waiting for me to initiate conversation.

"I'm here to apply for a tourist visa to the United States," I said.

"Who gave you our address?" she asked with affected disinterest.

"A hairdresser friend of mine from Tarija who lives in Washington."

"What did she tell you?"

"That you know all the secrets to writing a strong application. She said you're well connected in the U.S. consulate and she spoke highly of your professionalism and your attention to detail."

"Does she still live in Washington?"

"Sure does. She's raking it in with that hair salon business of hers."

"So, you'd like to travel as a tourist?"

"For a few months at most. My son lives in Florida."

She stared me down for a few seconds without saying a word. "Now and then we give good friends of ours a hand with their visa applications. What's your last name?"

"Alvarez, from Oruro."

"Do you have a valid passport?"

"Yes, plus a round-trip ticket."

She stood up and tapped her knuckles against a door, the upper half of which was made of frosted glass framed in aluminum. When she opened it, I caught a glimpse of a fat man chatting on the phone. Seated in a swivel chair behind a desk, he looked like a businessman up to his ears in work. She whispered to him, came back out from his office, and declared: "Wait just a moment."

Before long, the fat man commanded her over the intercom to let me proceed.

"Eduardo Ballón, at your service."

The fat guy lit a cigar while I shook his soft, flaccid hand. His papers were scattered all over the place. The way he obsessively organized and reshuffled them suggested that he wanted to appear stressed out. He was in his shirtsleeves and his belly had just about busted through his trouser buttons: the fat rose up through his chest, gathering in his neck and jowls. His diminutive mouth looked out of place in the middle of his pear-shaped face. His distinctive nose stuck out like a pig's snout, casting a shadow over his tiny eyes.

"So, Señor Alvarez," he said, "some lady told you we could fix your problem . . ."

"A hairstylist who lives in Washington."

With an elbow propped up on the desk, he rested his cheek on the palm of his hand. He kept looking at me. "I don't remember her," he said.

"A sensual, well-endowed, light-skinned lady from Tarija," I invented.

"Sensual?"

"Big-breasted; her breasts could knock you over they're so big."

"Wasn't she the one who didn't like the consul?"

"That's her."

"She got a green card."

"That sounds right."

"So you want to follow in her footsteps."

"As soon as possible."

"Have you been to the consulate yet?"

"No, I came straight here. I just got in yesterday from Oruro."

"Let me see your passport." He leafed through the document while chomping on his cigar like a stevedore. "That hairdresser wasn't lying to you. We have connections, friends who help us speed up the paperwork every now and then. If everything's in order, the visa isn't a problem," he stressed. "But usually everything isn't in order; an expired document here, an undated deed there . . . You know what I mean?"

"Yes, of course."

"All these people in the consulate ask for is a few pesos. They help us and we help them."

"How much?" I asked.

"Eight hundred dollars." Pushing off with his stumpy legs, he rolled backwards in his chair. Taking note of my horrified expression, he immediately added: "If your paperwork's in order, then all we'll do is book your flight. Go on to the consulate. You can go there yourself, you know?"

"That sounds like a lot of money just to speed things up," I said. "All my documents are in order: I've got the deed to my house, my bank statements—"

"Good for you. If that's the case, just go to the consulate. They'll look over your papers and return them to you in a few days. If all goes well, you'll get the visa; and if not, you'll have to go through Mexico like everyone else."

"Crossing the border on foot?"

"Or in some coyote's trunk." He laughed and bit hard into his cigar.

"I hear it's dangerous. Raymond Chandler used to say nobody's better than a good Mexican and no one's worse than a bad Mexican."

"It's up to you, Señor Alvarez. That border is a no-man's land. Let's just say, unexpected things happen there."

"Eight hundred dollars is a rip-off."

"It depends. If for some reason you don't want to show them your papers, then it's a good deal. Keep in mind, Señor Alvarez, that the gringos are meticulous. One slipup and it's over. If they deny you the visa once, forget about emigrating."

"But I don't want to emigrate!"

"Whatever, it's all the same. This is your first try, right?"

"Yes."

"You're not young, but you're not old either. You're right at the cut-off age. Maybe if you can get on the consul's good side . . . What's your problem anyway?"

"I'm just worried some jackass will deny me the visa and then I won't be able to see my son."

"Or the hairdresser."

"Hairdresser . . . ? Oh right, that hairdresser is a real piece of work."

"It's up to you, Señor Alvarez."

"Eight hundred?"

"They put their jobs and their integrity on the line even though all they're doing is making sure your papers don't get lost in the pile or filed away until Christmas. The consul himself looks them over, signs them, and stamps them with his official seal."

"No problem then?"

The fat man smiled as he squashed his cigar like a cockroach. "The visa is totally legal. We just expedite the paperwork to keep those private detectives from sticking their noses where they don't belong."

"And Mexico?"

"It's cheaper, but you'd have to start praying those hoods don't bust your balls."

"That would be worse than eight hundred dollars," I replied.

"Some people don't care about their virginity; all they want is to make it to the other side. Think it over, Señor Alvarez. That's the price and not a cent less. It's worth it, especially if you find a job in the States and stay there for good. Goodbye, Oruro, hello good life!"

"I'll think about it," I said.

The fat man smiled like a good-natured asshole. "I'll be in La Paz until Friday. Then I'm making a trip back home to Vallegrande."

I couldn't think of anything better to do than take refuge in the first dive I saw. Ever since I was a kid, I'd been in the habit of using personal setbacks as excuses to get plastered. After Antonia left me, I think I spent a whole year hitting up watering holes until one day I stepped off a curb, completely wasted, and got run over by a motorcycle. I was later resuscitated in the part of the public hospital where they send patients who are about to die. For a few years I survived on soda pop and coffee, until a brainy lady got me drinking again. She was a high school biology teacher who watered her plants with beer. But I only turned into an occasional lush, the kind who can still control his neurons. My hangovers used to keep me in bed for days—vomiting, with a splitting headache.

I barged into an enormous underground bar where they served only beer. Just inhaling was enough for the acute smell of malt liquor to make my head spin. The place had forty tables, but at that early hour there weren't a lot of customers, just a few regulars playing dice games; either they were retired or they were public employees. Several dozen beers adorned their tables. The waiter, a thin man with a sour look on his face, escorted me to a secluded table reserved for deep thinkers with serious problems.

"How many?" he asked.

"One at a time."

I got up to take a leak as soon as the waiter disappeared. A good piss is the only way beer drinkers can purge their bladders of toxins. A white-haired man about sixty years old was resting both palms against one of the bathroom stalls, futilely trying to shoot his spray into a gutter that was meant to be a urinal. His penis hung out of his fly profanely, ridiculously. He was so wasted that if he'd taken one hand off the wall to try and redirect it, he'd run the risk of hitting the cement floor face first.

Once the old man realized someone was there, he turned to look at me and stammered, "Hey . . . fucking give me a hand, will ya?"

I was heated and in no mood for charity. So I stepped up to the end of the gutter farthest from the old man. It was a terrific photo-op; the guy just stood there, completely motionless.

"Fucking fogey," I blurted out as I left the room.

An ice-cold beer awaited me at my table.

"You'll have to pay up front," the waiter said.

"What? You can't even trust a decent guy?"

"Sir," he protested faintly, "it's not that we don't trust you. The thing is, we get cheated every day. They'll have two dozen and say it was one, or five and claim it's four. We don't ask you to pay up front for nothing, sir."

I paid and got to thinking. Things were looking murky. The consulate would find out about my fake papers for sure. That guy at the agency just wanted to hustle me out of eight hundred dollars. What a bunch of crap. I'd saved exactly what I needed for a week in La Paz and to pay the airport departure tax, and I'd set aside a hundred dollars for my first few days in the United States. Before leaving for eternity, my father had given me a few gold nuggets, about ten grams worth. He told me they would "multiply like the loaves in the Bible and bring you luck." Instead of spending them, I'd held on to them, hoping they'd multiply. But they still weighed the same as they had eight years before.

I downed my beer in the time it takes a rooster to let out a morning crow. *Why don't you kill yourself?* I thought. If I could just chug twenty beers and then go to sleep, they'd find my cold body the next day. It was the only death a screw-up like me deserved. The law of life states that he who cannot rise should make way for others. The world's small and useless people are better off underground where they can't be heard, awaiting the last judgment. That's the day we'll all be equal. Who was I kidding? Where had I gone wrong? When had I gone so far downhill? I was asking myself these questions for the thousandth time.

Born into a comfortable middle-class family, my father had been an inspector for the Bolivian Railway and my mother the only daughter of a wealthy tin mine owner. My maternal grandfather was selfish, reactionary, and had been alone in the world ever since his wife died young, years before. He'd wanted for his little girl to climb the social ladder and never approved of her marrying a modest railroad inspector. My father secretly hated his bosses, Brits every last one of them. And he hated his father-in-law so openly that, just to spite him, he joined the MNR*, back then a progressive party with a statist platform that made landowners and mine owners' hairs stand on end. I was born in Uyuni, then an important railroad town, along with my brother Osvaldo, who's six years my senior. I came into the world in '52 just as the revolution changed my family's fortunes for the worse. The ruling MNR nationalized the mines, ruining my grandfather.

At the time, my grandfather had been living comfortably in an affluent neighborhood in Santiago, Chile with a sweet, down-to-earth Chilean girl. He hadn't suspected that the Indians would one day reflect on their bad lot in life and decide to take over the land and, by extension, the mines. He'd wasted all the money he earned from his mine's profits on extravagant parties and trips to Paris. He didn't despair when the money stopped rolling in, though, landing a gig as the headwaiter at a restaurant in Santiago, on Huérfanos Street.

My father, on the other hand, benefited from the new social order. He resigned his post as a railroad inspector and got into the flour importing business. We moved to Oruro, and then a few months later my mother's kidneys gave out and she died before we even realized what was going on with her. It was a terrible blow for us. Flora, my

*Since 1950, the Movimiento Nacionalista Revolucionario (Nationalist Revolutionary Movement) has occupied the Bolivian presidency more often than any other political party.

mother, had been a quiet, well-mannered, selfless woman, wholly devoted to family life. She was no beauty, but had delicate, distinguished features. My father, Jacinto, the only man she'd ever had, was strong and light-skinned, with a logger's moustache and a serious face lit up by two youthful, sensual brown eyes.

Still young and good-looking when my mother died, my father didn't waste any time in starting after a girl who was fifteen years younger, a seamstress with the most eye-catching backside in all of southwestern Bolivia. The two lovebirds moved into an apartment together, leaving me and my brother Osvaldo alone in the old house. Osvaldo, who had always fought with my father over everything, couldn't think of anything better to do than join the Bolivian Socialist Falange.* He started going through hell—beatings, detentions, a month behind bars—until he was finally exiled to Chile. He made his way to Antofagasta, where a Peruvian woman fell madly in love with him and gave him the money to start up a bakery. Osvaldo was the spitting image of my father, though dark-skinned. This Peruvian lady was so fascinated by the way he would get drunk and beat her that she bore him five kids. I last saw him eight years ago in Arica, Chile. He told me he'd sold the bakery and was working in construction. We went out to dinner a couple of times, and I found him changed. He was far more closed than before and he didn't care about politics anymore, only money. He asked halfheartedly about our dad and then swore he'd never return to Bolivia.

In '64, General Barrientos took power and the revolution's glory days came to an end. With the MNR no longer calling the shots, my father lost all his government connections. Practically overnight, he became an unemployed, impoverished, spiteful old man. As soon as his

*The principal right-leaning political party opposed to MNR rule during the 1950s and 1960s.

woman realized he didn't have any money, she left him for a lieutenant with a promising future. I was still attending Bolívar High School, the cream of the crop in Oruro. I was a hard-working student with a lively imagination. With the new military "order," we'd fallen from rising middle class to borderline destitute. My father had forgotten how to earn an honest living with the sweat of his own back and, just like my grandfather, had failed to save enough money to pay for his own funeral. Without pomp or circumstance, he found work at a tire importing company.

He didn't make much and he started drinking heavily. Since he didn't have the money anymore to attract rich women, the best he could do was make love to half-breed harlots from the north side of town. He spent his weekends sunbathing and playing chess. Meanwhile, as soon as my eighty-year-old maternal grandfather found out that his political enemies had been defeated, he decided to return to Bolivia to revive his old mine. But luck would have it that, right as he stepped onto the train at Río Mulatos, his blood pressure shot through the roof and he ended up dying at a run-down hospital in town. They buried him at the local cemetery.

As bad as things were, I managed to graduate from high school with a diploma that made my father cry. "I suppose you'll go on to become a doctor or an engineer," he declared. When I confessed to him that teaching was my calling, he sunk into a depression that only worsened when, a couple of days later, I introduced him to Antonia, my new girlfriend. Antonia studied education and dreamed of teaching Spanish. I wanted to teach English, a language that had fascinated me ever since I saw my first Leslie Howard movie.

We both got our education degrees, and as soon as we'd finished our obligatory one-year teaching assignments in the countryside, we were married in a simple but joyous ceremony at a friend's house that started off discreetly but ended with several of our guests behind bars. Antonia's father, who worked at a bank, helped us secure a two-thousand-dollar loan with which we bought ourselves a four-room, one-bath bungalow with a fifty-square-foot rose garden in Oruro's Chiripujio neighborhood. I bought a bicycle and dedicated my heart and soul to teaching. I was hopeful about the future. I lived modestly, but I wasn't hard up. I was healthy as a buck, my wife was a dedicated worker, and we had plenty of friends. Combining our two salaries, we were sometimes able to put aside savings. We dreamed of emigrating to Córdoba, Argentina and kept a collection of brochures, newspaper clippings, and letters from people we knew describing the city's beauty and pleasant climate.

Within a year our son was born and we baptized him Luis Alberto Carlos. He came out pearl-colored, with his mother's black hair, bawling like there was no tomorrow. Antonia was attractive, thin, soft-spoken, and discreet. You barely noticed her during the day, but she used her imagination, repressed by years of studying at a Catholic girl's school, to fill our nighttime lovemaking sessions with surprises. In spite of living in a poor, unstable, troubled country, I couldn't complain. I had a satisfying existence—low on means, but high on hope.

My only real worry was my father's decline into a state of profound neurosis. He started getting irritable and any old thing ticked him off. One day he took me aside and confided to me that he'd lost his virility. I told him it was just a temporary problem that a good sexual-enhancement drug could fix, which consoled him.

My little boy was growing up, happy and healthy. After working for four years as a teacher, I bought myself a motorcycle and became the envy of the neighborhood. How did it all go to hell? I remember that my wife always used to come down with colds, and then one day she had to go to the hospital with a fever and a nasty cough. The doctor who took care of her told me she had a spot on her lung, but that it wasn't serious and she'd get over it with a little rest. After leaving the hospital, she quit working and tried staying home for a while. But as soon as she started getting active again, the symptoms reappeared: fatigue, night sweats, and a cough as stubbornly persistent as a leaky old roof. I blew all my savings on medicine, and before I knew it I was in debt and drinking more than usual. Bolivia was in bad shape back then; it's always been in bad shape. I sent my wife away to Tupiza Valley to stay with an aunt who owned a grocery store, and to breathe warmer air. With the passing months she got noticeably better; she started to gain weight and she got her good looks back. Her sense of humor returned and so did the color to her face.

The tragedy is that although the spot did disappear from her lung, Antonia no longer felt anything for me. At first she didn't want to make love because she wanted to recuperate. Later, she needed time to feel like herself again. In the end, she just didn't love me anymore. She didn't even want me to touch her. My caresses were pure torture for her. I was too dumb to realize she'd latched onto another guy, a new-wave, right-wing, pro-military, boot-licking politician who'd gone from opportunistic trade unionist to labor advisor for the Armed Forces. While I taught English at a public high school to a bunch of do-nothings, she spent the whole afternoon in bed with that rich bastard. I couldn't bring myself to kick her out of the house because our son was still so young. I swallowed it . . . I swallowed it, anxiously hoping that Antonia would get bored with that guy. I used to see him from time to time in town, strutting around with the other politicians, regular louts and sleazebags every one of them. I thought about buying a revolver and putting a bullet in his head, but killing him wouldn't have solved anything. I would have gone to jail, my son would have died of hunger, and Antonia would have found somebody else.

I went from brothel to brothel screwing tarts until I started getting an ungodly discharge that I was only able to cure with a mail-order medication from Germany. I became a self-denying cuckold who was still hopelessly in love. My teacher's salary wasn't enough to cover even our basic necessities anymore, and so I left the rich and precise language of Keats to work in contraband, a line of work that's looked down upon but that brought in three times more money for me.

That still wasn't enough to get Antonia's attention. She slept alone in a separate room and couldn't have cared less whether or not I went out whoring. One day she declared she was leaving for Argentina to reflect on her future, on the essence of her womanhood, and a bunch of other nonsense. When she said goodbye, we clasped hands and she kissed my son on the forehead. I haven't seen her since. Years later, people told me she was living in Mendoza with some guy who sold empanadas on the road to Chile. One Christmas, I got a photo in the mail of her beside a lake. Poor thing . . . she revealed that the trip was helping her find herself. With her callow, empty bumpkin's mind, I don't know what the hell she was going to find. Luis Alberto Carlos had become an easy-going, handsome, dark-skinned kid and he was getting bigger; soon he'd grown taller than my shoulder. I did a brain-washing job on him to make sure he didn't feel anything for Antonia. He burned all her pictures and proclaimed that she was dead to him.

After graduating from high school at the age of eighteen, my son got the preposterous idea of moving to Canada and nearly pulled it off. A cousin from my mother's side owned a fur shop in New Orleans and was married to an American. He came down to Oruro on vacation once and hit it off with my boy. He told me that Bolivia was going nowhere and that if I wanted a better future for Luis Alberto Carlos, he could take him along to Louisiana as his helper to teach him the fur business. If the kid felt like studying, he would have the time and the money for it. The idea hardly made me jump for joy, but it was a good option for my son's college education.

My relationship with my son was based on mutual respect: He was my companion, my friend . . . and sometimes my confessor. I didn't have a lot to give him. Contraband sounds romantic, like a lot of money, but that's only true for the guy who puts down the dough himself and then sells the merchandise. I was just a middleman, a ten-percent-plus-travel-expenses kind of guy.

I let my son go even though it meant I'd be as lonely as a priest in the boondocks. It was best for him to take his chances on the American dream. Just like Borges, the Argentine, I've always had a weakness for Anglo-Saxons. Not so much the Brits as the Americans, most of all because of their crime fiction.

So the fur dealer had his helper, and my son promised to write often and to send me a ticket as soon as he could scrape a few bucks together. Back then it was relatively easy to do the paperwork to go to the United States. I don't think my son had to go through as much agony as I did later. In spite of his promise, I didn't hear a peep out of Luis Alberto Carlos for three months. Then one day I received a four-page letter in small handwriting that read like a last will and testament. He explained that he'd left New Orleans because my cousin was exploiting him like a Chinese laborer and paying him a pittance. So, it turned out my cousin was a real son of a bitch. Luis Alberto Carlos set off for Chicago, where he worked in a gas station and later in a hotel. He said the winters were freezing there with biting winds. The manager of the hotel, an old Armenian hag who smelled like olives, wanted to get into his pants, so he was planning to head back east and relocate to Miami, a tropical paradise inhabited by a teeming mass of Hispanics.

Another six months passed before I received a second letter, this time two pages long: He was studying Business Administration in college and waiting tables at a seafood restaurant. His tips were outstanding and his female coworkers had no inhibitions. Six months later came a third letter, one page in which he wrote that he'd had a successful first semester at school, that he'd been promoted to headwaiter and all he ever did was serve shrimp soup to fat-cat ruffians. The fourth missive didn't contain a single word, just a round-trip ticket. One week later, the fifth letter: five lines in which he announced he'd found me a job at the House of Pancakes in Miami and told me to work on getting fake papers to dupe the gringos for a visa. In the postscript, he wrote that he didn't have a stable address for the time being but that he'd stop by the House of Pancakes every week to look for me. Next, the address of the House of Pancakes where I was supposedly going to work, and that was it. My boy was off his rocker, but what else could I do? It was my frustrating destiny . . .

"Another drink?" the waiter asked. Just walking from table to table, the guy must've lost two pounds each night.

I got up to pee for the second time. The john was packed with boozehounds trying to figure out how to avoid pissing all over each other. I realized I'd reached my limit and that another drop of beer would send me into uncharted territory. It was time for me to leave.

"Thanks. You're all set," the waiter said empathetically as I left.

The afternoon had changed color: a sea of gray clouds obscured the sun and threatened to smother the city like a blanket.

My drunken high led me straight home, where I fell asleep for a few hours. After sobering up with a cold shower, I went down to the lobby at around 7. I felt dejected and I was still a bit out of it, but the cold shower had brought me back to the reality of my insoluble problems. I ran into Blanca in the lobby. Wearing everyday clothing of T-shirt, jeans, and no makeup, she exuded a kind of youthful sparkle. Without her harlot's guise her bawdy sensuality was a thing of the past. She could have passed for an everyday girl from eastern Bolivia. She looked five years younger and like she didn't have a care in the world.

"How'd it go?" she asked.

"Bad."

"Your breath reeks. You've been drinking, haven't you?"

"Just beer. I was hoping the alcohol would cheer me up, but all it gave me was a wicked hangover. I could use some aspirin."

"I was going to get some Chinese food for dinner," she said. "Wanna come?"

There are some looks that only women can give you, and this was one of those, an unmistakable signal that we could be more than just bedmates. We walked down Evaristo Valle, past street vendors preparing for the nighttime rush, before arriving at Plaza San Francisco. When I traveled to La Paz with my father as a youngster, it was worth the trip just to lay eyes on that plaza, a magnificent, austere jewel that brought to life the grandeur of the colonial era and filled me with pride. Surrounded by a fenced-in garden, it had a distinctive nineteenth-century flavor. Romantic and autumnal, it was a place that evoked bygone times. But then some crackpot developers destroyed the garden, creating a gigantic, open cement terrace that became a hot-spot for boisterous missionaries, rock bands, street vendors, beggars, drunks, shamans, and hobos at all hours of the day and night. At one end of the plaza, an eccentric sculptor had erected a hodgepodge of curious stone statues that looked like the remains of a colossal set long ago deemed unsuitable for television. Heartlessly, and with a healthy dose of stupidity, the city had concocted an enigma for the amusement of foreign tourists. The church, meanwhile, had lost much of its shine and magic.

We plodded down the narrow streets around the old post office before stumbling across a cheap Peruvian-Chinese eatery. The owners recognized Blanca immediately and escorted us with Asian courtesy to a table for two. Blanca asked for the menu and I contented myself with a cup of jasmine tea. After getting up to buy a pack of cigarettes at the counter, I returned to find Blanca chatting with a guy standing beside her.

"I don't know who he is," Blanca said. "He's wasted and he won't stop yakking at me."

The man stared at me with watery eyes. "I'm a pilot," he declared.

"Excuse me," I said, "can't you see she's with me?"

"Who're you?" he inquired.

"Her man."

The pilot started shaking as if standing on the bow of a fishing boat on the high seas. He stared at me scornfully and repeated, "I'm a pilot."

"Get out of the way. We're about to take off," I said.

"What's her name?" he asked.

"Connie," I said. "Connie Cockface."

Blanca broke out in laughter.

Standing two hand-lengths from my nose, the man inhaled. "Some other time," he grumbled. "When I'm ready."

The pilot walked away, leaving behind a trail of booze stench. Blanca looked around indifferently.

"Every time I come I meet new Chinese people. I swear they're using our country to get to the United States."

"If only they'd show me how it's done!"

"They work together and always find a way."

A muscular bowlegged Chinese waitress dressed in a sweater and a skirt left an enormous plate in the middle of the table: a concoction of fish, chicken, and pork rind lathered in sweet and sour sauce, accompanied by a generous serving of Peruvian-style fried rice.

"I don't think you're getting enough calories," I joked.

"The way I live, I'll get burned out in a month if I don't eat well," Blanca said. "What are we gonna do about you? The gringos have ruined your appetite."

"Find me eight hundred bucks." I told her about my visit to the Andean agency.

She didn't seem surprised. "That stuff goes on everywhere, even in that consulate."

"It's all legal," I retorted. "They just speed up the paperwork."

She looked at me like I was a newborn baby. "So you wanna come to Villa Fátima?"

"I don't have any plans."

She raised her long curled eyelashes and studied me mockingly. "You can watch me work. I'm the best one," she bragged. "At least come and have a beer. You won't stop drinking this late in the game."

Outside, a police siren wailed in the distance. No doubt the cop was using it as a horn to get around traffic.

"Where's your wife?" Blanca asked out of the blue.

"She took a train to Argentina. I won't bore you with the whole story. I don't even dream about her anymore. These days my dreams are dark like the night."

"The men are gorgeous in Argentina, but they take off as soon as they get a few pesos out of you," she remarked.

"You don't have a special friend?"

"I haven't found anyone who's worth it. I'm not the kind of girl who gets desperate quick. If I don't find someone I like, I just take care of myself. Anyway, up in Villa Fátima they're all dirty half-breeds. There isn't a single white man."

My left hand climbed up her hard robust thighs.

"You'll make those Chinese guys blush," she said.

"They've been pale for thousands of years."

"They go up to Villa Fátima sometimes. The Koreans too; they pay well, but they're the biggest freaks. Haggling turns them on."

Blanca ate like a burly truck driver. She didn't leave a single piece of rice on her plate. The beer took care of my hangover and I stopped thinking about the American visa. Blanca devoured a strange dessert of chocolate and tropical fruit that looked like it could constipate a duck, and washed down her meal with three cups of jasmine tea.

"It'll take awhile to walk off all that food. You're gonna catch a cold, it's chilly out."

"You should see me at work in just a bikini and panty hose."

She paid the owner, an obsequious Chinese guy with a cynical smile à la Fu Manchu. He offered us a cigarette on our way out. Nightfall appeared behind tiny amber clouds that gently covered the city. We strolled in silence down Avenida del Ejército until we arrived at Las Velas, a bustling outdoor food court. The wind suddenly started to gust and shortly thereafter the rain came. Balls of hail began to fall and then a veritable scourge from heaven was unleashed upon Miraflores. As everyone ran for cover, we hailed a minibus headed for Villa de La Merced.

Blanca giggled like a schoolgirl at the deafening sound of hail smashing against the roof of the minibus. Streams formed along the edges of the sidewalks and the water rushed violently south. The driver barely managed to force the door closed. It was as if the passengers had all morphed into an amphibious mass. Blanca's buttocks were funneling heat into my lap. She smiled at me knowingly. The driver cussed in Aymara and Spanish as the minibus, a 1970s-era clunker, inched along painfully. Nobody dared get out. The water engulfed the tires and threatened to seep into the motor. It took us a whole hour to reach the red light district, where Blanca and I got off along with five other prostitutes headed for work.

The hailstorm stopped, but the rain kept falling. Villa Fátima looked like Oruro in its worst days, desolate and cloaked in shadow. Blanca walked up to a food stand and greeted a woman who must have been a twenty-year veteran of the pickup business. Her face looked sad and carnivalesque, like a painted mask. After eyeing me from head to toe, she told me she had never been to Oruro, but that she once worked in an exotic dance club in Caracas. For dinner, she ate a bowl of soup mixed with rainwater in which pieces of potato and a few strings of meat floated like tiny islands.

Blanca bought a pack of gum before we headed down an excruciatingly steep byway that dead-ended at a cliff by the edge of a garbage dump. In the doorway to the brothel, a drunken bouncer eyed me suspiciously. The house had an enormous patio, a lounge with a dance floor, and private rooms on all sides. Clearly, it had been built for only one reason. I could tell it was somewhat respectable because there weren't any half-breed tramps. About twenty guys leaned back against the walls, hands in their pockets, checking out the harlots.

"Those whack-offs come here every day," Blanca explained. "They stand there for hours without moving and don't spend a cent."

Blanca's arrival in the ring stirred up a small commotion among the regulars at the dive, which was called El Faro.

"I'll go change," Blanca said. "Wait for me in the lounge."

The lounge was strategically illuminated by colorful lightbulbs. This worked in the girls' favor, since you could only partially make out their bodies in that light. If you were to see them in the light of day, they were the kind of girls you would run away from. On one side of the room stood a mounted stage on which a band had set up the equipment. I made out an organ, a set of drums, three electric guitars, and a microphone. Several members of the band, dressed in cheesy blue tuxedos, busied themselves with hooking up the sound system. The lead singer, who was about the size of a jockey, smiled smugly as he tested out the microphone. In the middle of the room a half-dozen whores warmed their bottoms by the fire of a gas stove. Another dozen or so were crammed in back beside a small window, waiting for their drinks. The madam, an old wrinkly hag, kept watch over her pupils from a tiny bar situated in one of the corners, her lips forming a bitter and disdainful grin. She jotted down clients' orders in a notebook while energetically bossing around a pair of waiters sporting green jackets. She looked out for her business with a librarian's seriousness and the penetrating gaze of a Basque shepherd. She didn't miss a thing.

When a girl managed to latch onto a client, she would trade in a ticket for ten pesos, presumably the cost of a room. Sipping a glass of beer at the madam's side was the bouncer, who kept all the drunkards in line. He weighed about two hundred pounds and was an astonishing Afro-Aymara hybrid. He nearly had a fit when he saw me walk in with Blanca. As soon as he realized I wasn't a regular, his instinct told him that I wanted a piece of the pie. I took a look around at the ladies—they were of nearly all races and types. Their uniform was either a simple bikini or a miniskirt short enough to allow you to appreciate their miniscule panties. The girls giggled and shouted as they bounced from one end of the room to another, clicking their heels on the tile floor.

Blanca appeared a few minutes later in full battle gear: a see-through silk shell, a pair of shorts a few sizes too small, and her makeup done to suit the tastes and sensibilities of the clients. She was by far the sexiest and most striking of them all. She wasn't the prettiest one, but none of the others could match her tropical flair or her primitive voluptuousness.

Blanca came up to me and ordered a beer. "What do you think?" she asked.

"The brothels haven't changed in twenty years," I said. "Back in Oruro, I started sinning in a place that was cold and dark like this one."

"It's not the best, but these days it's better to work here than in one of the houses downtown," Blanca asserted.

"What matters is the quantity. Sex at wholesale prices," I suggested.

The band struck up a lambada.

"This business is all about the time it takes you to get the customers to finish. Most of them are young and already horny when they get here, so a couple of wanks and they're done. They like it when I do a little theater for them. It makes them feel macho."

"Did the madam use to be one of the girls?"

"She's sick with cancer. At least that's what they say. Maybe she made it up just so we'll feel sorry for her."

"And the tough guy?"

"Some half-breed they brought over from Peru. He snorts coke all day and has a dealer who stops by around midnight. But it's not all for him. They say the madam uses it as a painkiller."

"She could have cancer. She doesn't look very well."

"Who knows? Anyway, you want to see my room?"

"In this cold? No thanks. I'll be waiting in the hotel when you finish."

"So you don't care if I start working?"

"Nah, I'll just hang out here awhile. I wouldn't miss out on the band for anything," I joked.

Twenty-odd pairs of eyes ogled at the pendular swaying of Blanca's hips as she strutted away. A young guy who looked like a military recruit approached her and, after they murmured to each other for all of ten seconds, he followed her across the patio. Most of the customers were recruits, laborers, and hoods, the kind of people who couldn't afford more than twenty pesos a session. Blanca surprised me. She didn't waste any time. She did six different guys in the single hour I sat at the bar. She avoided the drunkards and the teenagers, but the rest were fair game. Blanca's good-natured charm and straightforward manner with the peasant migrants made them forget how inferior they felt. A white woman, unattainable under any other circumstances. The country's rotten economy was hitting the expensive hookers; for the common people, something good had finally come out of the recession.

At around 11 o'clock, Blanca swapped her original get-up for a bikini, stockings, and a pair of extremely high-heeled shoes. That was a trick to further accentuate the swaying of her buttocks. Her level of activity at that hour was truly impressive. She went in and out of the lounge, hardly pausing to breathe, and yet the pace didn't seem to affect her. After each excursion, she would quickly brush her hair and reapply some lipstick. Her idea of inviting me to see her in action seemed to be a subtle way of offering me a future cut of her nocturnal earnings. If I hadn't been so caught up in my visa problems, I would've considered it. The girl meant well and the money flowed into her like a slot machine. We wouldn't have had to pay any taxes, but then there was the risk of AIDS and other STDs. There's always a price to pay. You can't get something for nothing in this world.

When the madam saw that I was about to leave, she decided she wanted to get to know me better. After offering me Chilean cognac on the house, her pale, limp fingers handed me a plastic cup. The bouncer, who still hadn't had his fix, gently shook my hand. His name was Tolque and he reeked of cheap hustler's cologne. The madam's sister, an ashen old lady who repeatedly stuck out her tongue like a lizard, kept track of what each table owed. With the passing hours the place filled up with night owls, the kind who have one drink and then stare intensely at the whores without saying a word, allowing their imaginations to run wild. By midnight I'd knocked back half a dozen beers. It was definitely time for me to go.

Outside I encountered a brutal high-mountain chill. The sky threatened to unload yet another deluge. The few stars that had been visible were now obscured and the wind hissed as it ripped over the mountaintops. Villa Fátima, a jumble of bungalows interspersed among the bordellos, sits smack in the middle of a ravine flanked by arid slopes. I could make out the trickling of a stream off in the distance. Before catching a taxi I decided to take a walk down Lambaque Street, which runs parallel to Avenida Tejada Sorzana. Red lightbulbs pointed the way to second-rate whorehouses worked mainly by half-breed women. As I started down the street, a dive with three tables and a counter caught my attention. In the doorway stood two transvestites caked in makeup as thick as the face paint used by Amazonian Indians. They blew kisses at the peasant riffraff walking by who weren't welcome at more upscale establishments. Tawdry, thin like sugar cane stalks, and short-legged, the transvestites stamped their feet in a vain attempt at keeping warm. Behind them, an inebriated lady shouted profanities at no one in particular.

When I walked through the entrance to one of those hot spots, a fat light-skinned half-breed grabbed me by the arm and declared she'd make my night for ten pesos. An exotic treat for some English tourist, maybe, but I wasn't in the mood to lift up five flowing skirts just to grab a piece of some lady's backside. So I kept walking. Once I made it back to the main road, I caught a taxi to Plaza Alonso de Mendoza.

The plaza was just about deserted, except for a couple of guys trading kicks and punches beside the statue of the founder of La Paz. A few curious onlookers formed a circle around the rumble without the least intention of getting between them. It was an entertaining match. Neither one had the faintest idea how to land a good blow, so they ended up just grabbing each other by the hair.

I climbed Evaristo Valle up to Plaza Eguino, where a solitary street vendor was hawking Korean umbrellas for five pesos. Two scruffy homeless men, as happy as Arab sheiks, carefully settled themselves into the cardboard house in which they were preparing to spend the night. A hooker with a medium build and a serious face was loitering in one of the corners of the plaza. She opened up her flowery umbrella, put one leg forward, and waited.

The cold was growing unbearable. Chilled to the bone, I returned to the hotel.

Chapter 5

Before dawn I woke to a gentle, tickling caress. It was Blanca reminding me of our date. I had been fast asleep and didn't hear her come in.

"What time is it?" I asked.

"About 5 in the morning. I couldn't come any sooner because it started to rain."

"Rough day, huh?" I murmured under my breath. As she came closer a pungent alcoholic aroma blew into my face, shaking me wide awake.

"It's like a pigpen," she said.

"What?"

"The second patio."

She switched on the light on the night table and started to undress. When she snapped off her corset, her breasts popped out wildly. She stood there completely naked, her light cinnamon skin shuddering at the slightest touch. She wiped her genitalia with some lotion and a piece of cotton. Without her gaudy get-up, she was like a different person. Who would have guessed that in a couple of hours she had gone through maybe twenty guys?

She slipped under the covers. Her body radiated heat like it was on fire, and when she covered my body with hers, from head to toe, it felt like I was inside an enormous banana peel. She wasn't used to being touched affectionately or delicately. The guys at the whorehouse humped her without even looking at her. Resigned and disgusted at the same time, she put up with their crude jerking and shaking. She got used to five-minute copulation sessions where she didn't experience the slightest physical pleasure. She had learned to detach herself from any kind of pleasant sensation, and over time evolved into a peerless screwing machine. But this night was different. I think she was discovering what it really felt like to be caressed and to hear sweet salacious nothings. Her movements stopped being automatic and she let my hands and my insinuations guide her. I witnessed a remarkable transformation. The word "spiritual" is too pompous to describe what I believe Blanca was beginning to feel. I can only say for sure that it was something she had sensed her whole life. It was always inside of her, but she had never before dared to experience it.

By the time the sun rose, Blanca was spent and sleeping serenely. That left me all alone with my angst, my ridiculous speculations, and my absurd answers for the puzzle in which I found myself. I didn't sleep. Instead, I stayed up listening to the thunderous pealing of the bells at Rosario's church and the early-morning shouts of vendors hawking hot empanadas. When I switched on Blanca's transistor radio, an announcer with a voice from beyond the grave remarked that the East Berliners wanted to put the Wall back up because even though they had lived poor, peacefully, and obediently before, now they didn't know what to do with so much freedom. I stood up and took a swig of *pisco* and soon dozed off.

Blanca gently shook me awake at 10 o'clock and made me a boiling cup of watered-down coffee.

"You don't look so hot."

"I feel like my hands and feet are tied," I said.

"Well, I slept like a queen," she proclaimed.

"Before I came back last night, I went for a walk on Lambaque Street. I had no idea so many half-breed chicks have flocked to the fornication business."

"They come here from the countryside," she said. "Because the economy's so bad, they put their asses out there for a couple of months and then go back home to be with their families and rest up. Then they come back here again as soon as the money runs out."

"It amazed me to see how well you know your business. I saw you make a lot of trips back to your den."

"That was nothing. You should see me on Fridays. By the time I finish I look like I've been beaten."

"I just hope you're saving so you don't run into the same problems as me."

She smiled. Her teeth shone as healthy as any I had ever seen.

"What does your dad say about all this?"

"Nothing—it would be a joke for him to try to teach me about morality. They eat with my money. Besides, money has no smell." She fluttered her eyelashes like Popeye's girlfriend. "How's the coffee?"

"A bit sweet, but good."

"What're you gonna do to get that money?"

"No idea."

"I'd never loan it to you even if I had it. I want you to stay here with me."

"Great, and what would I do?"

"You could take care of my daughter."

She tried to kiss me on the lips, but she didn't know how. She ended up just pressing her lips against mine.

"We've only seen each other three times. I could be a crook."

"My ex-husband was one of those. You're not like him."

"Who was he?"

"He worked in a sawmill in Riberalta. That's where I met him. He was a distant cousin of my mother's. I fell for his sweet talk, and only later did I find out he was a womanizer and that he snorted a lot of cocaine. He's totally irresponsible. These days he ships drugs to Brazil and goes around having kids all over the place. I haven't seen him in two years."

"If he's in the cocaine game, he must do well for himself," I remarked.

"He spends it all on women and booze. He'll probably turn up dead one of these days."

Barefooted and wearing a simple linen robe, Blanca was strutting around the room stealthily, like a mountain lion. She stopped to stare at me for what seemed like an eternity.

"You need someone to take care of you. You're gonna crack up. It's not good to be alone. Loneliness kills," she said.

She sat down on the edge of the bed and embraced me. Having seen her perform in Villa Fátima so naturally, it would be easy for me to think of her as just like any other tart: indifferent, uncouth, bitter, and beaten down by her tough life. But the girl lying on my lap didn't have a thing in common with those other high-altitude harlots, those boneheaded twenty-peso bimbos. Sure, her body had passed through hundreds of buyers, but her internal essence was still that of a country girl from the sweltering savanna. She was innocent and devoid of the slightest tinge of malice. The classic concept of sin did not exist for her. Her job was a simple business. Getting in bed with a new stranger every fifteen minutes didn't infringe the least bit on her morals. Her livelihood couldn't corrupt her little girl's soul. Her desire for affection was immense and she thought the only way to get it was by asking me to be her pimp. Ironic as hell, but life can be funny like that. Life makes a mockery of us all in the end.

The announcer for Radio Fides reported that striking miners were crucifying themselves in front of the public university.

"Where'd they ever get an idea like that?" Blanca asked.

"TV," I said. "*Spartacus* was on the other day."

An hour later I walked out to the patio. Don Antonio was having a foamy hot chocolate with a piece of bread, which he would dip and then grind with his bare gums. The solitary tooth left in his upper gum looked like a lighthouse in the middle of a reef.

"Alvarez, dear friend," he greeted, "how would you like some delicious chocolate?"

"Thanks, but if I mix that with the watered-down coffee I just had I won't feel any better than those wretched miners from Potosí."

"Look what we've come to!" he exclaimed. "The heroes of the national revolution crucifying themselves so that they don't get laid off."

"It's a great way to attract attention."

"A veritable banquet for the human rights folks," he stated. "I'm sure it's part of a plan hatched by the Bolivian Mining Company's foreign consultants. It is true, though, that our miners have always had a finely tuned sense of the pathetic. I'll head down there around 2 o'clock to cheer them on. We the dispossessed need to give each other a hand." He paused for a moment. "How'd it go with the agency?"

"They can get me a visa for eight hundred dollars."

"They went overboard. I don't think the lady from Tarija had that much dough. They must have thought you were a millionaire."

"If they look good, women don't need money to fix their problems."

"So you don't have eight hundred?"

"Not even close."

"Try mooching."

"The one who might eventually cave is my godfather, the barber. But he's so damn stingy . . . Mission impossible."

"And your son?"

"I don't even know where he is."

"Damn!"

"No one in Oruro would loan me the money. I owe a few pesos to the bank and to a shark, the one I gave a bad check to. I'm going straight to jail the minute he sees me."

"There's got to be a way."

"I'm going to pray to the Lord Jesus of May."

"Where is the Lord Jesus of May?"

"In San Agustín."

"Has he performed any miracles that you know of?"

"They say his shrine is filled with thank you notes."

"You've got to be kidding, Alvarez. I don't think of you as much of a believer. I see you more on the side of the agnostics or the atheists."

"I have faith. Only a miracle can save me."

"Lucky you. The Lord knows I've never been a believer." Changing the subject, Don Antonio added, "My intelligence service informs me that you've been receiving conjugal visits."

"No secret's safe around here."

"The manager would have a heart attack if he found out. In his fantasy world he's the Lord Byron of Illampu Street. He wouldn't allow for any challengers. The poor guy is obsessed."

"Where are the other guests of the second patio?"

"Gardenia is asleep. After a night that you could call hectic, it's a good thing he didn't bring any special friends back. The goalie rushed off to pick up the memorandum that will probably transform him into the new manager of the Customs Union in Santa Cruz, and the wine salesman is busy running around the city. The guy's a relentless walker, a pro at selling and even better at saving . . . I have a question for you, Alvarez. Could you spare five pesos?"

I handed them over to him. He kept his eyes on me, trying to discern my reaction.

"Tomorrow I'll be getting some cash from the hotel owner. I proofread an article he's writing about the Pacific War." Don Antonio served himself a second cup of chocolate. I noticed his asthma had intensified, perhaps because of the added humidity from the previous night's rain.

"I'm heading over to the university to check out the crucified miners."

"Careful the police don't whack you over the head. They're all on edge. Watching people crucify themselves is enough to knock anyone off his rocker."

An odd atmosphere pervaded downtown La Paz. Thousands of onlookers headed toward San Andrés University. On Avenida Montes, a column of police marched in pairs, helmets strapped on and army boots pounding against the pavement. An ancient fire truck sounded off a languid siren. Nobody could get into Plaza Venezuela; it was totally roped off. Hundreds of busybodies crowded against the statue of Marshall Sucre on horseback. You could make out the suffering miners from there. A Red Cross ambulance was parked in front of the Health

Ministry, ready to intervene in the event of any fatalities. The crucified miners had covered their bodies with tin cans that brightly reflected the sun. A police lieutenant was pointing and barking orders for the officers to take their positions in case the racket got out of control.

On the terrace in front of the university building, a red hammer-and-sickle flag was burning. Enormous portraits of Marx, Engels, and Trotsky hung from the windows of the top floor of the building. I hiked up Landaeta Street and then approached the university on J.J. Pérez. At the beginning of Avenida Seis de Agosto, a police cordon blocked the onlookers from getting any closer. The anti-strike dogs, a peculiar cross of native breeds and German shepherds, were kept on lockdown by the police. Egged on by the atmosphere of confrontation, the dogs barked as if they were staring at a hundred full moons. A couple of students on the university terrace tested the officers' patience, tossing stones at them like Palestinians in the Intifada.

The crucified miners were mortified by the unrest around them. If the cops set the dogs on them, the students would make a dash for the university building, leaving the miners for dead. The stalemate lasted about a half-hour, until the students got tired of throwing rocks and went home exhausted. A slender police officer with sunken cheeks ordered the troops to withdraw. The dogs retreated and the mass of people moved toward the terrace, where the miners had tied themselves to the fences surrounding the university garden. The spectacle was painful to watch and also, to a certain extent, laughable. The miners could have passed for actors in one of those Australian science fiction flicks. A veritable concert of banging metal pans and revolutionary songs started up. A photographer from a German television station set up his video equipment smack in front of one of the miserable crucified miners, just as the anchorwoman, a young Teutonic lady dressed warmly enough to scale Mount Illimani, smiled at the camera with a take-charge look. The crucified guy, a bearded miner, looked like a Thracian slave about to expire.

"How arre you doink?" the interviewer asked.

"Bad, really bad. Very cold. Nothing to eat."

"You spent ze whole night outside?"

The miner assented with a slight head nod.

"Can you hang in zere for anozer night?"

"We'll die here if the government doesn't give in."

"Vat do you vant?"

"To get our jobs back. They threw us out of the mines like dirty laundry after we spent twenty years frying our lungs to make the bourgeoisie richer." The miner was communicating in proper Spanish and seemed to be in good shape in spite of the cold, the wind, and the rain the previous night.

"Vat is your name?" the German lady asked.

"Benedicto Condori. I'm from Huanuni."

"Ven vas ze last time you ate?"

"A bowl of soup three days ago."

"How mutsh ver you making ven zey laid you off?"

"One hundred fifty pesos a month."

The German lady turned to face the camera and explained incredulously that that sum didn't even add up to two hundred German marks. The conversation came to a close and the camera crew ran off to look for more suffering miners. Another crucified guy was dramatically perched all alone on the edge of the university building's second-floor balcony. He was strung up loosely about two steps away from the abyss. The tin cans covering his body shook dangerously with the blowing wind. The guy didn't have a beard, but he did have a full head of hair that was tangled in the shredded wooly ropes lashing him to a flagpole. I figured the guy could tip over at any moment and, like a metal bird, come crashing down twenty yards below. Maybe that's just what the crowd was hoping for—a tragedy to put an end to their boredom.

A few minutes later, the terrace had become devoid of police and rock throwers and metamorphosed into a kind of outdoor fair. The miners elicited sentiments of pity and respect from most of the people, and in a few cases astonishment and mocking smiles. Classical music that would have been the delight of Bela Lugosi or Boris Karloff was blaring from the speakers on the fifth floor, serving as a kind of backdrop to that Pasolinian stage.

I walked along the railing to see if I knew any of the miners. After all, I was from mining country and I used to visit the great state mines four or five times a year. I soon noticed a guy named Justo Rojas, a deep miner who had been in the army with me. We were stationed together in an inhospitable barrack on the dry, frozen Andean plateau near the Chilean border at 16,000 feet elevation. Justo was graying and his bronze face had wrinkled, but otherwise he looked exactly the same. He recognized me as I got closer.

Chapped by the cold, his skin had acquired a violent tone. He was covered by part of a gasoline barrel that he had probably cut out himself and a few newspapers. A bowl-shaped sombrero crowned his head. Twenty years earlier he had been a sad, lonely guy. Maybe we had become friends because I honored his silence. I was the one who dragged him out to his first brothel, and I was the one who got him into his first fight in boot camp with a sadistic and racist sergeant who gave him an awful beating. A good Indian is a quiet Indian, and Justo started to talk too much. He'd been a Communist ever since he was a kid because of his father, a miner from Potosí who read Pablo Neruda and handled dynamite sticks like they were nothing. He first went to the mines to work at age twenty and returned every single day for the next twenty years. He studied the classical Marxists, and as far as I knew he never softened up like Gorbachev. Stern and proud, he was never an intellectual type or a yakking leader. He was always close to the grassroots, his feet firmly planted. I hadn't seen him in ten years. His black eyes brightened when he saw me.

"Hi, Justo."

"Hi."

"I thought I might run into someone here from the old guard."

Lost in a chasm of disquietude, his little eyes were ringed by heavy bags. He never could grow a beard. He was smooth-faced like most Indians, but he did have that long Amazonian tribal chief's hair running halfway down his back. His coca-chewer's breath elicited memories that I had long ago forgotten.

"I could get you some *pisco*," I said.

"Just water, friend. This is no party."

"I thought you were in Oruro."

"The mine is my destiny. I'm going to die there."

"A tough guy like you could stand this crucifying thing for a week, even if they nailed you to the fence."

"You're looking good," he said.

"I'm rotting on the inside."

"We're all rotting in this country. Only the dead are saved."

The onlookers milled around compassionately. One miner suggested it was about time he got taken to a hospital for rehydration, and a woman with a middle-class look to her bent over and gave him a piece of bread to chew on.

"If you want, I could bring the German TV crew over here," I said. "You'd be on display for all of Europe."

"I don't speak German," Justo said. A broad-backed woman wrapped in an alpaca poncho forced her way through the crowd. "She's my wife."

"Why don't you all keep moving? There are others worse off than my husband," the woman said. She was a housewife from Huanuni, nothing more and nothing less. Accustomed to suffering, resignation, and death. She looked me over sardonically.

"This is Alvarez, my buddy from the army," Justo murmured.

The lady sighed and then covered Justo's neck with a garment that looked like a scarf. "He told me about you," she said. "Would you crucify yourself?"

"Not for a miner's salary."

She smiled. "He catches colds that are like pneumonia. He's got bronchitis, so if he has another night like the last, it'll be over for him."

"Here's something for old time's sake." I handed the woman ten pesos, and she put them in one of Justo's swollen hands.

"It'd be good if one of us died on the cross," he said. "The political impact would be huge."

"There's no cross here. You're tied to a fence," I said.

"All you need is a little imagination," Justo replied.

A paramedic pushed me aside. He bent over to take Justo's blood pressure. "It's time for this one to go to the hospital," he announced after listening to his chest.

Justo's wife started to pray quietly. My friend stopped paying attention to me. I walked away toward El Prado, leaving all the hubbub behind.

The spectacle of the crucified miners left me sad and stimulated my appetite. I wandered the streets around El Prado until I found a dive in the basement of an old house that was about to be bulldozed. The windows on the first floor and on the upper floors had been boarded over. A couple of day laborers were busy nailing a poster in the doorway that announced the construction of a shopping center. The bar was the only sign of life in that decrepit adobe structure. I had hardly put a foot down in the place when a European-looking guy invited me to sit at his table. It was the owner, a Balkan, last name Landberg. He recommended the house specialty—suckling pig with a side of potatoes and salad, all for five pesos. A beer was the solution to help me digest the meat. After jotting down my order on a scrap of paper and handing it to a waitress, Landberg offered me his life story as an appetizer. He said that he was born in Riga, Estonia and had lived in Bolivia since the '50s. He confessed to me that he had helped the Germans during the Second World War because he was ethnically German and hated the Russians and the Poles. At first, while the Germans still had the upper hand, they had promised him a whole lot of land in the Ukraine after the war was over. In a shockingly sadistic manner, he told me about how he had dynamited a train full of Russians just as it was crossing over a bridge.

"A lot of people died," he explained seriously. "That's why the Germans awarded me a medal." He added that he made it to the outskirts of Moscow just as the rains started and got trapped in the mud, cold, and snow. He paused as the waitress set down a pitcher of beer. Later, they chased him all the way back to Germany, where he began to sense they would lose the war. He fled to Italy and then traveled to Argentina in the hold of a ship. The waitress put a piece of roast pig exuding a pleasant aroma right in front of my nose. Landberg waited for me to take a bite and then claimed it was impossible to eat pork that good, that cheap anywhere else.

"It won't give you trichinosis," he reassured me. "It's pork from Stege, nothing like what the half-breed girls here raise in the garbage dumps." After a moment, he continued: "I never got used to life in Argentina because the men there yell like Italians. So I decided to try my luck and got on a train to the Andean plateau. I had nothing to lose. I got married twenty days after arriving in La Paz. I got married three times and my third wife taught me how to cook. I landed a job in the Interior Ministry; this was back when the MNR was calling the shots. They needed guys with my kind of experience."

His story about the bridge reminded me of the one that Gary Cooper blew up in that movie about the Spanish Civil War, *For Whom the Bell Tolls*.

"Fucking Reds," he muttered.

"Is she your third wife?" I asked, nodding in the direction of the young woman working the cash register.

"No, that's Lola. She's just a friend who helps out around here."

"So they're going to knock this place down?"

"Not until they pay me ten thousand dollars to leave. If they hand over the ten grand, I'm gone the next day. If not, they can bulldoze this place over my fucking dead body."

"Don't you pay rent here?"

"Not a cent."

The pig went down like a piece of lead, and my conversation with Landberg didn't help any. Luckily for me, the Balkan gave me an after-dinner drink. It turned out that the guy had salami syndrome: First he tried to sell me an old car, then a television set, next a plot of land in Alto Beni, and finally a Hungarian salami.

I felt a little dazed and had a stomachache when I left the place. I headed over to the café at the Club de La Paz and gulped down three cups of coffee. The coffee reminded me of the American visa, and the America visa made me think about how pathetic my situation was at that moment. My other problem: I was nearly flat broke. I had fifteen pesos, fifty dollars, and ten grams of gold that, for all the good wishes of my dead old man, weren't multiplying for a damn. The Brazilians say, "If there's no solution, there's no problem." Aren't they smart! In Bolivia it's like we're all made of stone and whatever sticks to the stone, in time, turns into stone. I had a problem that was getting bigger and bigger with the passing hours, kind of like a giant snowball. Although I knew I didn't have any answers and that I was probably out of luck, a tiny light stubbornly burned on inside of me. Eight hundred dollars was the same as eight thousand or even eight million dollars to me. I thought about my godfather, and then about Blanca. My godfather was miserly and distrustful. Maybe Blanca could give me eight hundred dollars, bit by bit, under the condition that I protect and accompany her. As for my offspring, he wasn't giving any signs of life. That kid never did have his head on straight. Like father, like son.

I didn't feel like going back to the hotel or embarking on another drunken binge. My hangover was exacerbating my desperation. The best I could do was take a walk downtown to people-watch, window-shop, hike up streets, and then walk back down them again. I ended up sitting on a bench in the Plaza Murillo, staring at some pigeons munching on corn, and at congressmen and senators posing for the TV cameras. With their elegant attire, they looked happy and arrogant. A few were in full suits and the rest were wearing sporty dress shirts, unbuttoned at the top as was fashionable among the moderate left-wingers. I was lucky enough to catch a glimpse of a foreign ambassador climbing out of a limousine and entering the palace to meet with the president. He was wearing a morning coat. The palace guards paid their respects as the regiment's band started up with a tune that sounded something like a polka. A half-hour later, a group of peasants marched on the palace to defend their right to grow the millenarian and beneficent coca leaf, and not the damned coffee the gringos and their slaves in Bolivia's parliament imposed on them. They paraded in front of the palace shouting yays and nays, but nobody paid them any mind, not even the palace guards, who stood there straight as toy soldiers. An old pensioner, whose exact age was difficult to judge, started yakking at me about his sleepless nights in a public nursing home.

That was when I decided to head out. I left the scene with no set destination in mind.

Chapter 6

started down Colón, my hand braced against the wall so as to avoid falling flat on my backside. I walked all the way down to City Hall, took a seat on a dilapidated wooden bench, and asked a heavyset shoeshine boy to clean my boots. His face was swollen from too much boozing. He was talking up the new forward playing for Bolívar to another shoeshiner, who, being a fan of their rival, El Tigre, wasn't having any of it.

Next, I took off down Mercado Street and then, without thinking, out of pure boredom, stopped in front of a bookstore window. A fastidious bookseller was busy decorating the shelves, arranging in the shape of a fan several copies of a recently published book by an author named Mabel Plata. The book cover bore a seagull flying above choppy waters. I entered the bookstore and started flipping through some magazines. Their collection of publications ranged from *National Geographic* to issues of *Hustler* featuring bimbos striking raunchy poses, sometimes alone and other times beside heavily tattooed men. On the last page of one of the magazines, the amateur models had provided their addresses for receiving any sentimental correspondence. Though not aesthetically pleasing, the pictures were provocative.

I lost myself amidst gigantic shelves holding hundreds of books, ranging from children's stories to thick volumes on medicine, and a gamut of novels and short stories in between. I was never a fan of literature that talks about literature. I always liked noir novels about detectives and hoods that have clear beginnings and endings. Guys like Raymond Chandler and Chester Himes can change my life for a few hours, freeing me to see the world through the eyes of Philip Marlowe or Grave Digger Jones. Just then I stumbled across one of Himes's books, *The Heat's On*.

The first few lines had me hooked. I spaced out completely as the escapades of Coffin Ed Johnson and Grave Digger Jones lifted me away to the alleys of Harlem. Apparently, anybody who knows Harlem can tell you how hard it is to get out of that neighborhood. I didn't even notice that the bookstore employees had cleared the shelves, moved the furniture from one side of the room to another, and adorned the tables with placemats, where only minutes before there had sat enormous piles of books. They set out plates, glasses, flower pots, and pictures of Mabel Plata, a haggard-looking woman with protruding cheekbones and a sad, deep-set face. A waiter sporting an immaculate white jacket and black gloves was ceremoniously arranging bottles of Chilean champagne, as a plump balding man with a Nietzschean moustache barked out orders impatiently. I figured he was the owner of the bookstore and the organizer of Mabel Plata's book launch. I was just the party crasher.

I thought it would be prudent to make my exit, but not before taking Himes with me, hidden under my shirt and behind my belt. I hadn't stolen a book in twenty years, and I didn't want to lose the habit. I tried slipping away, but the street exit was roped off. The balding man approached me, Cuban cigar in hand, and then grabbed me by the arm with a big shot's self-assurance.

"This way," he said. "You're here just in time. I like punctual people. I'm hoping the rest of La Paz's bigwigs get here soon. Where do I know you from?"

"A long time ago I owned a used bookstore in Oruro."

"And . . . it tanked."

"How did you guess?"

"Books are a bad business in this country. Not a lot of people read and the few who do, they read about politics hoping that it'll be of use to them. What are you doing these days?"

"I don't make a good living. I'm planning to emigrate."

"To Australia?"

"South Africa. The white people are leaving because they're afraid the blacks will eat them alive now that they have the same rights."

"Do you like black people?" he asked inquisitively.

"I have a thing for black women. You've never seen a black lady lying naked on white sheets?"

"In Brazil, but I don't remember the color of the sheets," he said, laughing.

"The sheets must be white. It's the most erotic thing you'll ever see."

"I'm Salomón Urquiola. I own this place," he declared, holding out his hand, then averred, "thank God there aren't too many blacks in this country."

"That's why our soccer players aren't any good. They don't know how to move their hips," I replied.

Salomón Urquiola handed me a cigar and lit it for me. He seemed puzzled by my identity. He couldn't place me; he directed quick, polite glances in my direction. He was wearing a dark gray suit. His footwear, a pair of copper loafers that looked like they'd been run over by a steamroller, clashed with his brown socks.

Once the ropes were withdrawn, the guests, sporting their best party outfits, started to file in. They all greeted Salomón Urquiola in an orderly fashion as they entered. An older man with a fancy walking stick and wearing an English coat and an imported Borsalino felt hat strolled into the bookstore. His face rang a bell: Last name Mezquita, he was a famous right-wing man of letters who had been chummy with all the military dictators. A rather artless teller of Andean folk tales and legends, he was a writer of tepid prose but an excellent businessman. Successive military governments had used him to write long-winded newspaper articles extolling their virtues. Salomón Urquiola greeted him with a hug and some sweet talk to show what an incredible honor it was to receive such a distinguished guest. The guy thanked him and then cast a Napoleonic gaze out at the rest of the crowd. Once he determined there was no one else worth greeting, he became aloof like a celebrity trying to escape notice. As he made his way toward the back wall, the entire room broke out in applause. The guest of honor had arrived, the skinny lady in all the pictures. An indigenous-looking girl was escorting her by the arm. Mabel Plata was tired, but she mustered enough energy to acknowledge the crowd with a smile. She flashed a set of decrepit yellow-orange teeth as she extended a languid, pale hand to the owner.

"Dearest Mabel," Urquiola said in greeting.

"All those hills," Mabel Plata whined. "I don't know how I'd manage without Andresita."

Andresita, a peasant girl, was unable to repress the look of irritation on her face. At the end of the day, carrying an exhausted poetess on her back up and down La Paz's sheer streets was no joke.

Salomón Urquiola extinguished his cigar and raised his left arm. The chatting died down, the murmurs ceased, and he began. "Ladies and gentlemen, distinguished scholars. We are very pleased to be here today for the reading of Mabel's latest book of poetry. In light of the crisis affecting every level of society in this country, these are difficult times for the publishing business. But this book is destined to be the next big hit. We have all anxiously waited to hear what topic our beloved poetess will choose this time. Years ago it was *The Lost Love*, and next *Tremendous Solitude*, to be followed by that harrowing and magnificent story about alcoholism, and then that daring and painful confession about eroticism between two people of the same sex, reminiscent of Anaïs Nin, and now the sea . . . Yes, the sea that was taken from us by the treacherous Brits and the crooked Chilean bourgeoisie. The sea, so near and yet so far, the romantic and deep-blue sea that we all miss. It's a difficult topic for even the loftiest of pens, a challenge that Señorita Plata has bravely taken head-on. Out of this challenge a book of poems has sprung that is sure to make your eyes well with tears, while at the same time infusing you with the hope that we will one day soon return to our imprisoned Pacific coast. I must confess that I read it all in a single night, spellbound, as Mabel's magical pen whipped me away to the empty beaches of the Atacama Desert, which may not have received a drop of rain in three hundred years but are still filled with the tears shed by our immortal soldiers."

Salomón Urquiola capped his speech like an orator from colonial days, spreading his arms wide and gazing heavenward. He wiped away an invisible tear and immediately lit another cigar. A round of applause crowned his performance. Next, Señorita Mabel Plata released herself from the protective hand of her Indian servant and slowly, as if dragging a heavy chain, walked over to the podium. Standing with arms akimbo, she waited until it was so quiet that a fly's buzzing could be heard.

"My dear, lovely friends, I am truly grateful for such heartfelt words from the people's publisher, the most humane bookseller in our country. He said it well—a challenge it certainly was. The mere act of traveling to the beaches that were once ours in the distant past meant, for me, entering a hostile and ghost-riddled universe. My great-great-grandfather, Antonio de las Mercedes Plata, died in combat near Mejillones. To see the ocean, to be able to touch it, to rock in its waves, to gaze at the ships, to glimpse the tiny fishing barges, and to breathe the marine air was a truly sad and unsettling experience. Staring at the unruly ocean that used to belong to us, but that we lost thanks to our backstabbing mining oligarchy, shook the very foundations of my poetic sensibilities. I started writing in a hostel that faced the water and, like someone possessed, didn't put my pen down until the last sentence. Then a couple of Peruvian hooligans stole the pen from me on the flight back."

"Ahhh," the crowd groaned knowingly.

"I didn't stop writing until I ran out of energy and was on the verge of fainting. I didn't eat or sleep for three days and three nights. When I returned to my senses and freed myself from the lyrical demon that had possessed me, I fainted right in front of my Andresita and made her cry like Mary Magdalene. I had lost eleven pounds and only gained the weight back by eating seafood. So much seafood!"

The audience laughed earnestly. Once Mabel's imploring voice had faded into an inaudible whisper, they broke out in fervent applause. The right-wing writer, who seemed to be suffering from an excess of militaritis, whispered behind me, "Mabel's servant doesn't just cry like Mary Magdalene. She gets it on like her too."

"Get your mind out of the gutter," said an ageless lady who had wrapped her neck in a fox fur collar that smelled like urine.

"Lesbians have every right to love each other, ma'am. We've got to respect the feelings of others."

"People talk just because they're jealous," the fur lady interjected.

Once Mabel Plata had left the pulpit, several waiters appeared balancing trays that held sandwiches and empanadas. It occurred to me that if I stuffed myself with sandwiches, I would have a free dinner. But I hadn't taken into account how much our scholars can eat. The cheese puffs were gone in a flash, and I didn't get a single glass of champagne. A host of hands snatched up every last glass as if they were going for a rebound under a basketball rim. While I anxiously awaited the second round, I observed how the poetess, seated behind a desk, went about signing the books that the guests had bought. She showered them with angelic smiles while her companion, Andresita, curled up at her side, observed the buyers with an air of pity. Mabel Plata looked like she was flying high; money inspired her.

I finally caught sight of a food tray and, without hesitating, walked toward the waiter. I arrived in time to fill myself up with bread, jam, and caviar and make off with a glass of sweet white wine with a hint of resin. I sidled away from the distinguished revelers and tried to get my hands on all the booze I could. At such a high altitude, white wine is like poison, and within fifteen minutes I started to feel a throbbing pain in the back of my neck. While she babbled at her admirers, Miss Plata downed a bottle of red wine all by herself. The wine made her even more melancholy, and she started to shower each girl with kisses, caressing their hair with her dry veiny hands, which looked like knots. Everyone was delighted with her affectionate behavior, especially the bookstore owner, who was counting on the event to boost the sales of *Fresh Encounter with the Lost Sea*.

With all the guests packed together, you could feel the temperature rise. I felt distressed and started to experience the early symptoms of claustrophobia—anxiety and a racing heart. I cleared a path for myself through the guests and took a rest in the section with all the dictionaries and tourist guides. I was hoping the get-together would end sooner rather than later; that way I would be able to leave without arousing any suspicions. The Himes book was probably going to slip down to my private parts when I tried wriggling through the crowd again, and the store employees were bound to notice. They knew that the guests, for all their spiffy dress and high-society pedigrees, were always ready to rip off a good book.

I was trying to figure out the most subtle way to vanish from that place when I saw her enter the store. Tall and thin, her fine features looked like they had been carved by a virtuoso diamond cutter. Amidst that gray, insipid mob, she was like a mirage. She was about twenty-three years old with dark-brown hair, pearl-colored skin, and greenish eyes. She wasn't beautiful like a Hollywood actress, and physically she wasn't close to perfect in the classical sense. Still, there was something about her that made guys like me hold their breath; she made you feel like you were standing before someone from another planet. Mabel Plata lost her train of thought and sat there motionless when she saw her. The young woman walked up and planted a kiss on her cheek. The blood rushed to Mabel's face.

"What a wonderful surprise!" she managed to stutter.

"I wouldn't have missed it for anything," the new arrival replied.

Mabel Plata wrote an ethereal dedication on the first page of one of the books that Andresita handed her. Smiling, the young woman read the words that the poetess had scribbled and returned her kindness with another kiss on the cheek. Mabel Plata was transformed into a stalactite.

As soon as that exhilarating encounter was over, the young woman walked around, book in hand, greeting the people she knew. She was wearing an exquisite blue suit, black shoes, and, draped over her white blouse, a pearl necklace for which a mobster would have gunned down the entire crowd. My eyes followed her. I sensed that I would probably dream about her that night. After exchanging pleasantries, she ambled around the place by herself, leafing through magazines and pocket-sized books. She stopped about ten feet away from me. I was nailed to the floor like a tree, and not just because I could feel the aroma of her enchanting perfume: The slightest movement of my hips was going to send Himes crashing down my pants leg. Instinctively, like vultures eyeing a feast, the store employees wouldn't let me out of their sight. I smiled with the ease of an Englishman about to get strung up by a mob of irate Hindus. She took a cigarette out of a gold case and said, "Want one?"

"Sure, thanks."

"Oh, sorry, I think I mistook you for one of the clerks."

"That's okay." Her interrogating gaze gave off a hint of humor.

She lit a cigarette, passed me the package, and then took the most erotic drag I'd ever seen in my life. Her mouth lit up like a rose about to receive its first drop of morning dew. I tried to look tough when I lit mine, à la Philip Marlowe, but she wasn't impressed at all. My uptight-ness surprised her and she knit her brows deliciously.

"I wonder if they have Gramsci's complete works?"

Nobody was behind me, so I knew she had directed the question at me. "I have no idea. I'm here to see Mabel."

"Her trip to Chile didn't do her any good," she asserted. "Lately she's been feeling worse than ever. Apparently she didn't spend a single day at the beach. She's one of those people who hate the sun."

I took note of her languid, alluring eyes. "Who's Gramsci?"

"An Italian Marxist. I'm writing my thesis about his life."

"So what's a good-looking girl like you doing with a guy who's so out of style?"

"Are you joking?"

"Didn't all the Marxists get buried by the avalanche?"

She smiled. I felt old and incapable of receiving her smile. It wasn't mine for the taking.

"I always see the same people here," she said. "I mean, the same guests at the book readings. I've never seen you before."

"It's my first time."

"I thought you were Mabel's friend."

"I wish I was her friend, she seems so nice . . ."

"Together, Mabel Plata and Mezquita make a couple that would bore a Tibetan monk."

"To be honest, I'm trying to get out of here."

She stared at me with sudden interest.

"I just picked up a book by Himes and I don't plan to return it."

She gazed down, looking for the briefcase in which I had hidden the book.

"It's in between my legs. I'm not joking and I'm not trying to be crude."

"Why don't you just buy it?"

"It's fifty pesos!"

"Are you serious? You're hiding it in your pant leg?"

"I swear by the Virgin of Urkupiña."

"I'll help you leave."

I fell for her idea. If I left in the company of that baby doll, the clerks wouldn't even dare glance at me. I followed her as she exchanged smiles with the guests. She bade goodbye to the poetess with another kiss on the cheek. Mabel Plata's entire body shook. As soon as we were out on the street, she said, "I'm Isabel Esogástegui."

"I'm Mario Alvarez from Oruro. Where are you headed?"

"My car's parked a half-block from here."

"I'll walk you there. You saved me from looking like an idiot."

"Why did you lie and tell me you knew Mabel?"

"I don't know. I guess I wanted to impress you."

She walked slowly, her waist oscillating with distinction. Passersby, male and female alike, stared at her with either fascination or jealousy, but none with indifference. As for me, I had miraculously liberated Himes and I was trying to feel uninhibited. I was dressed like a Korean: pants, an open-necked shirt, and a drab jacket. If I'd been twenty years younger, it wouldn't have been so pathetic. Isabel wasn't the least bit embarrassed.

"Did you see the miners get crucified today?" I asked.

"I stopped by this morning. We're organizing a collection at the Catholic University."

"I was born in Uyuni and I used to hang around the mining camps when I was a kid. One of the guys who crucified himself is a friend of mine."

We crossed Colón Street. She entered a pharmacy, bought a rose-colored pill, asked for a glass of water, and swallowed the drink.

"My nerves are shot," she said. "Family problems."

"I've got problems too, but instead of pills I drink moonshine."

"What's that?"

"Cinnamon, cloves, extract of cacao, and alcohol. It's a poor man's drink."

"Where do you get it?"

"In the upper barrios; from Plaza San Francisco on up."

The sun's last rays fled behind the mountain range. The night was sneaking up on us. The skies were clear and there was a light wind, so light that it allowed me to inhale a whiff of Isabel's perfume. In the parking garage, a boy wearing overalls raced to bring her car, a Honda that glittered like it was right out of a TV ad. She handed the kid his tip and, settling into the driver's seat, asked me if I was headed for the southern part of the city. I thanked her for asking and tried to hold my ground. My knees were trembling as if I were about to take a penalty kick. She sped away, leaving me standing next to the kid in overalls. The little squirt exuded such a filthy odor that if I'd stayed any longer I would have felt sick for the rest of the night.

"So, she comes here every day?"

"Sometimes," he said. "But she's always with someone."

He let out an insolent laugh, just to make me understand that I didn't stand a fighting chance.

"Who the hell asked you if she came with anyone?"

He wiped the jackass expression off his face, did a one-eighty, and then vanished into the security hut.

I retraced my steps back down Mercado and stopped at the corner of Ayacucho Street to wait for the next minibus. Three of them overflowing with passengers raced by without stopping, and then the fourth one pulled over. Inside, I was greeted by a menagerie of odors. We made the trip to Manco Kapac Street pressed together like sardines.

Blanca was watching a soap opera while she waited for me in the lobby. She had caught the attention of a sleepy-faced man seated on the sofa who preferred the view of her rump to the hysterical shouting of the Venezuelan actors.

"Wanna eat?" she asked.

"I already pigged out on sandwiches in a bookstore, but I stole this book."

She flipped through the pages until she realized there weren't any pictures. "We're going to get a lot of customers tonight; there's a soccer game for the Liberators Cup. Do you know who's playing?"

"El Tigre."

"What's your favorite team?"

"The great Oruro Royal, may they rest in peace. There's going to be some serious celebrating if El Tigre pulls off the win."

"You mean that if they win, the men will all go out drinking."

I noticed that the redheaded manager was staring at us out of the corner of his eye. He clearly wasn't happy about the thing Blanca and I had going. Not because he had conservative beliefs about how hotel guests ought to behave; it probably annoyed him that someone could screw one of the whores without paying. That right was supposedly reserved for him.

"The manager won't stop looking at you. He's so horny that one of these days it'll make him sick," I said.

"He's disgusting. His skin is like the belly of a toad."

"He hates my guts," I added.

"Listen, if there aren't a lot of customers, I'll come back early." She took one of my hands in hers and played with it for a moment. "Your hands are cold. We've got to warm you up."

"I need some *pisco*."

"You're still thinking about that visa."

"I'm just thinking about taking care of you while you're still working," I said sarcastically.

"I wouldn't say anything I didn't mean."

"It's the first honest proposition I've heard in years."

"We'll talk about it tonight." She said goodbye to me. The clacking of Blanca's heels echoed as she made her way across the lobby.

The manager followed her movements with the expression of an idle executioner, then shot me an interrogating glance. I walked over to the second patio, where I found Don Antonio stretched out in a rocking chair, chatting with an unusual-looking fellow. The old man introduced us as soon as he saw me.

"Alvarez, friend, this here is the best wine-and-cheese seller in the city, the tireless, early-rising Rommel Videla." The salesman rose wearily from the tiny stool on which he'd been parking his skinny backside.

"How's it going?" I greeted.

He was a fifty-something guy, scrawny and with dry, wrinkled skin that made it look like he was convalescing after a recent illness. When I shook his hand, I sensed that he was transmitting all of his apathy and sadness to me.

"Rommel Videla, at your service," he said.

"Our buddy, Rommel, who was named in honor of the famous Desert Fox, is a tireless walker. Going door-to-door in a city that's shaped like a rollercoaster is a feat in and of itself," Don Antonio explained. Rommel Videla was a white man, but his impassivity was like that of an Aymara.

"Do you drink wine?" he asked me.

"I'm mostly a beer drinker. Wine is bad for my blood pressure."

"That's a shame," Videla said seriously. "I represent the Paz y Paz wineries in Tarija, and for cheese, the San Ignacio estate in Santa Cruz."

"Alvarez, have you read Omar Khayyám?" Don Antonio asked.

"I don't remember."

"He was a magnificent Persian poet who used to sing verses praising the virtues of wine."

"Unusual for a Muslim," I said.

"There are lost sheep even in Allah's kingdom."

Rommel Videla looked at me as if I were easy pickings. "If you know anyone who needs any cheese or wine, let me know," he exhorted.

He had a thick, ceremonious radio broadcaster's voice, which didn't at all match his slight, atrophied frame. I nodded and then left for my room. I wondered to myself if the gold my father had given me was still in the little bag at the bottom of my suitcase. It was. I grabbed the sack with the nuggets and returned to the patio.

"All of these comings and goings are for the visa?" Don Antonio asked.

"It's more complicated than you'd think," I said.

"If you take this thing too seriously you might end up with a visa to the cemetery," Don Antonio said. "Alvarez here is planning a trip to the United States."

Videla swiveled his head as if it had been wound up like a toy.

"You know where I could sell a couple of pounds of gold?"

The salesman half closed his eyes. "I could call up a friend of mine, if you made it worth his while."

"Ten grams," I clarified humbly.

Videla smiled with the top half of his lip, while the bottom half remained motionless. "If you head up Max Paredes, you'll find hundreds of buyers."

"I haven't laid my eyes on gold since the '50s. I gave up my last chunk in Valparaíso, in Chile, in exchange for an unforgettable night," Don Antonio mused.

"Max Paredes," I repeated.

"You can't miss it," Don Antonio said. "The bottom of that street is crawling with Koreans."

Chapter 7

spotted Koreans in the doorways to their fabric stores. Father, wife, and kids, they worked industriously as a family unit to run small but efficient businesses. They shouted at the top of their lungs and always seemed to be engaged in verbal altercations. Before arriving at the sprawling indigenous encampment that made up the Black Market, I began seeing *We Buy Gold* signs pointing the way to modest stores—hole-in-the-wall offices in tiny patios or at the ends of narrow alleyways, in which jewels and silver objects were sold. I observed that half-breed women monopolized the gold trade. You could find them seated behind shabby little tables, handling rusty scales and estimating values with their pocket calculators. Even though I was carrying just a small sum of gold in my pocket, their scornful, foul-tempered expressions didn't exactly inspire my confidence. Some of them conducted business behind makeshift stands facing the street. They didn't seem to be afraid of muggers or even petty thieves. I looked around in vain for a police-man somewhere in the vicinity, but the coppers were glaringly absent.

I ended up on Ortega Way, which links Max Paredes with Tumusla. It was packed with people browsing amidst the tented vendor stalls, which rose up on both sides of the passage. As in nearly all the narrow corridors in La Paz's working-class neighborhoods, Ortega Way was divided into sections. I cut past stands offering notebooks and all kinds of school supplies for sale. Next up were the stands selling shoes, undergarments, liquor, eggs, and garlic, followed by booths that over-flowed with used clothing.

I needed a hard drink or two to get through the afternoon. I walked into the Luribay, a hostel with a grimy dive on the first floor. The place had a spacious counter, plenty of stools, and a bartender who looked like he'd had his face smashed in a hundred times. I asked him for a double moonshine. He kept them lined up on a shelf behind the counter. They cost one peso a pop and there were different kinds for people who were just warming up, people who already had a good buzz, and people who were about to black out. According to a vagrant swaying drunkenly beside me, the bartender's last name was Yujra, and he was once the pride and joy of Bolivian boxing back in the 1960s. He was a raging alcoholic who kept in shape by giving a whipping to the bums who made a ruckus in his bar.

I sat at a table next to a window with a view out onto the alleyway. I was just finishing my second moonshine when, by chance, a house facing the bar from the other side of the street caught my attention. A gold dealer had an office on the second floor. The building's façade was worn and chipped, but the floor with the gold business looked spacious, clean, and prosperous. I noted the presence of a neatly dressed woman who managed the transactions from her desk, on which an array of gadgets sat at her disposal: calculators, the indispensable scale, two telephones, and a computer. The lady was dealing with a man who seemed to be a gold runner. He handed her a little bag, which she emptied onto one of the arms of the scale and then carefully weighed the gold. She jotted down the price in a notepad and showed it to the man. He accepted and the lady led him to a small safe that was built into a wall. She twisted a knob from left to right and then from right to left several times, opened the safe, took out some pesos or dollars, and, after counting them, paid the man, who stashed the dough away in his jacket pocket.

The seller left. The woman picked up the phone, said something, and then hung up. After fixing her hair, she lit a cigarette and pressed a buzzer. Immediately, a half-breed appeared with a bundle tied to her back. They exchanged pleasantries and then the half-breed untied her colorful bag and handed over a small box fastened shut with braided rope. The lady removed the box lid and I thought I saw a couple of bars of gold. She repeated the operation with the safe and the money, except this time my eagle-eye, still sharp after all these years, spotted a fat pile of greenbacks changing hands. My mouth started to water. It was in that crazy moment, I don't know whether from heaven or from hell, that the idea came to me to plan a robbery. Unfortunately, I wasn't a professional, or even an amateur with a poor track record. The most I had ever stolen was the leather jacket from the Slav I used to work for. I had been crossing the Chilean border at Tambo Quemado, when I opened up one of my suitcases containing contraband goods and spotted the jacket. I wore it with the intention of returning it, but since the guy never said anything, I just held on to it.

The retired boxer, who by that time, nearly 8 o'clock, had already given three troublemakers the boot, asked me if I wanted a fourth moonshine.

"I'm going to sell a few grams of gold and then I'll be back," I whispered under my breath.

The old boxer had been hit in the head so many times that he was deaf as a fence. "What's that?"

A coarse light-skinned woman—the kind you would call white trash in North America—shouted, "He says he's going to sell some gold and then he'll be back!"

Twenty drunkards did immediate one-eighties. They stared at me as if Paul Getty himself had descended from the heavens.

"Try Señora Arminda's place, they pay dollars," Yujra said.

I tiptoed out of the bar. With Yujra staring them down, none of the vagabonds dared to move.

I crossed the street and pushed open a heavy door. To my left, a cement staircase led up to a mezzanine. I climbed the steps and knocked on the door. A young man opened it and greeted me with a surprised expression on his face. His dark brown eyes penetrated me like lasers.

"Yes, señor?"

"I'd like to sell some gold," I said.

"We're about to close," he replied.

"It'll just take five minutes. I'm leaving on a trip tonight."

"You should have gotten here earlier. This way."

I entered a small lobby where a man and a woman were waiting. The woman guarded an enormous purse against her chest and the guy, judging by the way he was stooped over, looked like he stood about 6'5". The woman was dark-skinned with Arab features. She was wearing a sports jersey that read *Dodgers* on the front and tennis shoes, the kind that the American basketball players made fashionable. The man was staring at a photo album. He had a briefcase trapped between the boots that Santa Claus had loaned him. Everything about him was astronomical. Instead of getting pulled from his mother's womb, he must have exploded out. I had never seen a guy like that before. He was wearing a raggedy sweater and jeans that only reached down to his shins, leaving exposed his thick wool socks.

The buzzer sounded. The young man told the lady with the purse that she could proceed into the office. Meanwhile, the giant dug up a little bag of peanuts and dried beans from one of his pockets. It's not easy to peel dried beans, but he squashed them just by rubbing them between his thumb and index finger.

"You from Guanay?" he asked me.

"Oruro."

"Gold runner?"

"I only have ten grams, a little something I inherited."

"Doña Arminda doesn't buy jewels."

"They're gold nuggets."

"My name's Cabral. I'm from Tipuani. All I got on my last trip was a two-pound piece I bought off a gold-mining expedition. Sometimes I go to Guanay or to Mapiri. You know the area?"

"I've only been as far as Caranavi."

"Gold country is real beautiful. It's a true paradise."

"Two pounds is ten thousand dollars," I calculated out loud.

"Just about," the man said.

When he stood up, he looked like an NBA basketball player. His arms were so long he could scratch his knees without bending over an inch. He cracked open peanuts and wolfed them down with the speed of an ape as he walked pensively from one side of the room to the other. His face, with its prehistoric features, looked like something that had escaped from an archaeology museum. He had a Neanderthal's head, crowned by a mop of hair big enough to shelter a serpent. When he breathed, he inhaled such large whiffs of air that if they sealed off the room, I imagined we wouldn't last twenty-four hours.

He passed me a fistful of peanuts and remarked casually, "Nothing better for a good hard-on."

"I always thought it was chili."

"That's Indian bullshit," he said.

Admiring his colossal stature, I asked, "How'd you get so big?"

He smiled like a spoiled young boy. "It's in the family. My father's a 6'4" Peruvian from Chimbóte, two inches shorter than me. He came to Bolivia and got married to a big-boned descendant of Spaniards from Alcoche. You gotta be made of good wood to handle life in the tropics. My brother Carlos is 6'5" and left for Argentina years ago. He used to be a professional wrestler until they broke three of his ribs. Then he became a pizza delivery man and now he lives in Tandil. Between you and me, buddy," he whispered, bending over, "my cock is eight-and-a-half inches long. When I go out whoring, they charge me a hundred pesos. Nobody wants a piece of me."

"You must like being on top," I quipped.

"I've been in the gold business twenty years. Gold fascinates me, but I never hold onto it. It brings bad luck. Gold dealing is interesting work, but it's risky. Everyone wants to cheat the other guy, so you gotta know how to buy. It's dangerous. There are a lot of bad apples out there."

"A person would have to be crazy to try to rob a guy like you. It would be like ripping a ring off Mike Tyson's finger."

"Don't believe it; it's happened twice. The first time a mixed black-Indian guy from the Yungas and a Brazilian, both armed with knives, tried to rob me at night in Tipuani. I split the black guy's head open with a rock and smashed the Brazilian in the balls until he started to sing the national anthem."

"His or ours?"

He ignored my comment and continued: "The second time, I was coming back from Caranavi in the back of a fruit truck. When we were passing by Unduavi, some prick gave me coffee laced with sleeping pills. I woke up the next morning at the public hospital. They had thought I was done for. The guy who gave me the coffee vanished into thin air with my pound of gold. How about that?"

"It was the only way he could have robbed you."

Somebody knocked on the door. The helper guy opened it cautiously. In came a small peasant carrying an egg basket. He counted out three dozen and the helper paid him.

"Arminda's husband is from down east, and for breakfast every morning he has four eggs and a couple of steaks."

"Poor liver! If all that food goes down, he must be your size."

"He's pure flab, a hundred and ninety pounds of fat."

"He doesn't come by to give Arminda a hand?"

"She works alone with Severo."

"He's the helper?"

"Yeah, her husband is an antique coin collector. He makes his rounds on Sagárnaga Street at around 11 in the morning. Doña Arminda is the main gold buyer in the city. Haven't you seen her ads in the paper? There are four different people with four different phone numbers. You call and they all give you the number of this place. She monopolizes the bulk purchases."

"What does she use it for?"

"Who knows."

The woman with the purse exited the office. The big guy stood up, waited for the doorbell to ring, and pushed open the door. I heard him greet someone. Severo was reading the Spanish magazine *Gente*; he was smaller than me and weighed about twenty pounds less. I could have maimed him with a couple of punches . . . unless he was a karate master. Even so, it couldn't hurt me to have a lead club handy. A blow to the lower neck would knock him out cold. And yet, something was bothering me. If Arminda bought so much gold, she had to have at least a couple of guys watching her back. Severo wasn't much protection, so if Cyclops was telling the truth, this robbery was child's play.

"What time are you open till?" I asked Severo casually.

"Until 8, sometimes 8:30. Depends how busy we are." He looked at me askance; he clearly didn't like my questions.

"That's the first time I've seen a giant with so much gold. Usually they're off in the circus working for pennies," I said.

"That guy's no freakin' joke," he replied.

"Couldn't hurt to have him here for security."

Severo punished me with a weary and disdainful glare. "We don't need anyone," he said.

What did he mean by that? That he was alone or that undercover bodyguards were lurking around in case they needed a hand? I prudently shut my mouth. Severo was going to get suspicious if I kept interrogating him, so I left him alone. He was quietly reading out loud and his cologne, which smelled like marijuana, was starting to make my head spin. Before five minutes had passed, the behemoth emerged, smiling from floor-to-ceiling. I noticed a fat wad of greenbacks nestled in his jacket pocket. When he gave me a goodbye shake, my hand disappeared inside his paw.

"Come in," Severo indicated.

I was greeted by a woman in her mid-thirties with blackish hair and white skin. Though not graceful, her features were pleasant. She had a full, sensual face, and her eyes, which were the same color as her hair, shone nobly. Her lips looked like those of a figurehead on a ship's prow, forming a faint, friendly smile. She was wearing a sky-blue blouse covered by a blue sweater, and a skirt that left exposed a pair of finely sculpted legs. She had the hands of a woman who liked to please and they were shaking nervously. Blushing, I handed her my tiny stock of gold. With precise hand movements, she took the lid off the bottle as she had before and picked up a testing saucer on which she deposited the gold. Next, she dumped acid on top and awaited the result.

"Twenty-four karat gold." She placed it onto one of the dishes on the scale. "Ten grams at ten dollars makes one hundred dollars, or three-hundred and eighty pesos. Okay?"

"I won't get very far with that," I said.

"Depends how far you want to go. Are you a dealer?"

"No. When my dad handed this stash down to me, he told me to make it multiply like the loaves in the New Testament. But with the economy as bad as it is, it's not so easy to recreate the Lord's miracles."

Doña Arminda shot me a good-natured smile and pulled open one of her desk drawers. She counted five twenty-dollar bills, piled them on her desk, dumped out the gold into a case the size of a shoebox, and put it away in another one of her desk drawers. The safe that I had glimpsed from the Luribay was half-open. With my heart in my throat, I saw bars of gold and small silk bags of various sizes, which surely contained nuggets or gold dust. Not even Captain Flint's treasure chest would have gotten me so worked up.

"Very kind of you," I said. "I'll stop by sometime later with a few more grams."

"From 9 o'clock on. We close for lunch."

Surrounded by a modern Japanese décor, Arminda gave off an impression of omnipotence and total self-confidence. I don't know if it was the smell of so much money in the air or the sight of the magnificent calves of that gold queen, but I started to feel a gurgling in my bowels. I left her surrounded by her treasures.

Out in the waiting room, Severo was vacuuming the hardwood

floor and whistling a tune by the Kjarkas. He hurriedly showed me to the door. "Good night," he said.

I didn't respond, simply because my mind was off somewhere else. The thought of what a racket life is—the way it showers a select few with riches and leaves the rest of us with just dreams—was eating away at me. I crossed the street and rested against the frame of an old door to a fruit store. With a theatrical flair, a trembling and sorrowful half-breed woman offered me a bunch of bananas. I lit a cigarette, returned to my senses, and went back to the Luribay.

It was a rowdy time of night. The stench from all the vagrants' breath was strong enough to launch a space rocket. I saw a half-breed lady dressed in rags and wearing a tight cap on her head yell at someone behind her, "How dare you lift up my dress!"

"Shut up!" the barman shouted back in Spanish and in Aymara. "Shut the hell up!"

The half-breed lady stared at him with a glazed look in her eyes. She lowered her head. Yujra stuck out his disfigured face and asked me, "Another one?"

"One double moonshine with lots of cinnamon."

I walked up to the window that had become the perfect lookout. From there, I continued studying Doña Arminda's harmonious routine.

My espionage didn't last long. She closed the curtains to her office, leaving me hanging. Doña Arminda was presumably starting to tally the day's inventory.

I felt the same kind of feverish excitement that I had experienced decades earlier when my father took me to see the ocean for the first time. Just like then, the horizon suddenly seemed to clear out and all of those gray clouds that hovered over my life dissipated. A magical

and energizing sensation rushed over me. With some smarts and a little bit of luck, maybe I could put an end, once and for all, to that heavy
frustration that had plagued me ever since I received the first letter
from my son, in which he proposed to meet up with me in the land to
the north.

The problem was that, frankly, I didn't see myself as a competent
outlaw. When I used to play cops-and-robbers as a kid, I always wanted
to be one of the good guys, and if it was my turn to play a gangster, I was
a terrible actor. I had always been a sorry and repentant ruffian. Years
later, after Antonia's one-way trip, a few buddies of mine asked if I
wanted to work as a mule and carry two kilos of cocaine to Buenos
Aires. I turned it down out of the fear of ending up behind bars, dis-
graced. I preferred to be an easygoing middleman without any ambi-
tions, a guy who doesn't have to put himself or his money on the line.
For the first time in my life, however, I now felt that I was ready to put
all my cards on the table.

In reality, I didn't have much to lose. If they caught me, they'd lock
me up in the slammer to bask in the sun for about five years, to drink
their horrendous coffee and bread, to stuff myself with their dog meat,
and to rub elbows with the most miserable riffraff in La Paz's underworld. But if I managed to get my hands on a few thousand dollars, or
at least the eight hundred to pay the guy at the travel agency, my life
would change completely.

Get a move on, Alvarez: Time for Operation Lazarus.

I anxiously finished my fourth moonshine. I was about to ask the
boxer for a fifth, when I saw the lights go off in Doña Arminda's office.
I rushed to pay and then cleared a path through the throng of boozers
crammed into the Luribay. Once outside on Ortega Way, I hid between
two vendor stands, beside a half-breed lady selling imported shoes who

could have played Emperor Nero without wearing any makeup. It had never occurred to me that Arminda and Severo, weighed down by all that gold, might make the trip home without a hired gun. They had to have a trick up their sleeves. There was bound to be at least a third man, armed to the teeth, to walk them as far as Tumusla Street. I calculated that it was a distance of about two hundred feet. Another route would be for them to walk to Max Paredes, which was only a hundred feet away.

Nightfall arrived dark, overcast, and silent. Ortega Way was deserted, surely because of the soccer match. The biggest show in town, El Tigre, was playing. Despite the numerous bulbs hanging from lampposts, the street lighting was relatively scant, perfect for an abrupt and violent heist. My imagination was a series of noir films in which I was the guest villain.

To my utter surprise, they were walking down the street alone. She was carrying a James Bond–style briefcase, and Severo, a standard duffel bag. It all looked way too naïve; everyone knew they had a fortune on them. I followed from a safe distance, concealed among the street vendors and the passersby. I walked bent over, as though looking for dropped coins.

They arrived at the corner of Ortega Way and Tumusla Street. *Elementary, my dear Watson*, I said to myself. A vehicle must be waiting for them. While hiding behind the back of a homeless man wrapped in a mass of rags, I took a chance and got to within ten feet of them. Arminda was chatting about the bad weather that was on its way, without showing the least bit of precaution. Severo looked up at the starless sky. Suddenly, he raised his arm and hailed a passing taxi. He opened the front door of the car for his boss, who sat down next to the driver, and then settled in beside her in the window seat. A pair of lovebirds was curled up in the back, leaving room for a third passenger. Without thinking twice, I hopped into the vehicle.

"Corner of Ballivián and Colón, please," Arminda said.

"And you?" the driver asked, looking at me through his rearview mirror.

"I'll get off around there," I said in a fake voice.

La Paz is a peaceful city. In spite of all the misery and alcoholism, assaults and robberies aren't as commonplace as in other South American capitals. It's unusual to hear news of a bank getting held up at gunpoint. That being said, Arminda and Severo were extremely unwise to go for a taxi ride loaded down with gold and dollars in the upper barrios of the city. They were tempting the Devil, and at that moment the Devil was me, scared stiff but lying in wait.

The driver looked like a bronze bulldog. Tormented by the traffic jam, he took out his frustrations on his change box, smashing it sadistically. At the Plaza Murillo, he said: "You can get off here. I'm headed to Miraflores to drop off the taxi."

"No problem," Arminda said. They got out and headed for Ballivián Street. The driver frowned at me in his mirror.

"I'm getting out too," I declared.

They were walking hurriedly, as they should have been. I had a tough time keeping up with them. When they paused at a traffic light, I went up to a kiosk and bought myself a pack of gum. In spite of the thick jacket covering her body, Arminda's derrière swayed provocatively. They hung a right at the corner of Colón Street. I sped up to keep pace. To my surprise, halfway down the block they vanished into the doorway of an ancient-looking, two-storied house. Hundred-year-old adobe blocks jutted out of the crumbling stucco façade. I waited at the corner, weathering the wind and cold. It was an uncomfortable time of night to be an undercover sleuth. I consoled myself thinking that those four shots of moonshine had prepared me for this very moment.

I lay in wait for barely five minutes. Empty-handed and with the smile of a job well done, Severo suddenly emerged from the doorway of that big house. Without hesitating, he headed off down the hill and then made a pit stop at a cheap eatery. He pushed open the door, but not before shooting a snooty glance at the menu nailed to a wall. Arminda had obviously stayed behind. I walked away from the corner and crossed the street, heading for the big house. Just inside the spacious doorway, I found myself in a sort of corridor that ended in a small colonial-style patio. At the center of the patio stood a dry, cracking fountain covered by a yellow tarp.

Halfway down the corridor, a shoemaker had set up shop behind a wooden stand. The shoemaker, a tiny and slovenly man with a throwback Rudolph Valentino–style hairdo, was busy resoling a shoe. A lightbulb stained black by buzzing flies lit up the stand. The shoemaker was so focused on the task at hand that he didn't even notice when I passed by two feet away. The striking of his hammer made enough noise to smother the sound of a charging rhinoceros. Ringing the patio was an old-fashioned railing that supported a wall of glass. On the first floor, a series of old signs pointed the way to entrances to stores that had already closed for the evening. A stone staircase led to the top floor, which was divided into two apartments. In the patio a bunch of kids, both boys and girls, were chasing some poor bowlegged dog. One of the apartments was shrouded in silence. Arminda surely lived in one of the two. If Arminda was the mother of that host of screaming dwarfs, then things weren't looking good. Robbing the home of a family of six in La Paz was an impossible task. On the other hand, if she lived in the other apartment, who knew what surprises awaited me?

I lit a cigarette and mentally retraced my steps. There wasn't a whole lot to think about. My plan was completely ludicrous, the frustrated dream of a harmless guy who read Raymond Chandler, Chester Himes, Dashiel Hammett, and Manuel Vásquez Montalbán as if they were prophets. I didn't have the balls for the job. And yet, a wicked force inside me that I had long ignored pushed me to continue with the adventure, which seemed more like a quixotic farce than a serious and thoroughly planned professional robbery. I resolved to return to the street, and as I passed by the shoemaker and his shoes, I spotted a beautiful blue Mercedes easing to a stop at the opposite end of the corridor. The passenger door opened and a man dressed in a fine gray coat stepped onto the sidewalk. His raised collar covered half his head and I couldn't make out his face. I moved closer to the shoemaker's hut and played dumb. I listened to the guy's footsteps, to the shoemaker's gruff greeting, and to a raspy voice responding with an elegant high-society grunt. The guy from the Benz didn't even notice me standing there, concealed beneath the sinister light. He arrived at the patio and climbed the left staircase. He tapped on one of the doors three times, as if it were a secret code. A woman's hand emerged and then, like a caress, with a slow and sensual movement, dragged the guy into the apartment. It could have been a scene out of a movie by the British filmmaker Carol Reed. Despite not hearing very well, the shoemaker evidently had the radar of a bat; without looking up, he asked, "What can I do for you?"

I sat down on the bench in front of him and responded: "I'd like you to give me half a sole."

"That'll be fourteen pesos."

"Per shoe?"

"Of course," he said without batting an eyelid. For the first time I noticed his eyes, cloudy like those of an aging cat. I handed him one of my shoes and he turned it over and over again, studying it. He was badly nearsighted, and his eyeglasses were the size of two magnifying glasses.

"When did you get these shoes?" he asked.

"I first used them during the '78 World Cup in Argentina."

"Bolivia didn't even qualify."

"I said I bought them, not that I played with them. They're classy shoes, Plus Ultra."

"That's a good shoe. They don't make them that way anymore. How many times have you had your soles changed?"

"I don't remember."

The shoemaker smelled like paint thinner. You didn't have to look at him twice to realize he was high off his ass.

"It would be best if I put in some neolite rubber soles. Otherwise, they'll crack at the heels."

"This house is one of the oldest in the city," I said, changing the subject.

"They say it used to belong to Don Ismael Montes. They can't knock it down because it's in the historic district, luckily for me and the other artisans here. Rents have gotten so high in the city!"

"The guy who just walked in is the owner, right?"

"Him? Nah. The owner is an old bat who lives in Arica. The guy with the Mercedes is a tenant. Of course, he doesn't live here. He just uses it as a den for bringing back chicks. I've seen all kinds go through there. Lately he's been with this chubby lady who always spends an hour with him."

"What time do you work till?" I asked.

"Today it took me awhile to finish these Texan boots for a friend who lives in New Mexico. But usually I go home at 8:30, sometimes earlier."

"Some bachelor pad," I affirmed.

"He does her twice in an hour," he said, then twisted his jaw in a mocking sneer.

"These rich guys won't do it more than once," I suggested. "They're too selfish to put in the extra effort."

He broke out in laughter and then started to pound my other shoe. While he worked away, I took a quick stroll around the patio to see if I might discover anything interesting. Silence imposed itself once the screaming little ones went in for dinner. Meanwhile, the guy with the Mercedes and Arminda were moaning and getting it on upstairs.

Ten minutes later the shoemaker handed me my boots. It cost me almost thirty pesos! All my fucking around was getting expensive.

I left the house and walked down Colón. The shoemaker was right: Without the neolite soles I'd have busted my tailbone on La Paz's steep streets. I passed right by Don Otto's, where I saw Severo devouring a succulent pork chop with a jumbo-sized serving of french fries. While he ate his dinner, he didn't miss a second of a soap opera special on TV. A bottle of beer accompanied his feast. To get more comfortable, Severo had taken off his jacket and rested it on the back of his chair. At first, I thought that the thing sticking up out of the lining of his sport jacket was his leather wallet, but a second look convinced me that it was the butt of a revolver. So the sidekick was armed. No two ways about it, he was all the protection she had. No one in his right mind would pay three cents to look like that ugly stuck-up prick, but the guy was no doubt a legitimate thug disguised to look like an accounting assistant or an errand boy. That asshole could probably shoot a gun just as naturally as he swept up dust in the office.

I kept walking and then dropped anchor at the corner of Colón and Comercio. I was as confused as a Saharan on the high seas. For starters, because I'd never been so close to so much money before; second, because I was playing along with a game that was threatening to become reality; and third, because I was scared to death just thinking about it.

I walked back up Colón. I tried getting into Our Lady of Carmen Church, which faced the old house, but the entrance was closed. There were just a couple of inebriated beggars outside. The cold was growing more intense by the minute. Off in the distance, I could hear the roar of the crowd jammed into Hernando Siles Stadium. Crossing Ballivián Street, I came upon an open pharmacy. The pharmacist, a balding man with an optimistic look about him, was fixated on the soccer game on the radio. An aging, nearly toothless prostitute was wandering about with little hope of reeling in a customer. She approached me and asked what time it was. I told her.

"You don't want to talk for a while?" I asked.

She observed me as if she were having a close encounter of the third kind. "What about?"

"I'm not from around here and I feel lost," I explained. "I haven't said hi to anyone for a week."

She smiled, hiding her teeth. Thirty years prior she must have been a very beautiful woman. "Where are you from?" she asked.

"Uyuni."

"Where's that?"

"Down south. It's colder there than it is here."

"*Brrr*. I'm from the Chaco. It gets hot over there. You've never been to the Chaco?"

"What is there to do in the Chaco?"

"Go fishing in the Pilcomayo River."

"You're going back there when you retire?"

"Retire from what?"

"You don't work?"

"Don't play dumb with me. What are you doing just standing here?"

"Nothing."

"You don't want to go for a walk?"

"With this cold, it would be useless for me to even try."

"I'll warm you up." She lifted up her skirt a little, revealing a soccer player's thigh.

"Looks tasty, but I can't."

"Twenty plus the room."

"You must have been really beautiful once . . . you still are," I said.

She opened up her purse, unzipped a pocket, and showed me a photograph. "This is from when I was fifteen."

I was right. She had been a precious little thing with a clean face, full of promise. I felt bad for having started up the conversation with her. The photo depressed me.

"It must be a long and sad story."

"Mine? Not so much. I don't regret anything. I had good times and bad. Things get tougher when you get older. The most important thing is to enjoy being young while you can. When you're old you only need a few pesos to eat . . . I'm gonna get going. If I don't find anyone, tomorrow will be a rough day."

She walked off with a certain Andean majesty. Years of wear and tear had taken a toll on her black coat, which looked like it weighed two hundred pounds.

Around 10 o'clock the Mercedes appeared like a beautiful cat under the moonlight, shining and stealthy. It stopped. The driver honked three times and then turned off the motor. I barely had time to take a leak on the side of a thick wall. When I returned, the opulent owner of that marvelous machine emerged from the house carrying Severo's duffel bag over his shoulder. He got into the car so fast I couldn't make out his face. The Mercedes roared, and then smoothly glided away.

The empty street seemed to exacerbate the night chill. The thunderous roar of fifty thousand shouting people broke out in Miraflores. The druggist lifted up his arms. Goal for El Tigre. Severo left the eatery and walked nonchalantly up Colón. He disappeared inside the big house and I was again left alone. My abdomen started to ache, and all of a sudden I had to go to the bathroom. That kind of luxury could wait. My nerves were playing a bad joke on me, so I entered the store and bought an Alka-Seltzer. The pharmacist handed me a glass of water.

"Two to one," he said happily. "Five minutes left."

Then Severo and Arminda emerged. She clutched her briefcase tightly under her right arm. They planted themselves on the edge of the sidewalk and hailed the first taxi passing down Colón. The comings and goings had ended, and now the questions began. I asked, and Mario Alvarez responded. Entangled in a web of deductions and suspicions and frozen stiff by the La Paz night, my mind short-circuited. The question was: *To follow or not to follow?*

"I need something to drink," I said out loud.

I headed up to the north side of town, where night falls amidst poverty, promiscuity, and despair.

Part Two

Chapter 8

All the noise and people in that Bolivian Calcutta were making it impossible to think straight. At the head of Figueroa Street, steps away from Plaza Alonso de Mendoza, I chanced upon El Yungueño, a small dive filled with lushes who were always celebrating something, be it their misery or their happiness. A tall, dark-skinned woman with a supple figure was standing and drinking beside the bar in the company of two lowlifes dressed in jackets and jeans. As I entered, the woman winked at me suggestively. The guys, cheap pimps for sure, stood watch over their charges and pretended not to see me. The owner of the bar was a hefty, slovenly lady who could easily have passed for the driver of a twenty-ton truck. She poured me a beer without even asking.

I started to mull things over. Time was short. To carry out my project, I first needed to acquire a lead club, a silent and efficient instrument. A gun was out of the question, since it was going to cost me at least two hundred dollars. Once I had the lead club, the second thing was to draw up a more or less rational plan. It didn't make sense to do the robbery during office hours because of all the gold sellers hanging around. The ideal thing was to catch Arminda when she wasn't with Severo; that way, the armed son of a bitch couldn't blow my brains out. I had a single window for finishing Arminda off with a crushing blow to the neck: between the moment her gorilla-in-training saw her to the apartment and when the rich guy with the Mercedes showed up.

I had it all figured out: Arminda bought the gold with the money the rich guy brought her. When they got together at her apartment, the gold was swapped for dollars, which in turn served to buy more gold. You didn't need the mind of Stephen Hawking to put two and two together. I wasn't interested in the gold, only in the dollars.

A second prostitute, a tiny and chubby girl with the expression of a graceless circus clown, joined the others at the bar. One of the pimps started to stroke her back with about as much tenderness as a bear. I needed an accomplice to help me tie up loose ends, but I had to act fast. As I lost myself in thought, a scandal broke out in the street. The police had detained a drunken pickpocket for trying to make off with a woman's purse. They locked him up in a car and then left with their sirens blasting, as if they had just caught some big shot from the Medellin cartel.

The air seemed to thicken. In the mood for some native victuals, I made my way toward the Uruguay Market. There, I settled onto a stool underneath a plastic tarp and ate an entire chicken. The chicken was so spicy that I was forced to drink a beer. A half-breed lady wrapped in an alpaca blanket and emerald flowing skirts served me a ladleful of potatoes sautéed in onion, which extinguished the fire raging inside my stomach. Riffraff and laborers were consuming two-peso dishes of tripe and lamb stew. When the half-breed lady served me a strong yet delicious coffee, I felt like new. If I was going to digest that late dinner, the wisest thing was to start walking. I chose Avenida Buenos Aires, the most diverse and exotic artery in La Paz and the one most crammed with people. I wandered past the sellers of raw meat and the fruit stands, past the tents containing coca leaves from the Yungas, past the music vendors, the glass dealers, the candy stores, and the grocery stores with dizzying quantities of rice, corn, and spices. I passed in front of the sellers of handmade leather goods, the bakeries specializing in wedding cakes, and the shoe stores.

At 11 o'clock, as I approached the Puente Abaroa, I observed drunkards trying to hide between enormous bags of bananas and pineapples as they awkwardly mounted half-breed whores. I was tired, but I wanted to get even more tired, stop thinking about the visa and the robbery, and fall asleep; "to sleep and sleep no more." Up ahead were three-peso barbershops, toilet paper sellers, leather workers, heavy trucks, porters unloading manioc and red peppers, sweetshops, and ice cream stores. I also saw vendors selling canned liquor, weaving shops, chicken joints, and cheap watering holes crawling with vagrant coke heads.

"Don Mario, Don Mario!" I heard all of a sudden.

An unusual looking young woman was motioning to me from a doorway. I touched my index finger to my chest.

"Yes, you! Don't you recognize me?"

A flesh-and-blood apparition, she looked far-out even in comparison with the rest of the street. The lady wouldn't stop smiling as she came closer, batting her eyelashes just like Pierrot before a circus act.

"It's me, Gardenia."

"Gardenia! What are you doing here?"

"I usually come here with my friends for *api* and empanadas before we go out on the town. Come in, it's on me."

I tried to bow out, but Gardenia, with an effeminate sweep of his hand, grabbed me by the arm with the strength of a teenager. Without further ado, he showed me around. The most fecund imagination could not have envisioned the scene before my eyes. A dozen or so transvestites decked out in bizarre outfits were occupying four tables and drinking *api*. Gardenia introduced me to the owner, a guy with whitish skin and curly hair.

"This is Don Félix," Gardenia said.

Don Félix appeared to be an older gay man who spent his days running a business frequented by young deviants, whom he managed to somehow control.

"Delighted," he enunciated slowly.

Chubby and well-dressed, he seemed obsessed with hygiene; his hair was parted in the middle and his skin was smooth. His gaze was both playful and mocking. I guessed that he was over sixty, but he had the sense of humor of a mischievous girl.

"Don Félix is going to make you some empanadas to die for," Gardenia said.

Don Félix invited me to sit down with Gardenia at a table. "Let me get you some *api*," he said, walking away.

"It's weird running into you here," Gardenia said to me.

"I ate an entire chicken for dinner. It was too much," I said. "I had no idea there were places like this on Avenida Buenos Aires. Where did all these transvestites come from?"

"Half-breeds dressing up like girls are a dime a dozen," Gardenia said knowingly.

"From what I can tell, you're the only white person and the only one who looks like a girl. The others look like carnival characters."

"Don't be so mean. You'd never know it with some of them."

"Maybe if the victim drinks half a bottle of *pisco* first . . ."

Gardenia let out a girlish giggle. It felt like I was seeing him, or her, for the first time. He was almost my height, about 5'9", and too pretty to pass for a guy. Nature had bestowed upon him a harmony of features that was incongruous with the male sex. He had light brown eyes that were practically covered by his eyelashes, long like the legs of a giant mosquito, and a pointed nose that complemented his finely chiseled face. His full lips over a wide mouth looked like those of an African fashion model. He was wearing a conservative purple sweater with white pants, worthy of a stroll along a seaside promenade. His delicate, graceful hands didn't remain still for a second. They reminded me of the hands of my cousin who used to embroider tablecloths.

"One glass of *api* a day, and say goodbye to your stomach," I commented.

"I think you've convinced yourself that you're an old man."

"I'm old enough to know not to overdo it with that stuff," I said. "I bet all the Indians here think you're a real-life angel. Don't tell me you'll get in bed with any of them for a few pesos."

"I come here to spend time with my girlfriends. But Don Félix's friends are good catches. They're old, married, and still in the closet, so they come up for air every once in a while. I actually work in a house in Sopocachi. Only classy folks go there."

"And these guys?" I asked, pointing to the other transvestites.

"They hang out at Plaza Kennedy, on Evaristo Valle, or at the Plaza del Estudiante. They're twenty-peso half-breeds." He laughed and covered his mouth.

"Don Antonio told me you're from the cream of Sucre."

"We have a solid pedigree. My family lives in Montevideo. We used to live in Sucre until they realized I was hopeless. They couldn't stand the idea that I was gay. They would've been happier if I'd caught leprosy. Years ago we used to be called fags because we were supposedly degenerates, but now people just say we're sick or sexually maladjusted."

Leisurely, Greta Garbo–style, Gardenia lit up his distinguished poison: a long cigarette in a golden holder.

"Do they at least send you money?"

"Three times a year, through an uncle of mine: on my birthday, at Christmas, and on Father's Day. They hold out hope that I'll get married to some birdbrained rich girl. What they send me isn't enough. My dad must think *salteña* pastries still cost fifty cents."

"As the Spaniards say, it's all in how you manage it."

"I've been living alone ever since I graduated high school. My parents sent me to São Paulo to study architecture. I fell in love with an American pianist who was touring with a rock band. I didn't like architecture; what I really wanted was to be a fashion designer. I'm good at drawing and I have good taste. When my dad heard about my fashion design plans, he stopped sending me money. Since I didn't react, he wrote me to say that I was dead to the family."

"So you're dead."

"I'm stuck between a rock and a hard place. You don't have anything against gays, Mario?"

"As a poor man, I can't afford that luxury."

"What's happening with your American visa?"

"I have a plan. If it works out, I'll probably leave. And if I screw it up, I think I'm going to commit suicide."

"Don't talk like that!"

"Twenty glasses of *api* plus forty empanadas would do the trick."

"That fucking visa!" Gardenia exclaimed. "I've been to San Francisco before. The pianist took me with him. On the way over from São Paulo, we stopped in Santa Cruz and picked up half a kilo of coke. We sold it in the States for a good price, and lived off the money for a year. He locked himself up in his apartment to prepare for a concert that unfortunately turned out like shit. I kept busy studying English and industrial textile design. I stayed illegal because I didn't want to live there. My dream was to go to Barcelona; it's a much cooler place."

"And what happened?"

"Even though we lived together, we were both free to stick our asses where we wanted. So one day when I was in a gay bar, I got busted by Immigration. They gave me twenty-four hours to leave the country. I wanted to fly to Spain, but they sent me here."

"Isn't San Francisco heaven on earth for guys like you?"

"Too many problems. Everybody has issues with drugs or violence. It's not my scene. I'm an easygoing guy; I could have enjoyed small-town living, but as soon as I got to Sucre my parents hired a priest to try and exorcise me. When the priest failed, they brought in a shaman who made me get into a tub of freezing cold water and then smoke-dried my body. It was fucking ridiculous." He laughed.

Gardenia was charming. I had a hard time picturing him hobnobbing with all those half-breeds.

"They wouldn't quit, so they set me up with a girl. I took her out to the movies. She would lift up her skirt a little to see if I'd touch her thighs. She was very pretty, and I didn't want to mess with her head, so I told her the truth. The poor thing cried, but later we became friends. As if that wasn't enough, a first cousin of mine dragged me to a brothel and forced me into a room with this fat whore who smelled like dirty underwear. The woman tried bending over every which way, but it didn't do anything for me. Eventually they all gave up and left me alone."

"Times have changed," I said. "Now it's cool to be gay. Look at all the gays in politics and business. Enough of this late-night debauchery; just find yourself a wealthy businessman and settle down."

"I like action," he said. "The action is in the streets."

"I hope you're watching out for AIDS."

"They say the virus can't survive at this altitude. Could that be true?"

"Don't believe it. Most of all, stay away from the foreign tourists."

"They're so damn stingy. They want everything for free. Even when it comes to sex, they're colonialists! If they lay a finger on me, they're paying. My goal is Barcelona. The world starts there."

"You'll do great for yourself. Not many Spics have your looks."

"Spics," he repeated, laughing heartily.

"Spain is far away," I said. "I hear they love Latinos on the other side of the ocean."

"I look French," Gardenia said. "I'm saving up; I buy German marks whenever I can."

"In my day, when I was still young, I had plans too. I was in love, my baby boy had just been born, and I dreamed of settling in Argentina, but it never worked out. My wife had other ideas."

The mixture of *api*, spicy chicken, and beer gave me a terrible surge of gas. There was no point trying to use the toilet; the transvestites were crowded in there applying their makeup. The call of nature could wait no longer, so I had to leave. I went outside and, after failing to find another bathroom, decided to make a dash for the wood sellers' stalls on Chorolque Street. There, I hid myself in an alleyway between two adobe walls. While a stray dog eyed me, I frantically relieved myself. I had eaten way too much street food, forgetting that I wasn't made of steel like when I was a kid.

The wind was ripping down Chorolque Street, stirring up mini-cyclones of dirt and papers beside the shacks of the leather craftsmen. A small group of drunken laborers were throwing rocks at hungry dogs scavenging for food in trash bins. A cab pulled up right in front of the alleyway and the driver invited a half-breed lady to hop in. Impressed by the car and ashamed at the same time, she appeared to be weighing the likelihood of a sexual assault.

I headed back to the *api* joint. Eagerly anticipating the moment of truth, the transvestites were making as much noise as a hundred caged parrots. Gardenia was polite enough to introduce me to his best friends. I met Lula, a huge guy who looked like a Mexican wrestler and seemed to be the leader of the pack. He was a two-hundred-pound half-breed guy who, as destiny would have it, had transformed himself into a two-hundred-pound half-breed chick. His face was swollen, his eyelashes were artificial, and powder and rouge were smeared all over his cheeks. He wore a leather jacket and tight pants that raised his Texas cowboy's backside. His punishing, baleful stares made it clear he wasn't happy to see me. Somehow, I had violated his privacy and that of the other transvestites who spent their days in a hostile environment in a city that was slowly turning into a large Indian village. The *api* joint had evolved into a refuge in which they were free to be themselves. It was a world all their own, removed from the morally totalitarian, hypocritical, and anachronistic world outside.

Gardenia's best friend was Lourdes, a fragile transvestite dressed in black from head to toe as if in mourning. "Lourdes designs his own clothing," Gardenia said. "He went to school in Rondonia, Brazil."

The combination of his leather jacket and black lamé pants, which left exposed a pair of bony and bruised calves, was something else. Truth be told, he looked like a vampiress out of *The Muppet Show*.

"Don Mario lives in my hotel. He's traveling to the States soon," Gardenia said.

"He looks really pale," Lourdes said.

"He's nervous about his visa," Gardenia explained.

"Visa? What visa?" Lula asked.

"Don Mario is afraid the gringos won't give him a tourist visa."

Lula started painting his nails a shiny silver. His coarse plumber's hands, attached to his effeminate gladiator's body, conjured up the Boston Strangler. "I know an army sergeant who could give you a hand," he said.

"Thanks, but when it comes to visas the gringos don't even listen to their own conscience."

The odor of male perspiration reached our table. A tall and confused-looking transvestite, who walked as if stepping on embers, unexpectedly served me some chicken soup. "This will make you feel better," he said. He had dyed his hair dirty-blond, and a white lock jutted out from his forehead.

"The cops! Everyone quiet!" Lula yelled.

Through the window I saw a police truck arrive: It was the Vice Squad. A male officer with a moustache, who looked like he could hail from anywhere between Patagonia and the Rio Grande, descended from the cabin. He was a mixed-race guy with clouded eyes and a threatening gaze. Lula approached him and slipped him an envelope. The officer said something and then put the envelope in his pocket. He greeted Don Félix politely and left.

"Twenty pesos a head for protection, per day," Gardenia said.

"Just so you can do your thing without being afraid," I remarked.

"It's the witching hour. Time to go," Gardenia said.

The transvestites were putting on the finishing touches to their makeup before heading out on the town.

"Does Don Antonio know this place?" I asked.

"I brought him once. Good thing the old man has such a bad sense of direction; otherwise, he'd be here more often."

"But he's too old to join the other team . . ."

"It's not that, it's just that he'd come here every day to eat for free." Gardenia stared at himself in a small mirror hanging from a beam. He put on his lipstick and then shook his backside for us, Tahitian-style.

Don Félix said goodbye to them one by one. "Hope to see you around," he said to me.

The streets emptied as night fell. Off in the distance, a radio blared a Julio Iglesias song. Lula cinched his belt and clacked his heels like a bull gearing for mortal combat.

"Let's go, girls," he ordered.

"Where are you off to?" Gardenia asked me.

"I'm walking back to the hotel."

"It's dangerous at night," Gardenia said. "You could get mugged."

Lula hailed a couple of taxis. The transvestites giggled as they crammed in. Gardenia stuck with his friend Lourdes and waited for the others to get a head start. He had hired a separate taxi; apparently, he watched his back more carefully than Doña Arminda did her gold.

I started walking. Beggars and drunkards took turns getting in my way. On Max Paredes, I observed the Koreans locking up their stores after a long, hard day, while hundreds of half-breed ladies got their stalls ready for the next. Those who didn't have metal stalls that could be sealed with a padlock had no choice but to sleep among their goods. The informal vendors who had taken over the sidewalks in the higher reaches of the neighborhood fought over selling space. They would buy permits from City Hall and pay protection fees to various groups that extorted them. If they didn't pay, they would find their spots occupied the next morning. There was a shortage of public urinals on these godforsaken streets, so the vendors and riffraff urinated and defecated on the curbs. If the winds from the Andean plateau didn't blow in from time to time, the bowl-shaped valley in which La Paz sits would be insufferable.

Exhausted, I arrived at the hotel. In the second patio, the cheese salesman was listening closely to the ex-goalie as he described the marvels of the city of Santa Cruz. They were so immersed in conversation that they didn't even notice my presence. I walked right past them, entered my room, and fell asleep within minutes.

The next morning, I paid a visit to a hardware store on Eloy Salmón Street. When I asked the owner, a frowning, potbellied Arab, if he could sell me a lead club, he answered in a sour voice, "Lead club? No lead clubs here. This is a street for working people, you know— construction workers, bricklayers, foremen. Go over to Sebastián Segurola, the street with all the crooks. You'll find lead clubs there." I was obviously in the wrong place; the guy just sold picks and shovels. "If you don't find them on Sebastián Segurola, you could stop by the jail. Some of the inmates there make them."

"How could that be?"

"They have to earn a living somehow," he answered.

The idea of visiting the San Pedro jail did not appeal to me. I couldn't shake the thought that once inside, I might never leave. Instead, I decided to head up Sebastián Segurola, a steep street lined with market stalls on both sides. Most of the vendors were small-time thieves, mean-looking guys lined up Indian file. I noticed that the buyers approached the sellers to make their requests; if the crook had what the buyer wanted, he would summon an eleven- or twelve-year-old street kid to go and fetch it. They worked with lightning efficiency; the deal took less than ten minutes, haggling included. From the looks of things, lead clubs weren't in vogue. I climbed all the way up the steep hill with no luck. I was about ten paces away from Avenida Buenos Aires and my spirits were beginning to sink, when a friendly-looking Indian boy approached me. He seemed to find me entertaining.

"What are you smiling at?" I asked.

"What are you looking for, sir?"

"A lead club and a glass cutter."

"We've got them both."

"Where?"

With an indolent gesture, he invited me to follow him. He approached a street vendor who sold porn videos and magazines from the 1980s. At his side, a lean man with a timid expression and a gash running from one ear to his jaw raised his eyebrows. It seemed to be his way of asking what I wanted.

"A good lead club and a glass cutter," I said.

He opened a bag at his feet and, to my surprise, flashed an extraordinary variety of clubs, switchblades, glass cutters, and knives. I selected a small but formidable club wrapped in leather. Just to prove he wasn't selling me garbage, the guy grabbed the club with one hand, held out the palm of the other, and gave it a whack that would have knocked my head off.

"You've got to hit on the neck," he instructed me. "If you smack him on the head, you'll kill him."

"How much?"

"Twenty pesos. Five for the glass cutter." He picked a piece of glass off the ground and nicked it with the cutter. His gaze rested on mine, and then he split the glass in two with a single chop. "You'll need a suction pad with the cutter. Otherwise, the glass can fall onto the other side."

I handed him three ten-peso bills.

"For five pesos I'll throw in a Peruvian porn magazine."

"Not interested," I said.

I stuffed the weapons in my pockets and walked toward the train station. At Plaza Kennedy, I entered a pool hall teeming with lowlifes, a sea of faces that would have made an SS boss nervous. I ordered a Huari beer. Behind the bar, a mirror leaned against the wall. There I was with a spaced-out expression; I recognized myself by my eyes, which seemed to be looking for an answer. I smiled but the image in the mirror stayed still. This meant the game was getting serious. It was no time for turning back or second thoughts.

I desperately needed some rest. After finishing my beer, I decided to head back to the hotel for a nap.

Chapter 9

By the time I awoke from my slumber, it was around 4 o'clock in the afternoon. On my way out, I found Blanca in the lobby flipping through a fashion magazine. I asked if she wanted to join me for tea and she answered with a beautiful smile.

We walked slowly downtown and entered a café that offered a wide range of creole dishes and cuisine typical of Bolivia's eastern provinces. I settled for a bowl of rice pudding, while Blanca opted for rice, fried plantains, eggs, and beef. The place was small and clean, run by an attractive and efficient lady from Trinidad.

"She makes a lot of money selling this stuff," Blanca said.

"You could start a place just like this in your hometown," I responded.

"I would need around five thousand dollars."

"I could get used to the heat."

"There isn't a lot to do, but the people are nice. You could run the cash register. I'm terrible with numbers."

"To grow old and die in a hammock, watching the wind blow over the *pampas* of Beni . . . it would be nirvana, Blanca. What else could I ask for?"

"Better than working like a dog in an American city."

"If it weren't for my son, I wouldn't doubt it for a minute. But first I have to see him."

156 ಕಿ AMERICAN VISA

"Doesn't he plan to come back?"

"What for? To be someone in this country you've got to get into politics, the drug game, or dirty business deals with the government. I'm a poor guy with no future. I can't do anything for him. I'll let him stay there. Even if he works as a laborer, he'll never run short of money in America."

"I want to make a decent living and take it easy," she said. "My life has been too hectic."

"You'd never guess it. You look like an aspiring schoolteacher who's about to get her education degree."

"The joke's on you."

Living with Blanca for the rest of my life wasn't such a bad idea; she would be a lover, a mother, and a nurse, all in one. It was easy to put up with her. She didn't say much and when she did, she didn't talk nonsense. She had within her the serenity of the great rivers that traverse her homeland, the repose of the savannas lulled by the Amazonian sun. It was relaxing to spend time with her. She wasn't very cultured, but it didn't matter. She was intelligent and simple, courageous and patient. If I had met her ten years earlier, I wouldn't be at the crossroads I was at now. Of course, I still had the option of convincing her with a single word and changing my future; I could trash my visa plans and stop writing my screenplay for robbing Doña Arminda. But the idea was already planted in my head like a shrub in the tundra, deeply and tenaciously rooted. It was a cursed obsession that was growing and beginning to suffocate me.

We stood on the sidewalk opposite the Foreign Ministry. From one of the windows on the third floor, an official dressed up like a stage actor watched us with disdain. In the Plaza Murillo, Blanca took me by the hand as if we were a couple.

She retired to her room as soon as we returned to the Hotel California. She said she was going to shower and then try on a new pair of spandex shorts. She invited me to see her in full battle gear, but I was too busy preparing for what I was up against that night. Since this was to be my premiere as a violent criminal, I lay down on my bed and tried to recall some movie or television series or detective novel that would give me a clue as to what I should wear. The English, who tend to dress formally, usually put on a casual get-up of a raincoat and overalls to rob a bank. Dressing down might be a good way to dupe the police. As for the Americans, they generally wear jackets in which a revolver can be easily tucked away. I was in a bind because my weapon was a measly lead club. I ended up settling on the outfit I'd bought in Oruro to impress the U.S. consul, the elegant Prince of Wales suit, which would turn me into an enigma. Doña Arminda, the crowd at Yujra's bar, and the shoemaker on Colón Street had all seen me dressed like an impoverished gold runner, so it was wisest to go for a refined look.

When I went to shave, guess what the magical mirror had in store for me? A light-skinned face, large thick eyebrows, a thin straight nose, a mouth without much personality, a prominent chin that made women swoon, a wide forehead riddled with wrinkles that converged in a kind of delta, black wavy hair with a few specks of gray, and skin that cried out for some moisturizer. My face was run-of-the-mill, the kind you forget almost immediately. And yet, there was something striking about it, something I had cultivated like an exotic orchid: a moustache that you don't find every day in these Andean latitudes, a French-style moustache that curled up, à la Hercule Poirot. It was my touch of distinction, the thing that drove the ladies crazy when I went down on them. It wasn't a Mexican, Argentine, Brazilian, or half-breed moustache; it was a French moustache, and for what it was worth, it lent my appearance an enigmatic quality.

I vanished from the hotel like a ghost. The hostesses watching a Brazilian soap opera didn't see me, nor did the manager who was sweating a river and trying to sell six Italian tourists on the merits of the hotel, nor did the bellboy who was busy booting a shoeshiner out onto the street. Perfect! No one had seen me leave. I walked down Illampu and within a few minutes reached Plaza Eguino. Eight o'clock was still an hour away, so I took a seat in the patio of a café called Stephanie. Actually, "patio" is a bit of an exaggeration; they had simply arranged two tables on the sidewalk facing the plaza. At one of them, a pair of lovebirds held hands. With their lips nearly touching, they shared a dish of ice cream doused in chocolate syrup. A girl wrapped in a greasy apron took my order.

"A beer, but I don't want it if it's warm."

On that windless afternoon under clear skies, Protestant preachers were singing a Christian rock song in the middle of the plaza. I thought about how within a few years, Bolivia and the rest of Latin America would cease to be majority-Catholic to make way for those singing missionaries who fought for their faith in the streets, mixing with the locals in an effort to disseminate simple but seductive beliefs. The money came from somewhere else, but that's the free-market era for you.

"Beer and tamales," the girl said as she placed them on the table.

"I didn't ask for tamales."

"They're free because it's the first day our oven is working," the woman reassured me. "But just for today."

Plaza Eguino serves as a kind of funnel through which thousands of people pass en route to buses headed for El Alto, the bedroom city that the MIR party naïvely baptized "The City of the Future." The hustle and bustle starts at 7 o'clock in the evening. Ninety-nine percent of the people are dark-skinned, but every once in a while you'll come across a native or foreign white person. You can easily pick out the tourists by their style of dress, their height, and their skin color. The blond people look like ears of wheat in a pile of charcoal. The tourists seem happy and unworried; compared with Europe or the U.S., it's cheap to shop in Bolivia.

I was growing mesmerized by the bustle of the crowd, by the chanting of the Christians and the blaring horns of the buses, taxis, and minibuses stuck in traffic, when I saw her . . . none other than Isabel Esogástegui. If she was a celestial apparition in the bookstore, here in the Rosario neighborhood she was galactic. She was accompanied by a tall young man who appeared to be in a bad mood. There was a certain unkempt elegance about him. At that hour, there weren't too many hoodlums or vagrants on those desolate streets, but a woman of her pedigree was still taking a risk. She was wearing a raincoat and loafers, with a plaid wool scarf wrapped around her neck. When they passed by Stephanie's, I stood up and called out, "Isabel!"

She turned around and looked over without recognizing me.

"I'm Mario Alvarez . . . from Mabel Plata's book signing."

"What are you doing here?" she asked.

I got a whiff of her expensive perfume. "I live in a hotel on Illampu Street. And you?"

"I came to pick up my brother. He loves hanging out here."

"Won't you sit down?"

"Thanks, but as a matter of fact, today is his birthday and I've got to take him to his party. There are a hundred guests waiting for him."

The birthday boy was a little older than Isabel, and, just like her, had refined, upper-class features. He was a handsome guy, with a lean yet robust build. He looked pale and had dark bags under his eyes, which wandered as if in their own far-off universe. From what Isabel had said and from his spaced-out expression, I gathered that he was high on some drug, probably homegrown Bolivian cocaine.

Without paying her any mind, the young man sat down and called for the waitress. "One dark coffee," he requested.

"Tamales are free today," the girl said.

He stared at her and then broke out in laughter. "What did she say?" he asked me.

"Tamales are on the house today; it's the first day they're offering them."

"A black coffee, nothing in it," he said. He flashed me an inquisitive glance, and Isabel had no choice but to settle in next to me.

I suddenly wanted her so badly that if the Devil himself had offered me five hundred years in hell in exchange for a relationship with her, I wouldn't have hesitated for a second. She looked gorgeous. She possessed the kind of beauty that seems unreal and invisible to poor guys like me; invisible because we don't even want to look at it.

"Hopefully the coffee will clear your head a little," Isabel said.

The guy smiled, straightened his tie, and ran his palm through his blondish hair. "My name's Charles," he said in an affable tone. "My dad is a serious anglophile. You don't get classier than the Brits. He went to school there." Charles paused. "Since you're from around here, you must know Virrey Toledo Street . . . ?"

"No."

"It's just past the train station and those shacks that the Bolivian Railway workers built to house the company bureaucrats." Isabel's face turned red. She tried to shut him up, but he continued: "You have to jump over a wall and the house is right there, a little yellow house. I didn't leave the place for two days. Know why?"

"I can imagine."

"Isn't it shocking?"

"Well, it's your birthday," I said.

"I had forgotten all about my birthday. Besides, I couldn't care less. My mother planned this great party for me."

"Go on, tell him your life story," Isabel muttered.

The waitress brought him his coffee. As Charles sipped away, his mind cleared up enough for him to remember he had come in a car. The problem was, he didn't remember where he had parked it.

"You're so irresponsible!" Isabel exclaimed.

"Where do you usually leave it?" I asked.

"Sometimes in front of the train station, sometimes at Plaza Kennedy."

"Drink your coffee and stop being such a pain," Isabel said. "Let's go look for it." She stood up and made as if to leave.

"I'm free until 8 o'clock," I said. "If you'd like, I can help you find it. What kind of car is it?"

"A Toyota Corolla," Isabel replied. "New and red."

"I thought I came up in the Nissan," Charles said in jest.

"Idiot," Isabel mumbled.

It took us fifteen or twenty minutes to find the car. We spotted it between two large dumptrucks, near Virrey Toledo Street, in a dark alley in which a few boys had created a makeshift soccer field with some rocks.

"It's a miracle nobody stole it," Isabel said. "Today's your lucky day."

Charles rested his arm on my back. "Isabel's always hanging out with boring guys," he said. "I like you. Where did you two meet?"

"In a bookstore. I'm not her friend, I've only seen her once before."

Isabel unlocked the car and sat down in the driver's seat. "Thanks," she said. "You don't want to come to Charles's birthday party? That is, unless you have something more important to do."

Charles pressed his palms together, as if in prayer. He took everything like a joke. The look on Isabel's face shot a chill down my spine like a centipede doused with morphine. I forgot that I had a robbery to attend to; there's nothing sex or love or the two together can't do. With my heart dancing a merengue, I hopped into the Toyota.

Charles fell asleep just as we pulled out. Isabel drove through congested downtown without saying a word, irritated by our slow pace. Only after we reached Avenida Seis de Agosto did she take a deep breath. She recounted for me the disturbing life story of Charles, her only brother, the apple of their mother's eye and their family's white knight. He had been a model child until the age of twenty-five. He graduated with honors from the Catholic University of Chile with a degree in Economics, and then returned to Bolivia with the energy and euphoria of a young lion. As soon as he arrived, he was lucky enough to land a job with an American company that paid him two thousand dollars a month. An elegant economist and graduate of a Chilean university who speaks English fluently, comes from a good family, and wants to rise to the top isn't something you find every day in Bolivia.

He worked like a Japanese executive for six months. Right at the one hundred and eighty day mark, he met a woman from a humble background who had money—a social climber, typical of the class that came out of the national revolution. She grabbed onto him tooth and nail, sucking the life out of him through sex and orgasms. One happy day they got married without telling Charles's mother, his sister, or his

father, who had been living in New York ever since escaping the condescension, haughtiness, and manipulation of his wife. It was a huge
scandal, and the Esogástegui line suffered a severe devaluation in the
ranking of La Paz's top pedigrees. They were forced to swallow it, and
then they got on with their lives. What the family didn't know is that
the girl was a huge coke head. She ended up getting Charles, for all his
sophistication, hooked on the stuff. At first they sniffed and soon they
started shooting up. She caught a strain of Hepatitis B, which landed
her in a hospital in São Paulo, where, despite her money and the doctors' best efforts, she died. Disconsolate, Charles was left a widower
and an addict. He got over her death but never the addiction. And
there he was, unemployed, down on his luck, and living off the family
fortune, with one foot dangling over the abyss.

"We don't know what to do with him," Isabel confessed. "I think
he's a lost cause."

They lived in a Provencal-style mansion in Achumani. I calculated
their property at a third of an acre. The house, which measured at least
seven thousand square feet, was ringed by a garden of exquisitely
trimmed grass and clusters of rose bushes. An illuminated pine tree
stood at one end of the garden. When Charles pushed open the gate,
a pair of mastiffs galloped to meet us, barking ferociously. They quieted
a little upon seeing their master, but my presence provoked distrust.
They wouldn't stop baring their fangs at me.

"Calm down," Charles ordered in English. The dogs obeyed and
awaited the next request. "They're bilingual," he explained.

"They'll go far," I replied.

Isabel showed us to the main parlor. There, an impressive number
of guests, ranging from twenty to fifty years of age, danced with aban-
don to the beat of a DJ who was harmoniously operating a collection

of multimedia devices. A colossal television screen showed a tantalizing black woman, none other than La Toya Jackson, gyrating on a dance floor to new age rock music, while a strapping black man with oiled skin mimicked a sexual act with a mulatta wearing a thong no bigger than a child's handkerchief.

Isabel approached a lady with the face of an Incan empress and kissed her on the forehead. I guessed that it was her mother. Isabel whispered in her ear, and the mother flashed an apprehensive glance at Charles. The young man's arrival was received with repeated rounds of applause. He greeted his peers confidently, and the older guests reservedly. His mother gave him a long hug. They made a champagne toast, and then Isabel motioned for me to come closer.

"My mother, María Augusta. Mother, this is Mario Alvarez."

Doña María Augusta was a miraculous Spanish-Indian amalgam. Her face was an Oriental bronze hue, and her lips, nose, and slanted eyes could have been drawn by one of those painters of the tombs of the royal mummies in ancient Egypt. She was a masterpiece of miscegenation.

"Mario helped us with Charles," Isabel said.

"What was wrong with Charles?" María Augusta asked with genuine surprise.

"He was a little drunk," Isabel continued. "With those punks he has for friends!"

"Charles has this ridiculous habit of getting mixed up with the wrong crowd," María Augusta averred. "I don't know who he inherited that from."

"Not from my father."

With a penetrating gaze, Doña María Augusta tried to size up my family tree. She asked me where I was from.

"Uyuni, in the Department of Potosí."

"Decent people used to live there before '52."

I tried to explain that my father had been a simple working man, but Isabel made a face that stopped me cold.

"Señor Alvarez is a literature professor," Isabel affirmed.

"How wonderful!" María Augusta remarked. "I'm a big admirer of Miguel Ángel Asturias. I can't stand García Márquez or Cortázar. Vargas Llosa got off track, but he's turned it around."

"It's because he spends most of his time in London," I said.

"The environment has a lot to do with it. You must have your favorites too . . . I imagine."

"I like José María Arguedas, from Peru, and Osvaldo Soriano. I also like Dashiell Hammett and Raymond Chandler."

"I've never heard of them. Are they new?"

"I think Soriano is still alive."

"You're an expert," she said. "You should visit us more often."

Isabel pulled me by the arm with a soft, irresistible caress. "How about a glass of real French champagne? It's nothing like what we had at the bookstore."

"You two met in a bookstore?"

"At the signing of Mabel Plata's poetry collection."

Doña María Augusta furrowed her brow like Jack Palance of yesteryear preparing to send a poor and honest cowboy to the other world. "I haven't heard good things about the sexual preferences of that woman," she said.

"Mom! Everyone has the right to be himself."

"I read in *Time* magazine that the problem is the hypothalamus, which regulates our sexual impulses. A little brain surgery and *zap!* You're cured," said Doña María Augusta, addressing me.

"Seeing is believing," I said.

"What do you think of my children, Señor Alvarez?"

"They're different."

"My husband, who lies buried in New York, was very handsome when he was young; he was blond, tall, and sexy."

"I didn't know that he had died."

"He's not dead," Isabel said. "He's alive and kicking. He works for a travel agency. To my mother, working in tourism in New York is like being dead."

"Of course," María Augusta stressed. "He used to be the CEO of an insurance company here in Bolivia. He made good money and enjoyed all the privileges of a man in charge. Then he got bored and ran off with fifty thousand dollars to New York, chasing after some girl. As was to be expected, he got robbed blind and ended up on the street. I'm glad; he didn't deserve any better than to have to start all over again from the bottom."

"I expect to travel to the United States in a few days," I said.

Doña María Augusta raised an eyebrow like a nineteenth-century aristocrat. "If you go with half-a-million dollars, maybe you'll fit in. Anything less, forget it."

"I didn't know about this," Isabel said.

"It came up at the last minute," I lied.

Isabel took off her raincoat. She was wearing a simple, beige, casually elegant dress. "I'm going to go look for Claudio," she said.

"Claudio is . . ."

"My official boyfriend; he was handpicked by my family."

She left and Charles reappeared. He had brought me a glass of Scotch, which I substituted for the champagne.

"I'm going to introduce you to some of my friends," he said. "They keep asking me who you are. I told them I have no idea. Who are you?"

"A guy who was born in Uyuni, an English teacher, and a lover of detective novels and films. I was raised on crime fiction."

"Did it do you any good?"

"Maybe. I'll know soon enough."

The room was so large that a tennis match could have been comfortably staged there. In back, a long rectangular table with white tablecloths was getting covered, little by little, with platters of food and bottles of imported wine. A number of waiters were serving the guests, who, as was typical at these functions, ate like a gang of shipwrecked sailors. To reach those delicacies, we first had to walk past some knuckleheaded acquaintances of Charles. They were high-society boys straight out of some Luis Buñuel dream: a prematurely balding ex–tennis player with sunken cheeks and a silly smile, and a chubby guy with an Argentine accent who was a former Minister of Economy. I recognized the ex-minister; his crooked ways had cost him his government post. Last name Sánchez de Bustillos, he looked like a Sephardic North African with his enormous backside, French beard, empty stare, and Mickey Mouse ears.

Enough is enough, I thought.

Charles took me aside. "The tennis player says he's friends with Guillermo Vilas, but he actually just sucked him off one night in Monte Carlo and hasn't seen him since. He also brags about banging all these Monacan chicks, but in reality he hasn't done a single one . . ."

"The guy couldn't score with a tied-up sow," I said.

"Exactly," Charles agreed. "This Sánchez de Bustillos is so stingy, he padlocks his freezer and his servants live all week on leftover noodles. He's a loan shark and charges seven percent a month. He's had all his best friends put in jail."

"Do you remember the name of that horrible woman from *Les Liaisons Dangereuses?*

"The Marquise de Merteuil."

"You better watch what you say," I cautioned.

"I just don't like them. They're the nouveau riche of our society, mediocre guys who have no class. With those assholes at the top of the pyramid, the poor people at the bottom are screwed."

Isabel returned with her boyfriend. Charles greeted him and then left to go hang out with his friends. Claudio, the boyfriend, was a sharply dressed, two-hundred-pound fire hydrant with a face like an orchestra conductor. He was devouring a whole trout meunière.

"Something to eat?" Isabel asked me.

"I'll have trout with a glass of white wine."

When Isabel headed toward the table with the food, the boyfriend asked, "So what do you do besides teach school?"

"I used to trade in merchandise from Chile. I was what you'd call a middleman."

He adjusted his glasses and burst out laughing.

"It's not a joke."

"How did you meet Isabel?"

"At a poetry reading about our lost sea."

"We got it back with the treaty that gives us duty-free access to the Pacific. Haven't you heard of the Ilo Treaty?"

"You've got a great girl," I said. I was getting tired of bullshitting.

"Did she talk about me?"

"Not a word," I answered.

"She's too perfect . . . intelligent, beautiful . . ."

"Do smart women scare you?"

"They scare the shit out of me. Are you married?"

"I was. My wife wasn't too smart or too dumb. She was average, but I liked her. She left me. I'm a free man."

"Don't you think there's too much intimacy in marriage?"

"You can do like the English and keep your distance."

Claudio praised the trout and then went for seconds. I had no choice but to accompany him. He was sweating profusely and I thought that if he didn't watch it, his cholesterol would force him on a strict diet for the rest of his life.

"That brother of hers, Charles, is such a screw-up," he said. "You came in with him; I'd like to know what you think."

"He can't help himself."

"He's a dope head. Everyone knows that. The kid has no decency. The worst thing of all is that his mother adores him and forgives him for everything."

Luckily, when Isabel returned she was relaxed and in a good mood. She had picked me out the best trout of the bunch. The wine, a Concha y Toro white, helped me understand why the Chileans had displaced the Germans in the U.S. market. Isabel had an easygoing rapport with her boyfriend, *comme il faut*. Claudio was a friendly, chic, high-society guy who was surely rolling in dough. Within a few years, Isabel would probably tire of him and turn him into a cuckolded fool. She came into the world to make a lot of men happy; it would be a waste to lock her up in some golden cage, surround her with kids, and wait for her to grow old. Hers was not a common destiny. As for me, I was hopelessly in love, so enraptured that I had forgotten all about the American visa and the robbery. Isabel seemed to realize that I was worked up about something, which is probably why she had me sit me down among four young wives who were animatedly trash-talking everyone who walked by. They showered me with wine. One of them, a dark-skinned lady with a detached gaze and thickly painted lips, shot darts at me with her eyes.

Within half an hour, I was mildly drunk and the wives had lost their inhibitions. Her name was Norha and she said the heat was making her feel sick. Her husband, who looked like an Italian mobster, was busy downing a bottle of Chivas and talking to imaginary friends. With each drink, Norha moved a few inches closer. At around 10 o'clock, our hands touched. I grasped one of her thighs.

"Mario," she whispered, "I have a car outside. We could go for a drive in Aranjuez."

"What's in Aranjuez?" I asked softly.

"Total darkness."

"I'm pretty hammered," I confessed.

That turned Norha on; a social nobody with a rock in his pants, no strings attached, augured only the crudest of adventures. With the guests dancing to a Juan Luis Guerra song, it was easy to sneak out. Sprawled in an armchair, Doña María Augusta was reciting a slurred, nostalgia-filled speech. Isabel absentmindedly stroked Claudio's arm, while he grinned like a doped-up sheep. You could tell Charles urgently needed a sniff of the white stuff because his nerves were acting up.

Norha left first, and I followed a few minutes later. Her car was an immaculate, brand new, cherry Peugeot. She was listening to an aria by Pavarotti as she waited. Tires screeching, we took off like an American police car. After crossing Calacoto to Plaza Humboldt, we hung a left and followed the edge of the La Paz Tennis Club before turning right onto a dirt road. The river was barely visible under the light of the new moon. Norha drove up to a discreet grove of eucalyptus trees, set back from the road. We still hadn't exchanged a single word; the great Pavarotti was the one making all the noise. She was hot, distracted, and impatient. Lucky for us, we were the only car there. She pulled over, turned off the motor, and lowered the volume. The moon, enshrouded by complicit clouds, softly illuminated the rugged mountains surrounding us. A gentle breeze blew. Compared to Blanca's burlesque, coarse, lecherous scent, Norha's perfume was a poetic invitation.

"What do you think? It's not so far."

"Only five minutes from your husband."

Norha lit a cigarette and placed it between my lips, all the while removing her silk taffeta dress with slow, firm motions. She had a slender girl's body, with graceful curves. I took off my jacket and tossed it onto the backseat. Then I unbuttoned her bra, breathed in the fine aroma of her naked skin, handed her the cigarette, and hung her panties on the ignition key. She turned on the heater. There was a terse, perverse silence. I heaved my pants containing the lead club and the glass cutter onto the dashboard and surreptitiously hid my poor man's underwear in the glove compartment. We were ready to go. She extinguished the cigarette in the ashtray and swapped Pavarotti for a Mexican *ranchera*.

She got on top of me and her smooth hands grabbed hold of my penis as if it belonged to Michelangelo's Apollo. She started to gyrate, slowly at first, and then smoothly accelerated to the cadence of a thoroughbred. Her moans reminded me of the civilized utterances of Mishima's Japanese hookers. I caressed her with one hand, while grasping her face with the other. Her eyes observed me distractedly. Before I realized it, she had spun around and her rear end was transformed into a kind of vertical smile, the hairs on her back standing up in a fan shape. I barely moved, leaving everything to her. She continued gently stimulating herself and oscillating her body with truly surprising tact. Suddenly, she entered into ecstasy and quickened her rhythm so violently that it felt like a pair of gigantic scissors was cutting into my phallus. She braked abruptly and let out a wolf's howl that greatly aroused me. Breathing heavily like a sprinter who just arrived at the finish line, she quieted down. I was only halfway there, so I stretched her out, as best I could, on the velvety seat of the Peugeot. With gusto, but without much style, I tried to finish as well. It just wasn't my night. I don't know if it was the damned murmuring of the river or the *ranchera* music or the dreadful passivity that had swept over her. What was certain was that despite my efforts, it was taking awhile and I was fighting against the clock. That's the bind I was in when a booming crash shook the roof of the car.

"What the hell!" I blurted.

Norha jumped up and pushed me aside, as if I were a small horse in a rodeo.

"They're throwing rocks," she exclaimed. "They're going to ruin my car!"

I opened the door, stepped outside, and shouted, "Fucking pricks!"

An avalanche of stones came crashing down inches from my steaming body.

"Get lost, assholes!" I yelled.

Norha turned on the engine and shifted into reverse. I didn't have any choice but to run after the moving car.

"What's wrong with you? Were you going to leave me there?" I got into the car and shut the door. Without responding, she turned the vehicle around. We sped out of the little grove and then stopped three hundred feet further ahead.

"You can't just leave me here!"

"My husband will kill me if he notices that they damaged the car. We bought it brand new last week!"

"What do I care?" I exclaimed.

Norha started to get dressed hurriedly. She glanced at me sideways and shouted, "Put on your clothes!"

"We could finish," I grumbled. "I don't like stopping halfway."

"Are you crazy? There's too much light here. Besides, my cousin Bebi's house is only half a block away. It's not my fault those Indian runts were throwing rocks at us."

"You said this was a safe place, but a bunch of cockblockers screwed it up for us."

"I'm sorry, darling. Please get dressed. You look ridiculous."

I put on my clothes, muttering obscenities under my breath.

"Look at the top of the roof and check the damage, please," she said.

I got out of the car and felt the roof. The stoning had left a scratch, but had not dented the metal. I told her there was nothing to worry about. She stroked my penis in appreciation.

"It'll have to be some other time. Isabel always invites me to her parties. Don't give me that face."

She reapplied her lipstick, fixed her hair, and then we headed back.

After parking the Peugeot in the same place it had been before, Norha lit a cigarette and looked up at the sky. "What a beautiful night!" she remarked. I didn't say a word. I felt angry and ashamed. The blue-blooded chick was discarding me like a piece of trash. Then she said, "I'll go in first."

I waited a few minutes in the garden, watching the bilingual mastiffs devouring pieces of leftover pork chops. A car stopped in front of the entryway. The driver, who was dressed like a jockey, hopped out and opened one of the rear doors. A man and two women emerged and entered the garden. The driver followed them.

"Tell them to give you something to eat from the kitchen. Be back here in an hour," the man ordered.

"Very well, Don Gustavo."

"I'll say hi to your sister and then I'm leaving," said the older of the two women, who appeared to be in her fifties and looked furious.

"There you go again," the man protested. "I was in Parliament. We were debating the upcoming privatizations. Sometimes the sessions go very late—"

"Please, Mom. There are strangers here," the younger woman said.

When the man saw me, he peered at me as if I were a bush. They entered the house.

The party was still going full tilt. Many of the guests were still dancing and the rest were chattering in groups, women on one side and men on the other. Don Gustavo's entrance caused a big stir.

"It's about time," one man said. "The future president of the Senate! We were starting to worry about you."

Don Gustavo exchanged greetings with the guests. The two women eluded the crowd and went to congratulate Charles. Isabel showed up with a pair of wine glasses in hand.

"This is red wine from Mendoza; it's Caballero de la Cepa," she said. "By the way, where have you been?"

"Your friend Norha took me for a ride. It was a disturbing and entertaining experience."

"She's so inappropriate. I'll bet she makes a good dessert; a little ditzy, but men like that."

Merely laying eyes on her was enough of a consolation for my anger to fade away. I forgot all about Norha the castrator and simply stared at Isabel. A few drinks later, I asked her to dance; her rhythm was sensual and enchanting. We talked about a little of everything. I would remember her for the rest of my life. It didn't even cross my mind to ask her to sleep with me, but not because her pedigree made me feel inadequate. It simply would have been mission impossible, like asking for the moon.

"We have a great library upstairs. It belongs to my father. One of these days I'll ship it to him in New York. I'd like you to pick out a few books to take with you. Think of them as souvenirs."

We walked up a carpeted staircase that might as well have been leading to a throne in some Disney cartoon. We passed through a hall-way lined with colonial-era paintings, each one as bad as the next. Isabel led me by the hand. Without her, I would have felt as lost in that house as if I were in the belly of a whale. The library was vast. It had at least two thousand volumes, most of them hardcover.

"Did you find Gramsci's complete works?"

"It's out of print. You have a good memory."

"Your father is a voracious reader. I've never seen so many books in one place before. Don't you miss him?"

"Day and night, but I can't go to New York. I have my studies and my mother here . . ."

"What does your boyfriend do for a living?"

"He owns a sawmill. He's a gold magnate and a coffee exporter. And I'm not even sure what else. He's very rich."

"And that works for you?"

"I think that money solves most problems."

"A poor man can become rich; all he needs is a lucky break."

"Maybe in Hollywood. In a poor country, you're either born rich or you get rich by stealing from the government."

"Your boyfriend is an honest businessman."

"His dad gave him two hundred thousand dollars to start with."

"My dad gave me two gold nuggets."

"Better than nothing."

I picked up a pair of Jack London novels; no better way to keep on dreaming than to read a dreamer!

At that moment, someone came in to join us. Cell phone in hand, Don Gustavo was preparing to dial a number. When he saw us he changed his mind and left the gadget on top of a desk.

"Isabel! What a surprise! You don't get out much these days."

He gave me a quick once-over, but couldn't quite classify me.

"This is Señor Alvarez," Isabel said.

"Such a pleasure," replied Don Gustavo. "Didn't I see you in the Senate?"

"I'm afraid not. I've never seen the Senate, except from the out-side. I live in Oruro."

"Ahh."

"He's a teacher," Isabel said.

"A teacher . . . a teacher?" he asked with a sneer.

Don Gustavo was decked out in a blue suit. He stood about a hand's-length taller than me and was dark-skinned, just like his sister María Augusta. His hair was straightened in the style of those blacks from Harlem in the 1950s who would put an iron to their heads to look more like white people. A smug-looking mestizo, his face had surely been softened a thousand times with fine creams. He was arrogant, unfriendly, and ostentatious. His rough, swollen hands straightened the reddish tie on his impeccable white shirt.

He began: "I wanted to talk with you alone for a moment. Your Aunt Alicia is being a complete pain. She's extremely jealous and she thinks that I have a lover. The truth is that I spend my time in Parliament. I've got more important things to worry about . . ."

"Is that right?" Isabel said with a smirk.

"Let me explain. For example, take the participation of U.S. soldiers in the fight against drug trafficking: Without the soldiers there's no foreign aid, and without foreign aid this country's going nowhere."

"Bolivia lives mostly off cocaine," I said. "It would be absurd to eliminate the coca crops."

Don Gustavo stretched out the corners of his lips into a grimace that would have looked funny if it hadn't been for the rest of his features, which remained funereal.

"Nobody wants to eliminate the crops, not even the Americans. Cocaine is a good business and the Americans like good businesses. They've created a theatrical operation in which we're like supporting actors; we unleash the mother of all battles against the drug traffickers, but that's just for the consumption of the media and the general public. Everyone agrees that if there's no cocaine, there's no money in the Central Bank, so they're okay with it. Since you're a teacher, I'll bet you're a lefty just like my niece."

"I'm apolitical. I didn't know that your niece was on the left."

"It's the truth, in spite of her money and good looks," Don Gustavo said. "You're one well-dressed teacher. How much did that suit cost you? Two hundred dollars?"

"I had it custom-made just for my visit to the American consulate."

"Big party?"

"I went for a tourist visa."

Don Gustavo laughed, shaking his head from side to side. "Isabel sure knows how to meet strange guys. She's always hanging around with these trade unionists, but at the moment of truth she picks a boyfriend from a good family with tons of money."

Isabel stared at him with snake eyes.

"They're more interesting than all of your right-wing friends in Congress," she responded. "My Uncle Gustavo belongs to the MIR. Before, he was an advisor to each of the military dictatorships, and when he was younger he worked for the MNR; he was even their ambassador to Belgium. Nobody's been around more than him."

"I'm on the side of history," Don Gustavo said, clearing his throat. "Now I'm a social democrat, an admirer of the Swedes and the Danes. I was a leftist when I was young because I wanted to learn all about scientific socialism and the dialectic. Marx was extremely useful to me in college. Luckily, that's all in the past. These days you have to look at the world differently. Darwin was right when he said that only the strong survive."

"It doesn't matter how," Isabel chimed in.

Don Gustavo strutted around the library as if taming a gang of wild animals.

"The perestroika was Kerenski's posthumous revenge; he always wanted a pluralist Duma. You don't have to eliminate the Bolsheviks—they're necessary. Without thermonuclear support, the Shining Path, Farabundo Martí and company are all harmless. They can wage guerrilla warfare for a hundred years and the earth won't stop spinning. Fukuyama called it the end of history. Have you read him?"

"Yukio Mishima is the only Japanese I've read," I replied.

"Political scientist?"

"He was a gay novelist who committed hara-kiri."

"Clearly another nutcase. I guess there's something for everybody." He paused and then continued: "Every now and then you've got to pay attention to the left-wingers. I do it too in Congress. They're good friends of mine. We get together for coffee, tell jokes, talk politics. They feel lost, but they make a thousand dollars every month, and that's good money these days. Let's hope they get enough votes in the next elections to return to the House. What would we do without them?"

Isabel was livid. Listening to a person that shameless was enough to get anyone riled up. The guy deserved to be blindfolded and hung in a well, but that would have been useless. Bolivia was plagued by Gustavos; they grew like a fungus and survived like cockroaches.

"Where did your brother go?" Don Gustavo asked.

"He's in the parlor."

"He's another one who wants to escape from reality, but through drugs. The kid is spineless, just like your father."

"Please don't mention him," Isabel snapped.

"It's a good thing he's gone. To him, we were all a bunch of stinking half-breeds. He thought he was better than everyone else."

"I said not to mention him, you jerk!" Isabel shouted.

Don Gustavo didn't turn red with anger simply because he was dark-skinned, and dark-skinned people don't change color even in the middle of a rainbow.

Isabel left the library. I picked up my Jack London books and was about to make an exit, when he asked me, "What's a teacher going to the United States for?"

"Pancakes," I said. "Have you heard of the House of Pancakes?"

"No kidding," he replied with a smile. He turned his back to me and made his phone call.

I went downstairs, where nobody paid any attention to me. I looked around for Isabel, but she had vanished. After one last glass of red wine, I walked out into the bitter night wind. A pair of policemen relaxing in a security hut watched me as I walked off in search of a bus to take me home.

A sleepless night thinking about Doña Arminda's dollars and Isabel's charms seemed to await me, and I wasn't mistaken. My acute desperation kept me awake most of the night. I figured I had blown my chance to ambush Arminda. I had stupidly wasted hours of my life with those rich stiffs, sipping blue-blooded liquor and unsuccessfully screwing a female castrator until she nearly made a biblical martyr out of me when we were hit by that volley of stones. I was a push-over; I was a lover of the impossible, a dreamer who never could choose his dream, an incomplete man. Deep down, maybe it was fear that had erased my will to steal and take risks. Nonetheless, I realized that the crime was the only thing left for me to do, the only way I could redeem myself in my own eyes, the one thing that would give meaning to my life. I acknowledged that if I didn't pull it off the following night, I might as well forget about it.

What would I do then? Screw Blanca in fleabag hotels in that neighborhood-from-hell, coexisting with a virus that might rear its ugly head any day? In a few years, we would retire to a tropical village to sell ice cream, kill mosquitoes, sleep long siestas in that all-consuming heat, gaze out at the rivers, and wait for the rains to come. It would be better to die for the American visa. I was in an idiotic predicament worthy of a Third-Worlder, but I wasn't the only one. There were millions of losers just like me. It was laughable but also real, so real that when I turned off the lights, my room was illuminated as if by a hundred bulbs. The solution was to drink some *pisco*, but there wasn't a single drop in my bottle. Fortunately, around 4 in the morning, Blanca returned, a little dizzy but happy. It's uncommon to see a sad prostitute; each night they bury their existential angst inside their vaginas. Maybe when God forgave Mary Magdalene he forgave them all, relieving them of their sadness and filling them with cheer.

"How did it go?" I asked.

"You're awake?"

"I just got back. I was at a party on the south side of town."

"Where?"

"Calacoto, Achumani . . ."

"I had a good night," she said. "I think that when the economy's bad, people stop buying clothes first, then they stop eating, and the last thing they give up is sex."

Since Norha the castrator had left me hanging, I made love to Blanca and thought about Isabel. She climaxed with the expression of a girl who has just discovered what an orgasm is. Immediately afterwards, she fell asleep and, naturally, started to snore. I did my best not to wake her; after all, she earned her daily bread through suffering. At 6 in the morning, I was lucky enough to see the parish priest climb up to the belfry and, with sadistic intent, ring the bells loud enough to wake up the entire neighborhood. He observed me from his perch. I gave him the finger, shut the window, and, as soon as the ringing ceased, fell sound asleep.

When I woke up at around 11 o'clock, Blanca was still sleeping like an angel. I went out to the patio, where Don Antonio was bingeing on chocolates.

"This is the best chocolate in Bolivia, Alvarez, my friend, straight from the *pampas* of Beni." Don Antonio held a bag filled with fresh bread rolls, still warm from the oven. He handed me one. "The owner of the hotel is in a diabetic coma. Let's hope he doesn't die on us. That would be a tragedy; we'd all be at the mercy of the nurse and the Scotsman. The old bat would boot me out onto the street within a week." After a pause, Don Antonio continued: "You don't look so hot. If you keep overdoing it at this altitude, they'll find you stiff in bed one day."

The salesman stepped out of the shower. He was much paler than usual and maintained an air of permanent sadness, of unfathomable bitterness. He had on a long-sleeved undershirt, long underwear, and old-fashioned slippers.

"Chocolate?" Don Antonio asked.

The salesman greeted me and, bending over, replied, "It's bad for my stomach. A bread roll and some coffee would be nice."

Don Antonio winked at me and scoffed, "Our tireless salesman sold out his entire stock of wine and cheese, a record for him. Even so, asking him for a loan is like asking for rain in the Atacama Desert."

"I don't borrow and I don't lend," the salesman said, retreating to his room.

"That's one lonely man," I said.

"The guy's a stingy, cold-hearted misogynist. The goalie tells me he's a huge masturbator. To be honest, I've never seen him with a woman, not even with one of the girls from the Tropicana Cabaret who don't exactly play hard to get. He pays for his room on time, eats two meals a day, and consumes an incredible amount of bread; our guess is ten to fifteen rolls every day."

The salesman returned with a small kerosene stove and began heating some water in a kettle. When it reached a boil, he mixed in a pinch of ground coffee and then added three tiny spoonfuls of sugar. After stirring the coffee, he put the cup to one side and, hands trembling, picked up a bread roll. With smooth and persistent gestures, he removed the crust, sliced the inside into small pieces, arranged them on a plate, rubbed his hands together, and began to drink the coffee. He sipped slowly, accompanying each slurp with a piece of bread. It was a true ceremony; we watched in silence for five minutes. He finished without speaking and then returned to his room.

JUAN DE RECACOECHEA ∽ 183

"A poor man's gourmet, but a gourmet nonetheless," Don Antonio commented, then changed the subject. "Today is a milestone: the last showing at the old Cinema Bolívar. They're going to turn it into a gambling hall. I used to get in for free. May the late owner rest in peace; the man was a good friend of mine and the ticket agents would let me sneak in when it wasn't too full."

"*The Last Picture Show*," I said. "Do you remember the movie?"

"We ought to see a porno flick; it'll raise more than just our spirits."

"Okay, what time?"

"Let's meet at 3."

"Sounds good. I'll take a nap and see you then," I said.

Chapter 10

The taxi dropped us off at El Prado and we walked slowly toward the movie theater. In spite of his physical and economic tribulations, Don Antonio was in a terrific mood.

"In my day, when I was still young," he began, "the United States didn't have immigration quotas for Latin Americans. If we wanted to go live there, it was no big deal. I never had the same dream as you. I wanted to go to Europe, to Paris most of all. If I had made it to the City of Lights, I never would have left. I'm talking about the Paris of the interwar period, the most brilliant Paris, the Paris of Picasso, Modigliani, Vallejo, and Henry Miller. Unfortunately, my MNR friends at the foreign ministry sent me to inhospitable places like Puno and Calama. I didn't have a bad time, but I would have preferred better postings. Valparaíso was very good to me; I fell in love with nearly all the hookers who worked at the port. I'd like to be buried there, but at the rate I'm going I'll end up encased in marble in the Alcorta family mausoleum. If you ever come back to Bolivia, you'll know where to find me. I'll be there until kingdom come."

"Don't talk like that. You look good," I said.

"Once you hit seventy, every day's a lottery. One bad fall, a year in bed, and then you're dead." Don Antonio ran his fingers through his silvered moustache and took a deep breath. "If I ever decide to kill myself, I won't need poison or even a pistol. I'll just catch a train to

Cochabamba, and within a week my asthma will send me to the other world."

Don Antonio bought some sweets at a street stand and started to suck on them delicately. He was wearing a fur-lined jacket meant for frigid temperatures.

The last showing at the Cinema Bolívar was an Italian production called *Nightfall in Istanbul*. Don Antonio flashed a friendly smile at the ticket agent as I slipped him a single peso under the rope. The theater was at near capacity with patrons from the middle class on down. The mixture of odors was impressive, but nothing I couldn't get used to. Don Antonio picked seats in the front row so he could catch every last detail of the erotic scenes. The plot was simple enough: A French couple, an older man and a woman in her thirties, were traveling to Istanbul on vacation to admire the Mosque of Santa Sophia. The man was impotent, and the woman, a nymphomaniac with a fetish for riffraff.

Just for fun, the husband would send his wife off to do guys in the poor neighborhoods. One afternoon, she screwed a Turk on top of their bed. Bottle of brandy in hand, the French guy sat in a chair at one edge of the mattress and ogled the couple's gyrations, amidst wild cries and Islamic invocations. Don Antonio confessed to having seen each of the previous three showings.

During the movie, I got up to go to the bathroom. There were two adjacent stalls in a hallway in the back. While taking a leak, I heard a fight break out between a man and a woman in the stall next to me. When they quieted down, the unmistakable cadence of lovemaking started up. I stepped onto my tiptoes and peered over the partition to find a couple of Indians entangled like a pair of larvae. The man was drunk, and the woman nearing ecstasy. They were humping standing up like a couple of animals, as if their lives depended on it.

"I'm the Turk," the guy stammered.

"Fucking Turk!" she cried.

I returned to my seat and told Don Antonio what I had seen.

"See Istanbul and die happy," he said.

During the course of the movie, Don Antonio ate a cold empanada, a dozen chocolates, and a tamale.

The film ended with the French couple's return to their ancestral homeland. They took back with them a Turkish sheepdog and a dimwitted, 230-pound wrestler with a shaven head, a nose like an anteater, and fleshy lips.

The show was over. It was 7:30 in the evening.

"I have to go," I said. "Wish me luck."

"Good luck," Don Antonio replied, "with whatever you're doing."

I left the theater and headed for Santa Cruz Street. Dusk advanced imperceptibly, as the sun began to hide its pale sphere behind the Andean plateau. In spite of the approaching night, it wasn't cold, nor was the wind blowing.

The north side of town had a festive air to it, as if it were the eve of carnival. I entered the first bar I saw and chugged a half-glass of *pisco* with a squeeze of lemon juice. I asked for a beer to chase the *pisco*, and then another *pisco* to chase the beer. I felt rejuvenated and ready to stop by Yujra's place.

Half an hour later I arrived at Ortega Way. The street was abuzz with vendors and people out for a stroll. I felt the weight of the lead club in my pocket. Serene and optimistic, I walked to the Luribay. I found the place nearly empty, except for three or four vagrants who were used to spending their waking hours plastered. As I entered the bar, the bartender ordered them to leave.

"Get lost, punks!" Yujra roared.

"Just one more, boss," one of the vagrants whined. "We'll split it and then we're gone. Don't be this way, brother—"

"I'm not your brother," Yujra retorted. "I don't have no bums for brothers."

"We got cash," another vagrant said. "We're going to Rafa's place then."

"She'll give you pure liquor. I don't sell garbage here."

"Don't tell me you were breast-fed expensive booze," the vagrant jeered.

Yujra lifted him up by the lapels and dealt him a well-placed head-butt to the face. It sounded like a truck running over a watermelon. One of the vagrants whipped out a pocketknife and said, "You were the heavyweight champ till that black Peruvian knocked you out. They had to take you away on a stretcher. You got hit so hard, it made you retarded."

Yujra went for the kill, but not fast enough. Right as he was about to get clocked, the vagrant stuck the knife into one of Yujra's buttocks. Yujra was so strong, he didn't seem to notice the wound; stepping forward, he landed a right hook that floored the vagrant. Yujra bent over and continued to pound the guy mercilessly.

"That's enough, pal!" the vagrant sputtered. "You're still the champ."

"I don't want to see you here again," Yujra snarled.

"Okay," the vagrant moaned.

Yujra returned to the bar and started to patch up his wound. I was afraid the police would show up and ruin my night, but Yujra continued to work as if he'd only been bitten by a mosquito. I asked for a shot of moonshine and then approached the window. I glimpsed

Doña Arminda weighing some gold nuggets. Her client, a guy with mud-colored skin and a straw sombrero, emotionlessly observed the operation.

The client departed, and Severo admitted an old man in shirt-sleeves, apparently a gold runner from the humid forests who didn't feel the chill in the world's highest capital. It didn't take long to weigh his treasure and close the deal. Once the old guy had left the premises, Arminda went about closing drawers, storing the scales, and scrambling the combination lock to her safe.

Next, they counted their money and put the gold away in bags. My time had come. I paid for my drink and slipped out of the dive. I'd forgotten to get something to conceal my face, so the first thing I did was buy a pair of panty hose in a little store on Ortega Way. To make sure I wouldn't lose track of Arminda and her companion, I parked myself next to a fruit stand, cloaked in the semi-darkness.

Minutes later, they emerged brimming with self-assurance and smiling broadly. My idea was to arrive at the big house on Colón Street before they did, which is why I hurried to reach Tumusla. I hailed the first taxi headed downtown. It dropped me off at the intersection of Potosí and Ayacucho. I climbed the latter in long strides, heart racing, and nearly ran out of gas. I was getting too old for this. In the Plaza Murillo, I stopped on the steps of Congress and took a deep breath. Congressmen and senators of the Republic passed by me ethereally. I kept speed-walking until Ballivián Street, where an evening mass was being conducted at Our Lady of Carmen Church. I stepped into the small foyer and blended in with the arriving parishioners. I stopped behind a column that bisected the church doors. From there, it was easy to survey the scene. I didn't have to wait long. Severo and Arminda emerged from Ballivián Street and headed down Colón.

When they reached the entrance to the old house, they disappeared into the passage at the base of the building.

The shoemaker was getting ready to pound a sole. Since he was working with his back to the passageway, he had no idea who was coming and going. That worked in my favor. Severo didn't take long to come out, sporting his smart-ass Indian smile. Just like the first time, he headed to the eatery for dinner. Doña Arminda was all alone in the apartment. I left the church, crossed the street, and tiptoed through the passage weightlessly, like a Russian ballerina. Unaware of my presence, the shoemaker hammered away with religious zeal. Upon reaching the patio, I stood in silence beside the fountain, closely observing Arminda's apartment. A dim lightbulb illuminated the scene. I checked my watch: it was 8:30. The rich guy usually showed up at 9, so I had half an hour, which was more than enough time. The prevailing darkness favored my plans. I awkwardly pulled the panty hose over my head, obscuring my face but also blurring my vision. I climbed the stairs and took out my glass cutter. Just to make sure, I pushed the door handle, but as I had expected, it was locked. My only choice was to nick the glass with the cutter. I had seen it done countless times. I delicately cut a small square into one of the panes on the lower part of the window covering the upper half of the door. This done, I stuffed the cutter into my jacket and pushed gently against the glass with my right elbow. Nothing happened. I tried pushing harder . . . and the glass broke, crashing down noisily on the other side of the door and shattering into pieces against the ceramic-tiled floor.

The sound was loud enough to wake up a deaf person. I froze in place like an invisible savage in the Amazon jungle. If Arminda appeared, I didn't know for sure what I would do, probably run like hell. Three endless minutes ticked by, but the gold queen wasn't giving any sign of life. I opened the door and silently closed it behind me, barely breathing. My eyes adjusted to the darkness. I realized I was in a kitchen that doubled as a laundry room. I started to walk down a hallway; to my left, I made out another door that led to a dining room, and to my right I saw a living room. At the end of the hallway there was a third door, from underneath which a sliver of light was emanating. Shivers of fear and anxiety raced through my body like electric eels. Still, I managed to muster my courage and continued toward the door under which the glow was coming. As soon as I opened it, I understood why Arminda hadn't heard the crashing glass. I had stumbled upon a spacious bedroom with walls covered by loud wallpaper and a budget hotel–style double bed decorated with two small pink cushions.

Against one wall, an old wardrobe, a pair of chairs on which some garments rested, and a bureau atop which I glimpsed, to my amazement, two leather briefcases. Arminda hadn't heard a thing because she was showering in the bathroom next to her bedroom. Praise the Lord!

The bathroom door had been left ajar, perhaps so she could keep an eye on the briefcases. I approached carefully, as if walking on egg shells, and tried to ascertain what was going on in the bathroom. A shower curtain covered the tub, and I could make out Doña Arminda's sillhouette. The steam had turned the place into a sauna; it was difficult to see clearly. I made a ninety-degree turn and picked up the suitcases. One of them weighed a ton. I placed them on top of the bed, keeping the lead club handy, just in case.

One of the briefcases was flush with dollar bills and the other contained gold. I wasn't interested in the gold, so I concentrated on the dollars. Tied in bundles, they lay there like paper diamonds. My eagle's eye counted at least twenty thousand dollars worth. I picked up one bundle, which amounted to ten hundred-dollar bills. It was exactly what I needed. But the greed of man is comparable only to his desire for self-destruction, and begging the Holy Spirit for forgiveness I stuffed a few more bundles into my pockets. *Give or take, it's all the same,* I thought, consoling myself. As I reveled in my discovery, I felt a puff of hot air come out of the bathroom. I figured that a gust of wind through an open window had collided with a small cloud of steam. What a surprise it was to see a human figure emerge from that mist, covered by an enormous towel. I immediately whipped out the lead club and got ready to whack Doña Arminda over the head. But I didn't have time; the towel slipped off the body of the airy apparition. To my astonishment, I discovered a figure covered by an impressive amount of body hair. Its skin had mysteriously tanned to a dark brown hue. The body of Doña Arminda, feminine, rounded, and curvaceous, had, through the work of the Devil, turned into a solid and muscular figure. Her sensual white face had transformed into a rough, masculine mask.

A hoarse voice brought me back to my senses. "Who are you?"

I didn't manage to respond. My throat went dry like that of a salt miner in the Atacama Desert. Through some strange process of transmutation, Doña Arminda had become Don Gustavo, Isabel's uncle.

He threw the towel to the floor and ripped the panty hose off my face with a catlike swipe.

"Teacher boy!" he exclaimed. "Teacher boy trying to run off with my money."

"Whaaaaaat!" Arminda yelled.

Don Gustavo grabbed me by the neck. Despite his age, he was much stronger than me. "What are you doing here?"

His dark frame was armed with a huge phallus.

"I need the money to pay for the American visa," I confessed.

He looked at me as if he were Lazarus's brother watching Lazarus sip tea after having had his eyelids shut forever. "Visa? What visa?"

"The American visa," I repeated.

"You think I'm an idiot? Put that money right back where it was!"

Instead of obeying him, I delivered a quick knee to his nuts, which looked like a pair of toasted figs. He let out a wolf's howl.

"Whaaaaat!" Doña Arminda yelled a second time.

Don Gustavo sprang to his feet with the ferocity of a panther, but he was naked and wet, just like when he entered this world. He slipped and fell anew. I tried to flee, but I had a pair of cement blocks for legs. Don Gustavo stood up and threw a left hook that could have toppled a bronze statue. I raised the lead pipe and slammed it over his wet head. He absorbed the impact and stood there as if paralyzed, eyes wide open and a look of incredulity on his face. Evidently, he hadn't expected the lead pipe. I made the most of his panic and attempted another escape. But the man was strong, so strong that in spite of the crushing blow, he still had it in him to grab me by the hair and hold on.

"You're not getting away, teacher boy," he snarled.

It was a good thing he had already lost half of his energy and couldn't quite keep a grip on me. I tried to free myself from his hands, like a squirming mongoose. We staggered across the room in slow motion, like a pair of mimes in swampy waters. I got a whiff of his breath, a mix of whiskey and homecooking, and heard him cursing me. Reaching deep into my soul, I was able to distance myself. I delivered another resounding blow with the club, this time to the forehead. He let go of me and leaned against one of the armchairs. It was the moment I had been waiting for. I pounded him numerous times until he collapsed to the floor. He stared up at me with hatred and resignation. I stooped over and met his gaze. And right then, the pall of eternity spread over him.

I shook him several times and tried in vain to make out his heartbeat. There was nothing but silence. Don Gustavo was on his way to far-off galaxies, to the cradle of the Big Bang.

"Hand me a towel!" Doña Arminda cried.

I watched the blood gush down the gray flooring, as if in search of the open sea.

By a trick of fate, I had become a murderer. It was one more detail in my life, the most important since my birth, the most transcendental; more significant than that morning my son was born or the day Antonia left. To me, murder had always been a literary or cinematic flourish, something that existed merely in fiction. Now, I had blood on my hands. I understood that my entire past was irrelevant and that I would endure whatever befell me day by day, hour by hour, until, like Don Gustavo, I stopped breathing and entered a state of permanent anesthesia.

"Towwwwwwellllll!" Doña Arminda cried out again.

I imagined the shriek she would unleash in a few moments, upon discovering the cold body of her lover and business partner. I left in a mad dash, but I was still lucid. Now things were getting serious. In the patio, I came across a small child playing hide-and-go-seek with a friend. The shoemaker was busy fastening a rubber heel onto a canoe-shaped shoe. A half-breed lady from Potosí, one of those who subsist off selling lemons, had set up shop in the doorway to the house and was preparing some soup. Three witnesses, all on another planet.

Once out on the street, I hurried up Indaburo. My nerves were jumpy as hell. Not a soul to be found. I thought about taking a taxi, but the traffic was heavy and slow-moving. Better to go by foot and not freak out. My mood was surprisingly stable, and my nerves were beginning to calm down. At Plaza Jenaro Sanjinés, I watched people gathering to attend a show at the Municipal Theater. A free adaptation of Bertold Brecht's *The Good Woman of Setzuan* was showing. Brecht wouldn't have approved of the murder, but Gustavo was bad news and expendable, just like the old lady Raskolnikov took out in *Crime and Punishment*.

I walked down Comercio. The people of La Paz, accustomed to the cold, were out for a stroll as if it were the French Riviera.

I passed by a fat panhandling street performer who was entertaining a crowd with jokes. A few hookers strutted around with about as much pizzazz as cows lined up at a country fair. Street vendors, young maids in search of a few pesos, newly uncloseted gays, and low-lying crooks all gathered in the Plaza Pérez Velasco. On the terrace in front of San Francisco Church, beside the raised sidewalk, I happened upon the eye of a storm.

I ditched the lead club and the glass cutter.

A group of obnoxious Christian rockers were making a racket in the middle of the plaza. Riffraff formed a circle around the band. My intention was to now head up Santa Cruz and get to the hotel as soon as possible to count the dollars that were burning holes in my pockets.

Cutting through the jamboree, I felt someone grab me by the arm. "You, sir, are the man I was looking for," said the stranger.

A young fellow dressed in black, with a white shirt and reddish tie, was smiling before me.

"What do you want?" I asked.

"You, sir, have been chosen to pick a card to show these people that I am not pulling their leg." He led me to a circle in which his traveling magician's wares were on display. He turned to the audience and said, "I've never seen this man before. Isn't that right, sir?"

"I've never seen him," I stammered. I hadn't yet come to my senses.

"He's not lying. I just arrived from Arequipa. I don't know anyone. I have no accomplices or friends; I'm no trickster."

He thrust a stack of cards before me and told me to pick one. I pulled out a queen of hearts.

"And now, ladies and gentlemen," he said, moving away from me, "it's up to me to figure out, through telepathy, what card he took. Sir, please look at the card in your hands." He backed up a few yards, paused to think with his head bowed, and then announced: "A queen of hearts."

The people applauded. The magician pulled out a shining gilt cigarette case, opened it, and offered me a smoke.

"I have great powers," he said. "For example, I can tell you blindfolded what this man is hiding in his pockets." He winked at me and smiled.

"Thanks," I said, "but my girlfriend's waiting for me at the merry-go-round."

The crowd burst out in laughter. I seized the moment and slipped away. I raced up Santa Cruz Street. No doubt the know-it-all Peruvian magician's ironic gaze was still following me. If that guy had guessed I was carrying thousands of dollars in my pockets, he probably knew I had also just knocked off Don Gustavo; typical amateur magician.

In the hotel lobby, I found Blanca accompanied by two girls from the Tropicana. She was dolled up in one of those dresses that black and Latina girls wear to nightclubs in the Bronx.

"What's the matter?" she asked.

"Nothing."

"You look pale. You shouldn't drink so much. What do you think of my dress? I bought it at a shop on Huyustus Street."

"Great."

She stroked my hair and stared at me lustfully. "I like you better when you're pale."

"I'm going to my room. I'll see you in a few minutes."

She looked at herself in a compact mirror. "Antelo's throwing a goodbye party," she said.

"See you there," I responded.

I asked for my key and went up to my room. I sat on the hard bed and placed the dollars on the bedspread; it was a good sum. I started counting: hundreds, fifties, and twenties. Fondling them, I added them up carefully. Two thousand three hundred and twenty dollars had been the price of my liberation and of Don Gustavo's head. I think that in the game of life, we were now even. Trembling, I stretched out on the bed and closed my eyes. The footage of the murder passed before my eyes in full color. I feared that the memory of the club shattering Don Gustavo's skull would become an excruciating, never-ending nightmare.

I stayed there for a while fingering the bills, throwing them into the air and letting them fall into a heap on my chest. As if carrying a strange spell, they represented that same blood-soaked nightmare.

"Doctor Alvarez!"

It was Don Antonio. What did the old man want?

I opened the door and saw his scheming grandfather's face. He tried to say something, but his cough got the better of him and he stood there choking for an entire fifteen seconds. He stopped and said: "Antelo sent me. We're having a party. He received notice of his appointment as Assistant Director of Customs for Santa Cruz, a gig that will make him a millionaire overnight. To celebrate, he bought bottles of fine *pisco*, wine, and beer. That soccer star is one lucky know-nothing."

"I'm coming," I said. I put the dollars away under the mattress and took out three twenties for spending money.

A number of hotel guests were at the bash: Blanca, Gardenia, Videla, Don Antonio, Antelo, and a couple of hostesses from the Tropicana, the ones I had seen before in the hotel lobby.

Antelo was flying high. With his tacky green jacket and white pants, he was ready for the tropics. He had shaved and put on some cologne, and was now smiling smugly, like a sheik before his harem. "Alvarez, my friend," he said. "I have everything I ever wanted. Now, I can ramble all I want and no one can make me stop. You should join me. Life is great down east; there are tons of beautiful girls. What do you say?"

"What would I do in Santa Cruz?"

"Customs can always use consultants; don't pretend like you don't know."

"Thanks, Antelo, but I don't even belong to your party."

"So? You can join. What's the big deal? Take the oath and we'll give you a membership card. With the card, no one can touch you."

"I got the money for the visa. My godfather, the barber, helped me out."

"North America is a safer bet, but at your age moving there is no joke," he said.

Gardenia was dressed like a man, in a leather jacket and jeans. Along with the hostesses, he was cracking jokes at the expense of the salesman, who was unable to wipe the sad Stan Laurel–like expression off his face.

Having had a few drinks too many, Blanca embraced me affection-

198 › AMERICAN VISA

ately as soon as the radio started playing. "Dance," she said. "Don't look so scared. Nobody's going to eat you."

"Do I still look pale?" I asked.

"The alcohol will bring your color back. What are you worried about?" She handed me a beer, we drank a toast, and she sighed. "I'm independent. If I feel like it, I'm gone . . . or I could stay for a man. But you're not my man. You're just a crazy guy who doesn't need anyone."

Everyone cheered when the bellboy arrived carrying two cooked chickens, baked potatoes, fried plantains, pickled vegetables, and hot sauce. Don Antonio said, "Gastronomic debauchery is the only kind of orgy I can handle at my age. What did you think of the film at the Cinema Bolívar?"

"I liked Istanbul. I'll bet that shacking up with a Turkish chick would be the best thing for someone on his deathbed."

"Sexual euthanasia," Don Antonio said approvingly. "It's not for a poor guy like me."

Blanca, who was two steps away, moved closer. "Enough about Turkish girls already! What do they have that we don't?"

"Ha ha," Don Antonio laughed. "At this altitude, jealousy is bad for your blood pressure."

Blanca took me by the hand and said, "You're trembling."

"I'm just so excited for Antelo. He's going to put a stop to poverty. 'Black Panther' Yashin couldn't do it better."

"You're acting really weird," Blanca said. "It's as if you aren't here." I grabbed her by the waist. She stood there for a moment and then rested her forehead on my shoulder.

Don Antonio suggested, "Take her with you to North America. You won't be lonely with a woman like that. Gringas are descendents of Scandinavians and Anglo-Saxons; it would be like learning to write all over again."

"I'm not going anywhere," Blanca said. "I love my country."

"Patriotic fatalism," I said.

Antelo swayed back and forth euphorically, like a fly inside a bottle. The hostesses from the Tropicana were busy eating; copperskinned Quechuas, they radiated a sensual mixture of Indian and Spanish. With the life they led, they would get old fast. They were in their twenties but looked about as burned out as harlots celebrating their fiftieth anniversaries in brothels. I tried not to get drunk, so that if the police came I would have enough time to gather my thoughts. The first thing the coppers ask for is your alibi, and I didn't have one. I needed to be able to justify the interlude between when I left the Cinema Bolívar, up until a half-hour ago. No way could I mention my visit to the Luribay, since the mistress of the late senator worked right in front. I thought about asking Blanca to tell the cops, in case they came after me, that she had been with me. The problem was that I had dusted off someone famous, and poor Blanca would flip her lid; deep down she was just a peasant girl, and if they pressured her, she'd panic. I decided that, if asked, I would simply stop the clock and explain that I went back to the hotel after the movie with a splitting headache that had me seeing stars, and I went to bed.

To ease my distress, I headed back to my room, took a few aspirin, and dozed off. I woke up and went down to the lobby, where I ran into Blanca and the others again. She hadn't seen me enter the hotel, but somebody might have. The manager always sticks his nose in everybody's business . . . Or the helper . . . the helper had handed me the keys to my room, but the guy's a drunk, a little absentminded, and, most importantly, bribable. A hundred bucks would shut him up. Yujra was another story. If the murder made it to the papers, which was likely since a senator was involved, it would get the ex-champ's attention. He would be able to link me to the gold queen; he had seen me in that dive two or three times. Against that pack of vagrants, a middle-class guy stood out. American detective protocol would have me take out the boxer to cover my tracks, but I wasn't up for another cold-blooded murder.

Besides, killing Yujra wouldn't be so easy. You had to watch it with that guy. If I messed up the first try, I'd be a goner. The wisest thing would be to wait and see if the police thought it had to do with a settling of scores with some Trotskyite group. I needed to hide the booty immediately in a secure place, and wait . . .

"Have a beer and stop worrying about the visa," Don Antonio said. "Money will buy you anything except your death. That's the honest truth."

Blanca asked sarcastically, "So you managed to get enough money? When are you leaving?"

"Very soon."

"Who loaned it to you?"

"My godfather, for old time's sake."

"A likely story," Blanca remarked.

One of the hostesses from the Tropicana came up to us. Her name was Fresia and she had a Polish last name. The blend of Quechua and Polish was something like a Molotov cocktail.

"Everyone's getting a little wild at this party," she said. "Except for you, Don Mario; you're already fixed up."

"Antelo's going to bring the house down," Don Antonio said.

"He doesn't have a single peso left," Fresia replied, looking at him askance.

I took her aside and whispered: "I want to make you a business proposal." She crossed her arms. "I want you to make love to Don Antonio. I'll pay for everything."

"The old man?"

"If he can't get it up, I'll still pay you. What do you say?"

"For fifty dollars I'll bring him back from the dead," she declared.

Don Antonio was savoring a piece of apple pie, courtesy of Gardenia. "Time for my Tedral," he announced. "There's an open pharmacy on Bolívar Street. It's going to be a long walk."

"There's still time for that," I said. "Right now, Fresia is here. She's from a UNESCO World Heritage site, the city of Potosí."

"Potosí," Don Antonio repeated. "I was there when Edward VIII visited Bolivia. Back then, he was the Prince of Wales. He stayed at the Governor's Mansion. Unfortunately, the mansion didn't have a single bathroom and his bowel movements ended up creating a diplomatic uproar. We had to escort him to a nearby hotel; once he finished, we walked him back. Let's hope he didn't mention it in his memoirs! This was in the 1920s, when I was starting out at the foreign ministry. I was a protocol assistant."

"This guy wouldn't stop talking if you taped his mouth shut," Fresia said.

I took Don Antonio aside. His eyes brimmed with curiosity. "What do you think of Fresia?" I asked.

"A Quechua concoction," he offered.

"She's ready to make love to you. It won't cost you a cent."

Don Antonio's face grew serious. He adjusted his glasses and smiled faintly. "Another one of your jokes, dear Alvarez?"

"I already talked it over with her. You have my word."

"I need the Tedral. Without the Tedral, I'm dead in the water," he said.

"I'll send for some. Are you ready?"

"It's been so many years . . . How much does she want?"

"It doesn't matter. Do you think you still can?"

"Of course. My prostate's good to go and my ass is as virgin as the deep Amazon. Wouldn't you rather give me some money to pay the hotel?"

"No, no . . . I want you to do her. None of this hotel nonsense."

"You're a cruel man, Alvarez, but if I have no choice . . ."

Gardenia was puffing on a pipe and blowing smoke circles, like Lauren Bacall in one of her movies from the '50s. "It's tough to pull together eight hundred dollars in this town. We'll miss you. We got used to having you around," Gardenia said.

"Barcelona's a great place," I hummed.

"Before I leave for Barcelona, I need to have an operation to get my little pecker removed."

"My advice to you, Gardenia," I offered, "is hold onto your dick. You just never know. I met an Argentine transsexual once who got the operation because he had a thing for young boys. A few years later, he started liking girls so he had to become a lesbian. It was tragic because there was no turning back. He couldn't get a penis implant."

Gardenia laughed. "Some story! That won't happen to me—don't jinx it."

"If you do go to Barcelona, watch it with needle-sharing and people without symptoms. I hear that the Mediterranean is an HIV paradise."

"A virus with class," Gardenia concluded.

Antelo approached us. His smile would have looked great on a jack-o'-lantern. "My party rose to the challenges of our times," he said.

"The MIR? They're the fair-weather party," Don Antonio jeered.

"With hands that good at catching soccer balls, now you're gonna make off like a bandit," Gardenia said.

"Don't come to me later asking for favors," Antelo scolded.

"Easy," I said. "We trust your honesty."

Antelo gave us all hugs and a whiff of his *pisco* breath. When he saw Fresia walk off to serve herself a piece of cake, he said, "Every last one of these hostesses works for the Interior Ministry."

"You think so?" I asked anxiously.

"They're such bimbos," Don Antonio said pointedly, "that they confuse plot with Pol Pot."

"Pol Pot?" Antelo repeated. "You lost me."

"The Khmer Rouge," Don Antonio said.

"Where's that?"

The lobby door opened and Rommel Videla peeked in with his withered face. His smile was faded and his eyes lit up like candles. "Cheers!" he offered. "If Antelo, my buddy from the Chaco, heads to Santa Cruz, I'm going with him."

"I'm not from the Chaco," Antelo grumbled. "I was just the goalie for Chaco Petrolero."

"They've been playing like shit lately," the salesman said.

"They don't have any young talent," Antelo explained.

"In Santa Cruz, my peddler friend, you can sell your sadness," Don Antonio said.

"In Santa Cruz nobody would buy it. They're happy people," Gardenia responded.

Blanca took a step forward and raised her wine glass. "I propose a toast to Antelo's health. He suffered like a single mother for that job with Customs."

Antelo lifted his glass in kind. He shed a tear that got bigger and bigger as it rolled down his cheek. "You're all like family to me!" he stuttered.

Rommel, the tireless salesman, asked Patricia, one of the hostesses, to dance. She was dark-skinned and had the heft of a member of a traveling wrestling troupe. They put on quite a show; she danced salsa and he tango, as the radio blared a Dominican merengue.

Blanca pushed me into a corner. She was drunk. "You've been up to something. You look different. Where were you?"

"At the movies with Don Antonio and the barbershop with my godfather."

"The money . . . did you steal it?"

"You're crazy. He loves me like a son. I'm going to repay him every last dollar. I'm clean. Later I'll send you a letter asking you if you'd like to join me."

"That and the face of God are two things I'll never see," she said.

The party continued. We finished off the chicken, the potatoes, the wine, and the desserts. Gardenia and Patricia left at midnight to buy more booze. Fresia brought some cocaine, really good stuff, and we sniffed a few lines. Don Antonio observed us with curiosity. Videla started to cry as he remembered his father, who had plunged to his death off a bend in the road to the Yungas. Antelo was diving on a bed, clutching at imaginary soccer balls. Don Antonio fell asleep.

We carried the old man back to his room. When Gardenia and Patricia returned from their liquor run, I told Fresia that Don Antonio was waiting for her in bed. She asked me for the fifty dollars. I gave her forty, promising her ten more the next day. The *pisco* they had bought could have moved the bowels of a camel; we took turns going to the bathroom. After several fruitless attempts, Patricia finally managed to slip her hand inside the salesman's pants. He started to laugh like a hyena, baring his teeth. I remembered the money and left the party without anyone else realizing it.

Once in my room, I wracked my brain for a good hiding place. I couldn't think of anything better than to remove a loose piece of floor tile, stuff the dollars inside a nylon bag, dig a small hole in the dirt underneath the tile, and leave the bag there. I put the tile back in its place and tamped it down hard. After making sure it showed no sign of coming loose, I returned to the party.

Patricia and the salesman were arguing over the price of a bed-down. The salesman wanted to pay for the act of lovemaking in bottles of wine.

"How many?" Patricia asked.

"Two Concha y Toro."

"Keep the wine, jackoff!" Patricia snapped.

Blanca was tired and asked me to walk her to her room. She started to throw up as soon as we got outside. After I put her to bed, she made three separate trips to the bathroom. Then she fell asleep. I undressed and started to envisage the next morning's headlines: *Senator Beaten to Death in Secret Love Nest*, or, *Strange Circumstances Surround Politician's Murder*, or, *Police Hunt Gold Assassin*. It was impossible for me to sleep in peace. The alcohol kept me in an intermediate state between vigilance and somnolence. I would sleep a few minutes and then wake with a start, alert to the slightest sound. The crime was replaying itself in slow motion.

Absolutely nothing happened. It was an ordinary night, interrupted by the incessant barking of stray dogs and Antelo's inane proclamations. He started to sing drunkenly and cause a ruckus in the hotel lobby, coming to blows with the night doorman.

Blanca slept like a log. I envied her indolence and her little girl's slumber. With the first light of dawn, I got up and quietly headed for the shower. I washed up and shaved in the arctic air and put on a jacket and jeans.

Without waking Blanca, I used a penknife to lift up the floor tile and grab my passport and a handful of greenbacks to pay for my visa and an outfit worthy of an affluent vacationer.

The dazzling blue sky augured a sunny day. In the hotel lobby, the doorman was reading the newspaper. Once he noticed me, he shot me an irritated look. "That jerk Antelo, he raised hell all night," he complained. "Good thing he's leaving."

"Anything in the news?" I asked, trying to sound relaxed.

"I don't know. It just came."

Not a soul in the streets. I had to walk about six hundred feet to find a newspaper stand. I bought the four dailies and then went looking for an open café. In Plaza San Francisco, a solitary homeless man sitting on the edge of a curb contemplated the world with a pained expression. The small coffee shops at Pérez Velasco and on Comercio Street were still closed. It took me almost half an hour to find a place that was open. On Avenida Juan de la Riva, I happened upon a joint that smelled of freshly baked bread. A young boy with a contorted face served me brewed coffee and two warm rolls. With anxiety, fear, and excitement, I leafed through every page of the newspapers like never before in my life. News about the crime was nowhere to be found. I figured that since I had taken out the senator so late at night, there must not have been time to print it. But I wasn't convinced. I told myself that it was impossible, and true to the old saying that "the criminal always returns to the scene of the crime," I hurried up Colón Street. My curiosity was stronger than my judgment, and it led me back to the very house where it had all happened. In front, at Our Lady of Carmen

Church, the bells were ringing for the first mass. The house was as quiet as any other in the neighborhood. I didn't see a single policeman at the door, nor any signs of a disturbance. The gate was wide open. The small man in charge of cleaning was sweeping the patio with an old broom. It was the spitting image of petit bourgeois tranquility, of idyllic small-town life. For an instant, I thought that I had dreamt it all, that my imagination, dulled by age, had revived, as if in the confused awakening of a madman; when I felt the dollars in my pocket, I convinced myself that the dream was reality and that the money was indeed the product of a homicide.

At 9 o'clock, after wandering aimlessly down streets near Jaén, the city's hidden colonial jewel, I resolved to pay a visit to the Andean Tourism Agency. I had to wait there half an hour before fat man Ballón showed up, with a look on his face like he was choking on a scorpion. When he realized that I had the money for the visa, his expression changed. He smiled repeatedly and even offered me some coffee. He told me I would have my visa in two days. When I let him know I couldn't wait that long and that I was willing to pay a thousand dollars to have him grease the wheels at the consulate sooner, he explained that it was impossible. But when he saw the thousand dollars on his desk, he said he would do everything in his power to make sure that they gave me the visa within twenty-four hours. I said goodbye and left him happy, thumbing the greenbacks.

I took advantage of the morning to go shopping for a wardrobe that would go well with the art deco look in Miami. I got everything I needed at a Jewish-owned clothing store. It was important to put your best foot forward at the Miami airport, since they sometimes send you home if they don't like your face and you look like a suspicious immigrant. I spent more than two hundred dollars on a wealthy tourist

208 ⁀ AMERICAN VISA

get-up and bought a few magazines in English to get a feel for the latest American slang. English is so dynamic that in a decade, if you don't keep up, you'll need the help of a dictionary just to read an article in *Time*.

Around midday, I went to an Argentine steak house; it had been an eternity since the last time I ate a cut of beef that smooth, tender, and classy. The waiter offered me the house wine, a Mendoza red. At 12:30, as I was attacking a salad, the owner, a blond Argentine with an impatient manner, switched on the television that sat on top of a shelf wedged against the wall.

On the screen, a woman with an angelic face declared with a smile: *"We regret to inform you of the tragic death by heart attack of the honorable Senator Don Gustavo Castellón in La Paz last night at 9 o'clock."* Next, she read a long list of important government posts that he'd held during his precious and fertile existence, while the television cameras zoomed in on his grieving family surrounding the coffin, which was laid out in a room of what appeared to be an enormous, gaudy mansion. I recognized his wife, his daughter, Doña María Augusta, Isabel, and Charles. Decked out in black, Doña María Augusta was a living image of theatrical pain. Isabel was consoling her and trying, without much success, to adopt a distressed air, while Charles, who looked kind of high, was smiling and visibly content. The sounds of a funeral march served as background to the words of the reporter, who added that the remains of Don Gustavo would be moved to the Senate in the afternoon, where he would receive a final farewell from political and religious leaders and the country as a whole.

I froze. I thought I had misheard. I summoned the waiter.

"Excuse me," I said. "I didn't catch what they said the senator died of."

"A heart attack."

How could they be so wrong? Why such a lie? What was behind this false scenario? I hadn't dreamt it; I clubbed him to death. Maybe the police wanted to throw off the murderer; they invented that crude version of the facts to disorient him before they pounced. But Bolivian police were incapable of playing Machiavellian games for free. There surely existed some powerful reason for twisting the facts and presenting Don Gustavo's death as a natural occurrence. It seemed to work in my favor, since without a crime there was no criminal. Still, I didn't trust our lawmen. The word "imagination" may not be in their vocabulary, but when they smell money they move like ants. A lot of dough was at stake with what had gone down on Colón Street—dollars and many kilos of gold. The police would look for me, not to put a murderer behind bars, but to liquidate me as a potentially troublesome witness. If they said the senator died of a heart attack, then the lustful Arminda must be in on it. They hadn't even mentioned her. I was in mortal danger. If I didn't hurry up and leave the country, I would suffer the same fate as the senator, except they wouldn't bury me with honors and a marching band. I'd end up in the morgue, so that medical students could play with my balls.

In the hotel room, I found Blanca still asleep, murmuring incomprehensibly in the middle of her adolescent dreams. I woke her and she rose like a sleepwalker and left the room without even saying hello. She returned ten minutes later with a steaming cup of coffee.

"When I go to bed with someone, I like to wake up with someone," she grumbled.

"I had to go to the agency to give them the money."

"Ah. Are you happy?"

"I've never been to a First World country before."

"And us, what world do we live in?" she asked.

"The Third World."

"Damn. And who says so?"

"The people in the First World."

"And what do you have to do to belong to the First World?"

"Earn at least ten thousand dollars a year per capita, one car for every three inhabitants, social security, vacations in the South Pacific—all that good stuff."

"I don't want any of that."

"Yeah, I know, Blanca. You belong to the great savannas, to the jungle. You're a member of an endangered species. By the way, I'd like to have dinner with you tonight. We'll go to a nice restaurant. What do you say?"

"I'm working. I can't go two nights without making any money."

"How much do you make a night?"

"Depends. Up to three hundred pesos on Fridays."

"I'll give them to you. You don't need to go to Villa Fátima."

"Don't waste your money. When I like a man, I don't charge."

"I'll pick you up at 10."

"Maybe. I hope my headache goes away."

Her lips felt like a piece of bark baking in the afternoon sun of Beni.

Chapter 11

n the Senate, the mood was subdued. The occasion was the wake of one of the most corrupt and shameless senators in the country's history, and no one gave a hoot; the end justifies the means.

It was tough making my way up the steps to the interior of the building. The people in the crowd jostled for position: television cameramen, congressmen, senators, aides, bystanders, MIR diehards, and soldier-women who would have frightened an ETA henchman. Out of morbid curiosity, I wanted to hear the chit-chat circulating inside the halls of Congress. I had forgotten all about the danger that lurked around me—about the police, their gumshoes, and their homicide detectives.

I managed by pushing and shoving to reach the hall where the coffin stood covered with floral offerings. There were crosses of flowers and wreaths everywhere. A pair of rifle-toting soldiers stood watch at the head of the deceased. Later, I heard on the radio that Don Gustavo had been Defense Minister under General García Meza. I saw his entire family there: wife, daughters, brothers, aunts and uncles, nieces and nephews, and distant relatives, all hoping to reap some benefit from their presence.

"Hi, what are you doing here?" It was Isabel. She looked like a million dollars in black.

"I came to give you my condolences," I said, feigning sadness.

"How nice of you. Would you like to pray for his soul?" Isabel smiled for both of us. "I'd rather leave," she added, then took me by the arm. "I've already been seen; I've done my bit for protocol. I would be lying if I told you I was grieving over his death. The truth is I don't care."

We crossed the Plaza Murillo and walked silently down Ingavi.

"My uncle had an amazing life. He had all of the best government jobs. The only thing left was for him to be president. He would have pulled it off in a few years; he was always very lucky."

"Too bad the same can't be said of his heart."

"The heart story is bogus," she confessed. She looked at me out of the corner of her eye, waiting for a reaction.

"What!?"

"This is between you and me, Mario . . . Promise that you won't tell anyone."

"You can trust me."

"The truth is, they killed him in his lover's apartment. She was a gold dealer named Arminda. He was paying for the pad; it was right here on Colón Street."

"Who would have done such a thing?"

"Anyone. A lot of people hated him. Other people knew that she bought a lot of gold, every day."

"I don't understand this heart attack business," I said.

"It's very simple. My uncle was a senator and also the president of Banco del Norte. It's not one of the major banks, but they manage the accounts of the drug traffickers and the money launderers. With the consent of the general manager, they withdrew money from large savings accounts, bought gold, and sent it to the United States. They sold it there for good money. It wasn't stealing, but they did use the money without the permission of the account owners. They bought twenty to thirty kilos each week, and made five hundred dollars a kilo profit. A young friend of Arminda's would get his way paid to New York plus a thousand bucks each trip. They didn't smuggle the gold; it was all legal, they even declared it. In New York, the buyers would wait at the airport with a couple of armed bodyguards and then transport it to a bank."

"The price of gold is set by the world market," I pointed out. "How did they turn a profit?"

"Most of the gold around here, from Guanay and Tipuani, is twenty-four karat, and over there it's eighteen karat. Also, they don't always pay the international price. If the seller looks hard-up, they pay him less."

She smiled, unaware that her smiles were making me vibrate like the chords of a gypsy violin.

"That's a great idea—fifteen thousand dollars a week," I said.

"Without risks," Isabel noted. "It was a clean job, except the owners of the dollars had no idea what was going on."

"So that explains this funeral scene."

"Of course. First, politically, it would have been an unforgivable transgression for a candidate for the senate presidency and a member of the ruling party to be implicated in those kinds of dealings. Second, the drug lords and money-launderers wouldn't be too pleased if the authorities investigated the Banco del Norte. At the highest level, they decided that my uncle Gustavo died of natural causes."

"His wife and kids are there . . ."

"They were in on it. I don't know how much they got. She didn't care much for him."

"Maybe the mistress killed him in a fight."

"From what I heard, she says she found him dead. The police know he was beaten to death. It was probably a couple of hoodlums."

"How much did they take?" I asked in a perturbed voice.

"Around thirty thousand dollars cash and twenty thousand in gold. They didn't leave a thing. That's the true story that will never be known."

I took a nervous, ridiculous step forward, as if somebody had just pinched my bottom with a pair of pliers.

"What's the matter?" Isabel asked.

I was kicking myself for not having taken all the money. I was an imbecile. Two thousand or thirty thousand, it's all the same; guilt doesn't increase proportionately with the amount stolen. How could I have been so naïve to think of myself as only a partial thief?

"Nothing," I said. "The amount took me by surprise."

We walked up Yanacocha until Indaburo. The temperature was springlike, the sky a deep blue. The contours of the surrounding mountains looked as if they had been sketched by a giant caprice of nature: hostile, bitter, and sterile.

"I'm not glad that he died," she said pensively. "But it seems right to me. He did a lot of bad things, especially to my father. He humiliated him for his gentle character, tormented him because of his high culture and his class, and hated him for his aristocratic refinement. He envied my father's pedigree and the way he could send anyone to hell, including my mother and the money that came with her. I'll call my father tonight and tell him Gustavo died. He'll drink champagne and pray that my uncle's soul goes straight to hell."

I laughed. She looked at me tenderly. A single word of hers could have led me to tell her everything and confess my full love for her; my never-ending, futureless love. In the end, love goes bad and brings us all down with it. With Isabel, love must have been something short-lived, fleeting, and violent, like a tidal wave.

When we got to the used bookstores near Jaén, she bought a novel by Skármeta, the Chilean writer, which had been lost among volumes on medicine and back issues of *El Gráfico*. I asked myself if Isabel could make me forget about Antonia. *In a single day*, I answered.

"I've been looking everywhere for this book," she said. "It's about Neruda and Black Island. Do you like Neruda?"

"I prefer César Vallejo. He was a sad man. He used to say, 'I was born on a day when God was sick.'"

Isabel stopped and said in a shaky voice, "I'll bet you think my boyfriend is exactly the wrong kind of guy for me."

"I like him. He's a good a guy; a rich, stable guy who can give you lots of kids and lots of vacations."

"Please . . . before I get married, I need to get my ideas straight. I'm a little lost. Gustavo's death is like a change in the weather; it doesn't have anything to do with the way I feel. The truth is, I don't see myself taking care of a house and looking after little runts. I'm afraid of boredom and routine. Still, there's no escaping my destiny to become a housewife on the edge of a nervous breakdown. I think I'll go to Rome to take an art class or something. If I really need to, I'll come back. In Bolivia things are always getting worse, but that's nothing new. I don't mind living in a poor country as long as it's free; I mean politically free. I don't like living in the United States. I've lived in Boston and Los Angeles. I get tired of the Americans, except for the Jews. They're the ones who do the thinking for everybody else."

I felt like I was approaching the edge of a dark, bottomless well; still, I asked her, "If I were ten years younger and had some money, would you follow me to the end of the world?"

She smiled without saying yes or no.

"This is the last time I'll be seeing you," I said. I felt my face turning red, my legs trembling.

"I'll give you my address, if you want. You can write and tell me how things are going for you."

We continued on Pichincha. I felt serene and trauma-free. I had confessed my love the old-fashioned way, as if I couldn't care less, without a trace of romanticism. She was too much woman for me. You could feel the word "friend" in the air. Small consolation; a punch in the face would've felt better. Hatred can lead to rape, and friendship to coffee or the movies. That's what I was to her, a strange guy who had become her pal. She could tell me anything, her secrets, her confessions. Since I didn't have her social standing, conversation was a cinch for her. I didn't have the right to demand anything; love and sex weren't in the cards. I was just some forty-something, borderline-poor guy who served as human experience for her, as a complement to her college education.

On Yanacocha, hundreds of children were just getting out of school. They took over the sidewalks and part of the street, forcing the cars to roll by at five miles an hour. They were making happy, carefree chatter. I had been the same way in my day, shoulder-deep in youthful fury, with that explosion of life in my heart, that joy of being young and still believing in the future. Now, I found myself in the future and it was no great shakes. To be honest, I would have preferred to stay forever in the past.

"I'm going back to the Senate," she announced. "My mother is waiting for me."

"When is the burial?"

"Tomorrow morning at 11 o'clock. The procession leaves from the plaza. The president and part of his cabinet will be there."

"All the crooked politics around the murder are confusing me. Don't you think the police are playing both sides, publicly accepting the story about the heart attack as a compromise while they go after the murderer?"

"Who knows? Maybe."

"Arminda could be in on it with the guys who killed him," I said.

"If they go out looking for the murderer or murderers, it'll be on their own dime and it'll be criminal against criminal."

She stopped at the corner of Comercio Street and looked at me with those eyes I would never forget. I kissed her on the lips, quickly and somewhat timidly. The contact with her skin made my head spin like an undertow. She opened up her purse, looked for a card, and then handed it to me.

"Ciao . . . keep in touch."

"Ciao . . ."

I couldn't find Blanca in the hotel. I knocked on her door several times but no answer. I descended to the lobby—her key was in her box. Just to make sure, I went looking for her in the room where the Tropicana hostesses lived. The two of them were drinking homemade tea with rice bread. Patricia told me that Blanca had gone to meet a client from Santa Ana, a cattle man who called her every time he visited La Paz. The guy was crazy about Blanca; he had even proposed to her after divorcing his wife, a woman from Pando whom he detested.

"You're the favorite," Patricia said. "Blanca doesn't like really old guys. This one's around seventy."

"What time will I be able to see her?" I asked.

"Who knows. Sometimes he has her for as long as two days."

Fresia appeared, covered in a skimpy bathrobe.

218 ȣ AMERICAN VISA

"You owe me ten dollars," she said.

"Did Don Antonio get it done?"

"Not really. Afterwards, he told me that with the forty dollars we could go out for some pork rind. The old man's got some nerve. I didn't accept. He groped my legs for about ten minutes and then fell asleep."

I handed her the ten dollars. "If Blanca shows up, please remind her that we have a date."

"If she finishes with the cattle man, she might go up to Villa Fátima later."

I didn't feel like talking to anybody. I was nervous and close to losing my cool. I didn't know what to think about the way the coppers were acting. If Arminda had taken all the money, she must have told them that the killer ran off with everything. The police would get on that guy's trail—that is, on my trail—secretly detain him, and then finish him off. They were probably looking for a villain with a long record of stealing gold, jewels, and dollars, a professional assailant or a hood who, upon being caught red-handed, had turned into a murderer. The underworld was familiar territory to them; they bankrolled snitches and informants who had their ears to the ground. If that were the case, then I was safe. All the authorities had on me in their files was a drunken mêlée in Oruro and the time I ran into a motorcycle while driving my Yugoslavian boss's car; not a single major offense. Yujra was the wild card. If the ex-boxer put two and two together, I would be up a creek.

It wasn't hard to get the picture: My hide wasn't worth much. On the other hand, maybe Arminda had cut a deal and split the booty with the police. That would be better because then they wouldn't go looking for anybody. Regardless, it was best to keep my guard up. I needed twenty-four hours—if I was lucky enough to get the visa to fly north.

I left the hotel and entered a café on Evaristo Valle. I called Ballón to ask about the visa. He answered the phone himself. He calmed me down by telling me that my passport was already at the consulate. The visa was almost a sure thing. I told him to book me a seat on Lloyd Bolivian Airline's red-eye flight the following night.

"That'll be tough," he replied. "If you don't put down a few pesos, you won't even get a seat in a week."

"How much?"

"At least a hundred dollars. They're always upping the price."

"It's impossible to live in a country like this," I protested.

Ballón laughed. He said he would advance me the hundred dollars and charge me when he returned the passport. I told him that was fine.

I had dinner at a Chinese restaurant on Juan de la Riva. It was six pesos for the special and a beer. I asked them to turn on the TV. At 8 o'clock the Channel 2 news came on. It was more than fifteen minutes before they showed a clip of the wake at the Senate. The anchor interviewed Don Gustavo's wife, who explained that her husband worked too hard and that the "stress" had killed him.

"He dedicated his life to the community," she said. "He is watching us from heaven as we mourn him. That is his greatest reward."

He was probably watching me too, his killer, and thinking how much of an idiot I had been not to make off with the entire loot. So, the heart attack story was the official one. I ate calmly. The beer loosened me up somehow; it whetted my appetite for more beer. I paid, and after roaming about for fifteen minutes or so, ruminating and dillydallying, I came across El Putuncu, a watering hole on Potosí Street. Fifty or so drunkards were making a ruckus, imbibing beer and playing dice games. They seated me at a table next to a couple of quiet boozers, the kind that blurt out something after every drink. They were so tanked that when they turned their heads, they remained still like a couple of antique dolls and then struggled to bring them back to their original positions. Three-quarters of the way through a pint of beer, it occurred to me to ask them if the place was always so rowdy.

"It gets worse later," one of the guys commented. He kept his mouth shut for a whole half-hour, then said out loud, "How much money must these owners make?"

His companion fell asleep sitting up. Periodically, he shot suffocating blasts of his buffalo breath our way.

The clock struck 8 and I had to exchange some dollars to pay the tab. The waiter converted the money and took a cut for himself. I decided to call the hotel and ask if Blanca had arrived. The manager responded in jest: "Blanca who?"

I stumbled through Pérez Velasco. On the cement terrace, a policeman was busy emptying the pockets of the shoeshiners. Boys between the ages of ten and twelve years, high on paint thinner, were trying to hide the residue of various toxins in little boxes, hats, and shoes. Three gay vagrants, dressed in rags, huddled together on a bench and watched the rascals play cat-and-mouse with the cop. Onlookers made fun of the solitary policeman, who ultimately gave up and left. Around twenty shoeshiners emerged from the La Paz night and began to inhale paint thinner in a sort of group dance.

On the steps that link Comercio and Ingavi Streets, a scruffy-looking, completely intoxicated rabble-rouser delivered an impassioned speech to the masses. Nobody understood a damned thing. The man would laugh, shout, and, from time to time, point to his own behind. Through his shredded pants you could make out a pair of skinny thighs, black with filth. The unavoidable Christians wasted no time pulling together a chorus of paid spectators and a country bumpkin guitarist who started singing a ballad in praise of Christ. The La Paz night felt like a labyrinth around there. Thousands of the city's inhabitants ambled from place to place for no particular reason.

I escaped the crowd and took a taxi to Villa Fátima. The red lightbulbs showed me the way to the brothels. In the house where Blanca worked, the oglers were congregating. The madam, escorted by the Peruvian gorilla, was surveying the action with a crabby face. I asked her about Blanca.

"She should have been here already," the woman answered. "Today's the busiest day of the week."

The Peruvian stuck out his chin and added, "If she's not here by now, then she's not coming." I didn't trust that brute's judgment, so I waited a little while longer.

At 9 o'clock, El Faro was a market for sex slaves in constant motion; on Fridays, the whores of Villa Fátima worked from 8 at night until the break of dawn. Twenty pesos at a time, they filled their pockets with the wages of sin at the expense of dozens of lowlifes who had climbed the city in search of erotic detoxification. Unfortunately, the sessions lasted at most ten minutes. For the first time in the history of Bolivia, the Indians had access to white pussy.

A few years earlier, a white hooker wouldn't have slept with a peasant for all the gold in the world. But now, the fanciest clients were the Indians whose payments of ten to twenty pesos allowed them to earn their daily bread. The hookers had gotten used to these interracial exchanges, dispatching their clients with extraordinary speed.

Bored of waiting, I went back downtown. If Blanca had passed up the busiest night of the week, it was because she was walking arm in arm with that cattle man. I would have liked to see her, invite her out to an expensive restaurant, take her dancing, and seriously propose to her that if I was successful up north and she was willing, I would send her a ticket so that she could join me.

Whatever I had left of a conscience was bothering me. She was nowhere to be found. To kill time, I decided to go to the movies. They were showing a David Lynch film at the Cinemateca. I wasn't much in the mood when I got there, but within ten minutes I had forgotten my fears and tribulations. It was called *Blue Velvet*, and it revealed a micro-cosm of American society, with all of its innocence and perversity: the United States laid bare, stripped of the American dream. If I was escaping misery, it was only to fall into the complacency of the absurd. Lynch really knew the human soul—as much as Ingmar Bergman—so well that it could drive a person crazy.

Afterwards, I walked into a wretched bar, a refuge for local bums across the street from the movie theater. There were four tables, an owner with a face like he'd died and come back to life several times, and a waiter who resembled a French buccaneer. I chugged two shots of stiff *pisco* and walked out into the mist. The sky was drizzling lazily, as if it didn't really want to. I traversed the high reaches of the city, which day by day were getting deeper under my skin. I arrived at the hotel and threw myself on the bed. I waited for Blanca to finish up her date and come to bed to sweat out her troubles, though she didn't seem to have any. I fell asleep and started having nightmares, then woke up around 3. A dog howling like a wolf marred the silence of Rosario. My head hurt and my heart was pounding as if it belonged to somebody else. It accelerated on its own and then quieted down without my con-sent. As I was already dressed, it didn't take much for me to go out to the patio, immerse myself in that whirlwind of twisting and turning hallways, and come upon Blanca's room. First I knocked a few times; anxious, I started to shake the door. Seeing as I wasn't getting any answer, I resorted to kicking it. I woke up the entire floor. A foreign tourist came out of his room and, pointing to his head, exclaimed, "You crazy fool! Is late!"

He was right. I returned to my room and read the paper five times before going back to sleep.

At 10 in the morning, Don Antonio was waiting for me with a cup of hot chocolate and a bread roll.

"Seems like you've been seeing ghosts all night," he said. "You don't look good."

"I couldn't get to sleep. I was thinking about my trip. Have you seen Blanca?"

"She's a nocturnal creature," he replied. "But unlike me, she leaves the hotel, while I just stay up because of my damned asthma."

I thanked him for the chocolate and resumed my search. Blanca apparently hadn't slept in the hotel. Putting aside my thoughts of her, I decided to set out for the Andean agency. Though the drizzle had ceased, it was still a cloudy, gray day with that high-altitude melancholy that can depress anybody.

In the taxi, I asked myself several times, *What on earth will I do if Ballón hasn't been able to get the visa?* I didn't have an answer. I consoled myself by recalling over and over that the fat guy had assured me I would get the American stamp. I got out of the car, trembling. Ballón was in his office, chatting with a guy who had been cut from the same cloth as the tireless salesman from the Hotel California. The secretary was painting her nails and she asked me to wait a moment. A few minutes later, Ballón received me with a smile that settled my nerves.

"There was no problem. We had to do some arm-twisting with our contact at the consulate, but I told him that it was for you, a serious person. I had a hard time getting the plane ticket from Lloyd; I spent a half an hour trying to convince a deaf bureaucrat to do the heroic deed. The hundred dollars softened him up. Here's your passport with a multiple-entry type B-2 visa, valid for three months starting today, and your ticket for the flight tonight. Be at the airport by 8 o'clock. You owe me a hundred dollars." Upon receiving the greenback, he added, "Please, not a word about any of this. I don't want anybody to find out about the operation. People can be real nosy, know what I mean? They could screw everything up."

"Mum as a painting," I said.

"Have a nice trip. You'll be fine at the airport in Miami; everything's in order. *Adiós*, Señor Alvarez."

I saw it and I didn't believe it. Out on the street, I stared at the visa that had cost me a brutal crime. It had been expensive, more expensive than the visa you need to enter Paradise.

In the Plaza Murillo, a hundred people had gathered to see off Don Gustavo, the ex-ambassador, ex-congressman, ex-mayor, ex-rector of San Andrés University, ex–coup leader, and former crook. A military band was taking a break, waiting for the corpse to pass by. Political and military figures were amicably rubbing elbows. I positioned myself in the plaza under the shade of a tree. I managed to catch the arrival of several solemn police lieutenants with moustaches. Suddenly, everyone turned around toward the presidential palace. The president of Bolivia, accompanied by his entourage, was heading toward the Congress building. Minutes later, the band director raised his baton. A funeral march took control of the scene. A dozen congressmen carried the coffin in which Don Gustavo, all quiet and cold, was taking one last spin around a plaza that had been like a second home to him. Behind the coffin followed the entire family. There was Isabel, and Doña María Augusta covered with countless black veils. The president took the first step and the rest of the crowd proceeded down Ingavi Street. From the Foreign Ministry, somebody threw a bouquet of roses, which was quickly picked up by an Indian boy who had mixed in with the passersby.

I concentrated on Isabel; I was seeing her for the last time. She was dressed, fittingly, in black, without affectation, plainly, with the kind of class that is only God-given. It's one of the few things you can't buy in this world.

Chapter 12

I **got ready to leave.** I made some final arrangements, dug up the money, and stowed it away in one of the pockets of the new jacket I had bought from the Israeli. I then left my luggage in the lobby, before the sneering gaze of the manager. I didn't owe the hotel a penny. I took the pleasure of tipping the Scotsman's helper and the bellboy. I held out hopes of finding Blanca at the last minute. I went out to the street and walked past El Lobo and two or three gambling houses nearby without any luck.

Upon returning to the lobby, I bumped into Don Antonio, who was getting ready to leave the hotel for the used bookstores with a work by Tolstoy under his arm.

"I need something to read during the trip," I said. "I'll take it for fifty dollars."

"Always the jokester, Alvarez," he replied.

I placed a fifty-dollar bill in the palm of his hand.

"I'll always remember you," he stammered, clearly moved. "Read it carefully; the old man's got important things to say."

"I can't find Blanca."

"You've grown fond of her, eh? She loves you in her own way. She'll be sad too. Those girls have their soft spot. I'll tell her you were looking for her."

We embraced, and then I asked the bellboy to hail a taxi. Don

Antonio went out to the balcony and raised his hand with that gnomish, mocking smile of his.

"Smoking or nonsmoking?" the ticket agent for Lloyd Bolivian Airline asked.

"No preference," I answered.

The girl scribbled something down on my boarding pass and said: "Please go to immigration. The flight is delayed."

When I asked a Lloyd employee the reason for the delay, he answered that it had something to do with passports. After buying the magazine *Cambio 16*, I duly stood in line before the immigration windows. A man advanced in years, with a well-groomed white beard, commented with an Iberian accent to his wife: "I don't know what the problem is with the passports. What a bunch of crap!"

It was my turn to show my passport to a young man who was dressed like a city slicker. The man reviewed it meticulously and handed the document to a policeman in the office.

"Please, señor, would you be kind enough to follow him?" the immigration guy indicated.

"What for?"

"They'll explain it to you. Go on."

The game's up, I thought. Just as I feared. They know everything about the murder. They'll frisk me and find the dollars. They'll know the serial numbers for sure.

The policeman led me to an adjacent office, opened the door, and showed me in. Standing casually against the edge of a desk, another policeman observed me as I entered. Beside him, also standing, a tall suntanned man with blond hair and Anglo-Saxon features studied me with a certain benevolence. Seated on the sofa, a fortyish woman wearing an eccentric, flowery dress was crying and using an old hand-kerchief to dry her tears. Beside her, a young man about twenty years old, pale and visibly shaken, shot me a frightened stare. The police offi-cer was handed my passport by his subordinate, who called him "cap-tain." After giving me a quick once-over, he passed it to the Anglo guy, who was wearing a Bogart-style trenchcoat. The gringo leafed through it and carried it over to a beat-up computer, into which he punched mysterious figures. A cathedral-like silence prevailed. The Anglo returned and informed the captain: "This is another one."

The police officer cleared his throat and raised his chin, unbut-toning his shirt collar. "Señor Mario Alvarez?" he barked with the tone of a jailer.

"That's me," I said. "Is something the matter?"

"Where did you get your American visa?"

"Through a travel agency, why?"

"What's the name of the agency?"

"Andean Tourism."

The policeman and the Anglo exchanged conspiratorial glances. The latter smiled an imperial smile. "Did you pay money for the visa?"

I didn't know how to respond. The woman was sobbing and the boy was sending me vibes of metaphysical pain.

"A little something to speed up the paperwork."

"Like how much?"

"I don't remember; enough to cut out the bureaucracy."

"American visas are free. Did you know that?"

"Yes, I did, but Señor Ballón said that they would take two weeks to give it to me."

"He said the same thing to me," the señora pleaded.

"And to me," the young boy chimed in.

"Not only to you three, but to many others. He tricked you," the police official said, driving the point home.

I felt my heart in my throat. It wasn't about the murder; Ballón had pulled a fast one on us. He had taken our money when we shouldn't have paid a cent. He had ripped us off. Now what? "If it was free, then Ballón is a crook," I said.

"That's not the only thing," the American commented with a slight accent. "He falsified the visas. These passports never went to the American consulate."

My throat went dry. My backside stiffened. "That can't be," I said. "Nobody falsifies American visas."

"Señor Ballón is part of a ring of international counterfeiters," he explained. "Our immigration officials in Miami caught a dozen Chinese people with fake visas. It was a professional job. They had us confused for several months; the Chinese people got their visas at the Andean Tourism Agency."

"It's not my fault," I said. "I thought the visa was real. I was certain he sent it to the consulate; he assured me he'd done it to speed up the paperwork."

The American official took several steps forward and held out his hand to me. "My name is Jack Martin. There's nothing to be afraid of. If you didn't know what Ballón was up to, you're innocent."

"That's right," I stressed.

"Señor Alvarez, why didn't you go to the consulate yourself? Don't you know you're supposed to apply in person?"

"I went one day, but the line was really long. So I decided to look for a faster way, you know, a travel agency."

"Are your papers in order?"

"Sure, the deed to my house, my bank statements, everything . . ."

The American smiled to himself. "Why Andean Tourism? It's out of the way; there are other travel agencies downtown, better-known ones . . ."

"A friend who used them to go to Brazil recommended them to me. They seemed to know what they were doing."

"Didn't Ballón tell you that you're supposed to apply in person and that sooner or later you would have to go to the consulate?"

"Yes."

"How much did you pay him? We'll find out anyway."

"Ask Ballón yourself," I said. "Ask him or his secretary."

"What time did he give you the visa?"

"Ten, ten-thirty."

"Didn't he seem nervous?"

"Ballón? Happy as can be."

The señora, brimming with anger and frustration, got up from the sofa and stood face-to-face with the American. "Ballón knows everything. What do we have to do with it?"

The American took a step back, as if his face were being sniffed by a rabid dog. "Ballón escaped by a hair," the police captain said. "He beat us by half an hour."

"Some cop must've given him the heads-up," the boy said. The captain directed a sinister look at him.

"Do you have any relatives in the U.S.?" the American asked me.

"My son lives in Florida. He bought me a ticket to go visit him."

"What does he do over there?"

"He's in school."

"With a scholarship from the U.S. government?"

"No, I send him money."

"How much?"

"Sometimes five hundred dollars, sometimes more."

"You can't live on that over there," he responded.

"I suppose he makes ends meet with some job or other. The kid's really frugal."

"Then you must make a lot of money."

I wanted to tell him to go to hell, but I had to play it cool. "I'm a businessman."

He smiled again, smugly, arrogantly. "The police have to look into whether or not you knew what Ballón was up to."

The woman protested: "How could you think that? We fell for it like flies."

The young man, on the verge of exploding, added, "We're not idiots. What would we have given him money for if they were just going to find out when we got to your country?"

He was right about that. Silence reigned for a few moments. The American took the captain aside and they conferred in low voices. The captain scratched his head and said, "Ballón will fall soon enough. He still hasn't left the country. Until we have that bird in our hands, it's my obligation to deliver your passports to our American friends so that they can annul your visas."

"And then?" the young man asked.

"I'll keep all of you in custody until Ballón is caught."

"That could be years," I protested.

The captain was angry. He wanted chocolate but we had given him strawberry. "I said a few days. Once you've proven your innocence, you can go back to the consulate and start the visa application over again."

"Nothing could be simpler," the American said.

All three of us, the accused, let out a spiteful burst of laughter.

"How will I live in La Paz?" the young man asked. "I'm from Sucre."

"Go on back to Sucre. We'll send for you," the captain said.

The boy cursed.

The policeman arched his back like a cat. "You better keep cool, unless you want to end up behind bars."

"We're not under military rule. You can't detain me without letting me call a lawyer first. The days of bullying are over," the boy said.

The official peered at the American, who returned the look. It was the plain and simple truth.

"You can go now," he said. "There are no charges against you. Go on to the Lloyd counter and pick up your luggage."

"I want my money back," I said. "I want that asshole Ballón to confess. If you guys are serious about it, Ballón will be caught in a few hours."

"How much did you pay him?" the American asked. The guy was a stubborn bastard.

I didn't answer. The woman was crying. The young man was uttering expletives slowly, the way people do in Tarija.

The captain said, "Ballón will be ours in a few days at most."

"And his secretary?" I asked. "She must know everything, or almost everything."

"She was his lover," the captain clarified. "They ran off together."

The three of us, the surprised and angry victims, sat in resignation in the waiting room where international passengers get ready to board. The foreign tourists, mostly Germans and Frenchmen, savored their last Bolivian coffees for one peso each. Then they stood in the line that would lead them to the steps for boarding the airplane on the tarmac.

A beautiful young woman in a blue uniform collected the boarding passes, smiling and wishing them a good trip. The Lloyd jet roared on the runway. The colorful, glittering lights emanating from its imposing armor were hypnotizing. There went our hopes and dreams, the happiness we coveted. The waiting room emptied within a few minutes and we stayed there as if mute and paralyzed. The jet, like a gigantic bird flapping its wings, prepared to take to the skies and disappear into the night. Only when we could no longer hear the churning sound of its engine, which had been swallowed by the heavens, did we stand up. We went out into the vast airport lobby. Hardly anyone remained from that bustling crowd. Only a few taxis, the ones that hadn't picked up any passengers yet, were waiting at the exit doors. The señora got a small man to help with her luggage at the Lloyd ticket counter.

The young man started to count his money, his hands trembling and his expression sinking into one of profound hatred. "I'm screwed," he said. "I only have twenty dollars left."

"Enough to get back to your parents' place in Sucre."

"What parents? What do you know?"

"You're all alone?" I asked.

"I have a brother who's a Franciscan priest in Sucre. I got the money to travel by saving for three years. I have a job lined up in Seattle."

"I was planning to work at the House of Pancakes in Miami."

"That Ballón is a real son of a bitch. If I see him, I'll kill him. Could you loan me ten pesos?"

I handed him a bluish bill. The kid was still incensed. "Come with me to pick up our luggage," he said.

At the Lloyd ticket counter, we found the señora foaming at the mouth and on the verge of crying.

"What's wrong?" the young man asked.

"Our luggage left on the plane to Miami."

I couldn't stop myself from laughing.

"What's so funny?" the woman asked. "It's a disgrace—no papers and no luggage."

A taxi driver came up to us and offered his services for half-price.

"Luckily, I still have some money," the woman said. "Who wants to split the taxi with me? Our luggage got the visa. We won't get anywhere waiting in the cold."

"Go ahead, buddy," I said to the young man. "I'm going for a walk. I need to get my head straight."

The taxi left and the woman waved goodbye. I went on foot toward the toll booth at the airport entrance. Crossing a paved highway, I arrived at an enormous ditch. I took a leak and tried to think. I felt as empty as the black sky above me. The wind was lashing my face. I took a gulp of 13,000-foot-high air, climbed out of the ditch, and started down a dark and deserted street. A dog resembling a sheep emerged from a shack and started to bark. I threw a rock at it. Frightened, the animal took cover in the shadows.

I was in Aymara territory. I roamed aimlessly over muddy, shadowy streets. Suddenly, I found myself at a paved thoroughfare with heavy traffic. Apparently it was the road to Oruro. I was surprised by the number of stores open at that late hour. Dozens of heavy trucks were coming and going.

I was looking for a tavern, any tavern where I could drink *aguardiente* and stop mulling over my hard luck. Not until I reached Tiwanaku Street, which is actually a cross between a road and a market, did I spot a joint on the ground floor of a four-story building with an exposed brick façade. It was an Aymara tradition not to cover the façade with stucco or paint—to save a few pesos and conceal your wealth.

The tavern, curiously named The Swan, was located in the back of a hole-in-the-wall video store. Four tables stood atop a layer of cement. A waiter wearing a dress shirt and practically freezing to death served me a double shot of *pisco* with a slice of lemon. A pair of peasants were arguing with each other in their native tongue. You could tell they were bricklayers by the dried mud on their hands and the bits of wet dirt covering their shoes. Never before had I seen the City of the Future so up-close; I always used to cross it without stopping on my way from Oruro to La Paz. El Alto is the bedroom city you have to pass through before descending to the nation's capital. It's a completely Aymara city, the largest in the world and the only one built exclusively by them; three hundred thousand souls at 13,000 feet above sea level, and more peasants arriving every day from the Andean plateau, which was becoming as empty as a Martian steppe. You didn't hear a lot of Spanish. Harsh, choppy Aymara was the primary language, with the occasional Spanish word to round off a sentence.

At that altitude, *pisco* rises to your head almost immediately, and it took just a few minutes for me to feel its beneficial, comforting effect. Even though I didn't want to think about anything, thoughts crisscrossed my mind like restless flies. It was that son of a bitch Ballón's fault that my dreams had been thwarted and that I was now surrounded by this surreal reality. What to do? Go back to the hotel like a defeated man, like a clown? No way. I already had one city crossed off my list: Oruro. Now, I had crossed off a second one: La Paz. With a thousand dollars, I could survive for a year lying low among the restless people of El Alto.

Maybe fate would have me live here undercover until my money ran out, before I either put a bullet in my brains or drowned myself in *pisco* to the point of turning my liver into a useless sponge. Cirrhosis plus a heart attack and I'd be done. I motioned to the waiter and asked where I could get a bite to eat.

"On Antofagasta Street at El Trigo Verde there's a snack bar."

I ventured out into the frigid Andean plateau. Antofagasta is a wide road lined with an incredible variety of markets, hardware stores, car repair garages, pharmacies, and delis. It was El Alto's version of the Avenida Buenos Aires, without the smells that festered in that city buried in the valley below. The wind up there sucked the life out of every last smell and there wasn't a single mosquito it didn't leave dizzy.

El Trigo Verde was more like a refrigerator than a restaurant. The cold was so intense that the meat looked as if it was shivering on the kitchen counter. A copper-skinned cook served me a hamburger with french fries . . .

What the hell are you going to do now? I asked Mario Alvarez.

I don't know, he answered.

How about you drink and drink and then throw yourself over the edge of the cliff where La Paz's shanties begin?

I don't like empty space—I'm afraid of heights.

Then pay a butcher five hundred dollars to slice open your belly as if you were a cow.

The problem is the pain, said Alvarez. *I can't stand pain.*

With a lot of pisco *you won't feel a thing; it's a good anesthetic.*

Where can I find a butcher?

Ask the waiter if he can recommend one to you.

"Waiter," I called.

A skinny, stooped-over Indian man approached me. "Yes, sir?"

"I'm looking for a place to stay."

"Nice or so-so?"

"Let's say, the best in the neighborhood."

"In the Plaza Azurduy de Padilla there's a place called Primavera. It's first class."

Avenida Antofagasta seemed endless, and it started to rain. *Pisco* hits you differently at 13,000 feet; the reduced oxygen seals the deal. The alcohol boiled in my brain. My heart's throbbing reverberated inside my skull like the shaking of a Brazilian samba dancer. The sky turned dark in the wink of an eye and the wind began to blow with unusual force. I was dressed Miami-style: a linen jacket, T-shirt, and loose pants. Things were getting ugly.

I arrived at Plaza Azurduy de Padilla frozen stiff. The Primavera, located on a corner of the plaza, was a one-story building that looked like a shack on the Argentine *pampas*. Above the bright blue door, someone had painted the words, *Family friendly, budget prices.*

The lobby was plain and half-empty. All they had for furniture were a table and a pair of chairs. Behind the table was a fat half-breed who resembled an Italian friar from medieval times. She looked at me somewhat surprised. Her regular clients didn't roll in with that kind of summer wear. She had an unfriendly face, a hooked nose, and small, penetrating eyes. Her braids brushed against her back like a pair of mooring ropes.

"A room with a bathroom," I requested.

"It's a shared bathroom," she said. "Where are you from?"

"Nowhere."

"You're pretty drunk. We don't take drunks. The police come to check. Besides, you don't have luggage."

I took out a hundred pesos and placed them on top of her grimy folder.

"I'll pay up front, let's say for a week."

"Double bed is ten per night. The room has electricity."

"Hallelujah!"

"Do you have ID?" she asked.

I showed it to her. She reviewed it meticulously, then opened the grimy folder and started to write in tiny characters. "Previous address?"

"Hotel California, La Paz."

The woman looked up; her eyes seemed to be carrying the load of her bountiful body, which must have weighed around two hundred and twenty pounds.

"No women here," she stated. "The police don't allow it." She stood up and grabbed an enormous key hanging from a nail in the wall. I followed her colossal derrière through one side of a small enclosed patio in which a few half-starved dogs were playing. From the ceiling in one of the hallways hung a cage with an old, sleepy-looking parrot inside. As for my room, it was worse than the one I had at the Hotel California. That says it all.

It was so cold that I might as well have been in Tibet. On top of the bed there was a straw mattress, two blankets, and a pillow covered with grease stains.

"The bathroom is at the end of the hallway," she said. "Showers only until noon."

When she left, I sat on the bed and puffed on a cigarette. As I exhaled, the smoke was illuminated by a solitary lightbulb. I finished the cigarette and left the hotel in search of another bar. I came across a cabaret with a blue and red awning. The place was deserted; not a single patron.

The bartender, a black guy, didn't even notice I was there. I had to walk up to the bar. "A double shot of *pisco*," I requested.

The guy was almost invisible in that vast parlor, which was lit up by a series of colorful bulbs hidden behind peeling pillars and ugly flowerpots.

"Where is everybody?" I asked.

"The girls come at 10:30. You'll have to wait."

"Are you from the Yungas?"

"From Coripata."

I settled into a corner table, depressed and eager to transform my personality with the *pisco*. There was a wood platform set up in the middle of the club. I smoked one cigarette after another. I was on my third drink when the dancers appeared. They arrived in a group, babbling like a herd of terrified hens. There were four of them; their faces revealed the wear of a thousand sleepless nights. One of them yelled, "Turn on the stove, Robledo, or else they're gonna be fucking corpses!" The other three laughed as Robledo, the black guy, worked on lighting a battered gas stove.

Upon seeing me, the ugliest one walked up and said, "Hey there, hot stuff." Laughter all around. "We'll be right back," she said. "Wait for us and get your money ready."

They disappeared through a side exit, joking and bumping into each other. Fifteen minutes passed before they came back. The makeup had worked miracles; they looked more presentable. Huddled beside the stove, they awaited the arrival of the first shadows. Their El Alto clientele, who looked like the living dead, began to trickle in. Some of them would cautiously open the door, shoot a timid glance around, and then return to the street. At 11, the performance began. About ten guys dressed as if they were in Siberia sat at the tables closest to the platform. The show consisted of a fully clothed dance for the first song, a striptease for the second, and buck-naked gyrating, without grace or spice, for the third. Those part-time strippers had a lot of extra pounds on them; rings of fat covered their washed-up bodies at waist-level.

By then I was very drunk. As with nearly every other time I've been wasted, I sat there motionless with a serious look on my face. The world seemed to be spinning like a merry-go-round. I got up to pee and, zigzagging through the crowd, found a toilet at the back of what looked like a patio. While I urinated, a young man was combing his hair in front of a mirror. He shot occasional glances my way, as if to make sure I was still there. When he left the bathroom, the guy, who appeared to be about twenty-five years old and had a riffraffish, up-to-no-good vibe, commented in a casual tone: "It's cold." I assented without saying a word.

At the table, I asked for a soda. I wanted the storm in my head to die down. But then the lowlife approached and sat down uninvited.

"Pal," he said, "you're all alone. Can I join you?"

"I'd rather be alone," I replied.

Paying no heed to my words, he motioned to the waiter. "One cold beer."

The waiter left. Three young friends of my companion appeared. Each was brazen enough to take a seat.

"Hey, man," one of them asked, "did you come in a car?"

What did they want from me? Free drinks, perhaps? They were cocky, insolent bastards, but you couldn't expect angels in the heights of El Alto.

They drank a toast to my health and then started to make fun of a stripper who was struggling mightily to dance to a rap song.

"Get your ass to a nursing home!" one of them shouted.

"This one doesn't have HIV, she's got leprosy," added another member of the crew, who looked like a Russian *mujik*.

The lowlifes erupted in laughter. A skinny guy with a sick-looking face and sunken cheeks flashed me his cadaver's teeth.

"Buddy," said a fat guy with a scar-covered face, "where's your car? There isn't one on the street."

"I came in a taxi," I said.

"Our buddy here's a liar," said the skinny guy. "The really hot babes are by the lookout."

"The lookout?" I repeated.

"It's right here, two blocks away. The babes are first-rate. All the losers go there to check out the Argentine and Chilean chicks dressed up like half-breeds."

"I'm no loser," I managed to utter. I was now looking at the world through a clouded lens.

"You wanna go?" asked the large guy, who had a face like a drunken baby.

"We're your boys," the skinny guy offered. "If you buy us some beers we'll show you the secrets of El Alto."

"How'd you like to see a fortune teller?" the big guy asked. "You could hear about your future, your health, your job . . ."

"How do we get there?" I asked with evident fatalism.

"In canoes, brother," the skinny guy said.

When I paid, eight eyes opened wide like carnivorous plants. Because of my drunkenness, I hadn't realized that I'd whipped out an impressive wad of dollars. They elbowed one another. The fat guy got me up and led me out to the street.

It had stopped raining and there was utter calm. The street air made me feel a little less drunk, but not enough for me to control all of my movements.

"Let's go where there's light," I said. "Down Antofagasta."

242 ⁊ AMERICAN VISA

"Whatever you want, brother," the skinny guy said. We walked down the road and arrived at the market in La Ceja, where half-breed women selling meat and vegetables were locking up their stalls. Lighting was scarce, as were people.

"This way," the *mujik* indicated.

We entered a sea of tin shacks, one beside the other, forming narrow alleyways. The mud and the puddles slowed our lurching pace. We found ourselves in a passageway filled with aromatic smoke and fortune tellers. Some of the Aymara shamans, who were standing beside their tiny rooms under the light of candles, invited us to come in. Two pesos to read our fortunes in coca leaves.

"I know someone who can read your future. It's no joke, he's the real thing," the skinny guy said.

Near the end of the line of tin shacks, a young shaman wearing a poncho, a *lluchu* hat, and sandals was smoking a cigarette.

"This is the one," the big guy said.

The shaman led me inside his abode. "Coca leaves or cards?" he asked.

I sat on a bench facing him. Between us stood a small table, on top of which he had arranged coca leaves in three separate piles. The guy was a damn sharp peasant, even though he couldn't have been more than twenty-two years old.

"Coca is better than cards. Sometimes cards deceive," he said.

The piles on top of the table represented health, money, and love, respectively.

"I want to know my future; I don't care about anything else," I said.

"Just your future," he gurgled. "We need to mix the coca leaves." He stirred them together into a single pile, threw a handful of leaves into the air, and started to recite a tongue twister in Aymara. Then he threw second and third handfuls. He stirred the coca leaves together again before sending yet another good handful flying into the air. The leaves fell all over the table and he said: "Future, here it is."

"What do you see?" I asked. "A trip, a long trip?"

"There is no trip," he answered, rubbing the green leaves. "I don't see trips, just a calm life without surprises. Your wife will take care of you. Sometimes you'll do well with money, other times badly. Everything must be purified with sacred smoke—house, body, and soul."

I handed him two pesos and returned to the hooligans.

"What's the word?" the skinny guy asked.

"I don't know what the hell he's talking about," I said. "I don't have a family."

They laughed and one of them put his arm around my back. "Now we're going to the lookout," he said. "If you wanna bang a half-breed Argentine girl, it'll cost you fifty dollars. You got it?"

I didn't answer. We found ourselves in a wide-open space, at the entrance to the twisting alleys; the forking paths, as Borges would say.

"Where is this place?" I asked.

"Over there," the skinny guy said, pointing at the night sky. "Two steps from here."

In the near distance I could make out the back of the statue of Christ that blesses the city of La Paz. I felt somebody twisting my arm and tried to break loose, but as drunk as I was, it was in vain. The first fist hit me right in the jaw. Somebody kicked my stomach with the force of a mule, knocking the wind out of me. Next, I received a series of blows to the face. The guy who was grabbing onto my arm started to squeeze it with both hands. I suffered a kick to the ribs that knocked me to the ground. It was impossible to react.

The only thing I could do was endure the blows.

"Take him to the cliff!" one of them shouted.

They carried me to the edge of an enormous garbage dump. A shadow emerged from the jumble of papers and rags and began to run. A scavenging dog started to bark. They took my money, my papers, my jacket, my shirt, my tie, and my shoes. When they were about to take my pants, I managed to unleash a piercing scream that startled them. One final kick in the back and a shove sent me rolling downhill. I tumbled through what seemed like thousands of papers before I was stopped by a boulder separating the dump from the abyss.

Before losing consciousness, I glimpsed the lights of the city of La Paz, which looked like a gigantic Christmas tree laid to rest over the valley.

Chapter 13

A luminous awakening. The sky was a Caribbean blue and the wind delicately refreshing, like the breeze of a flamenco fan. Unfortunately, the odors I was inhaling didn't jibe with the picturesque landscape. It was the smell of excrement; I found myself in a narrow embankment that served as a toilet for hundreds of Indians from the City of the Future. Since I'd been hit between the eyes, I had trouble opening my eyelids. I tried to stand up, but it was impossible. I'd been beaten to a pulp and my entire body hurt, as if I'd been stampeded by a hundred terrified cows. I was resting, curiously, on an enormous rock shaped like a millstone that was planted vertically in the ground. About ten feet away, an unemployed defecator was squatting Hindu-style and reading a newspaper. A few minutes later, upon noticing that I was giving signs of life, he said: "You got so stinking drunk you don't know where you are?"

"In a shitting hole," I mumbled.

He lifted up his trousers after wiping his rear with the sports page and approached me. "Mother of God!" he exclaimed. "The hoods from La Ceja got you good."

"Help me," I begged. "I can't move."

"Good thing that rock stopped you on the way down. If not, you would have ended up a hundred and fifty feet below on the roof of some house. They would've found you belly up like a dead frog."

"It was four guys at the cabaret. I had a thousand dollars on me."

"And my grandmother plays center forward," he said.

"I have to go to the police."

"Without shoes?"

I glanced at my feet. They had spared my brand new socks.

"You probably know them," I murmured.

"Probably. How many were there?"

"Four."

"Did you catch their mugs?"

"What?"

"Their faces. Do you remember them?"

"One of them had a face like a wire fence. Have you ever seen him?"

"Rings a bell. What'll you give me if I sniff him out?"

"I'll pay you. If you find the thousand, you get half."

"Relax, man," he said. "It looks like you got some dough in your trunk." He accompanied the statement with a glance at my back pocket. It was the truth. I had a couple of tens left.

"I'm better off going to the police," I said. "Those bastards!"

The man advanced parsimoniously. You could tell he was a hopeless old bum from a mile away. He had a purple face dotted by dark stains and yellowish eyes. He was toothless and his lips were swollen. He was wearing a reddish sweater, green pants, and shoes that were probably stolen, as they were too big for him.

"If you go to the coppers looking like that, some asshole might give you a hard time. You should look at yourself in a mirror."

"Help me stand up," I said.

"I can't do it alone. Hold on while I get some reinforcements."

I waited a few minutes. He came back accompanied by another

semi-moribund vagrant. They struggled to lift me up and then dragged me over to the foot of the statue of Christ that casts a blessing over La Paz.

"Give this poor guy five pesos or something," he said. "He's been deaf ever since he found his lady in bed with his best friend."

"I want a hot coffee," I declared.

"It's a miracle they didn't chop you into pieces. Those thugs have no mercy."

I watched his eyes, which were like two black holes with death written all over them. "What's your name?" I asked weakly.

"People call me Suitcase. I used to rob luggage at the train station, until I retired because of my drinking." He doubled over in laughter and started to cough. When he finished, he proposed: "For twenty bucks, I'll take you to the guy with the scars."

We traversed those strange, narrow passageways between the tin shacks. I remembered that the thugs had taken me along the same route; I also recalled the shaman who had read my future in the coca leaves. As we crossed that world all its own, that Aymara Ukbar, I realized it would be difficult to picture his face in my mind. Even if I recognized him, he wouldn't spill the beans on the ruffians, because if he did, they would send him back to his village with the mark of Zorro on his forehead. Going to the police, as I had thought of doing before, wouldn't be such a good idea—if I broke down and lost my cool, I could see myself telling them about Don Gustavo. That would put me in jail forever. Better to suffer in silence, as the old bolero goes.

"I couldn't have survived a beating like that," Suitcase said. "You're strong."

He led me to a foul-smelling bar in the midst of that indigenous morass. He sat me down in a corner and went to speak with the owner, an Indian guy who appeared worn down by the altitude and the cold.

We ordered a couple of *piscos* and two coffees.

"If you don't want me to help you out, at least give me ten dollars," Suitcase said.

"I'm still strong enough to kick your ass," I said. "Get lost or I'll track you down later and cut your balls off."

Suitcase wasn't a fighting man. He didn't have it in him anymore. Thanks to alcohol, his condition was terminal. He left cursing and damming the thugs for not having finished me off. I fell asleep for a few minutes, only to be awakened by the pain, which came over me like a rising tide. I could feel all the places, from my ass to my neck, where they had hit me.

My testicles were throbbing with pain; they felt heavy as two steel balls. I urgently needed some painkillers and a couple of days in bed. I didn't consider looking for a doctor because I couldn't afford it. Even a local yokel from El Alto would cost at least twenty bucks, not including medication.

I summoned a kid who was panhandling motorists stopped in traffic. I asked him to hail a taxi for me and promised him a one-peso tip. The taxi came; the driver and the kid had to lift me into the car. At first the driver mistook me for a cripple. Then, halfway to the hotel, he bought me thirty painkillers and a couple of family-sized bottles of orange soda. When we reached the Primavera, the owner thought that I had been run over by a truck. She and her husband, a taciturn guy, helped me to my bed. Upon hearing what had happened, the half-breed lady started to complain: "I thought you were a problem when I first laid eyes on you. You should go to the hospital. I don't want you to die in my hotel."

"Don't worry; I don't plan on dying yet."

"You shouldn't be out on the street at night; there are lots of Peruvians around. They're cruel."

"The guys who robbed me were one-hundred-percent Bolivians. I would've preferred Peruvians."

The half-breed moved her head from side to side several times, like a horse shaking off flies. The husband said: "Get some rest and we'll see how you do. You're not going to die here. If you're still doing badly, we'll take you to the hospital."

They left, closing the door behind them. I swallowed three painkillers with a gulp of soda and tried to sleep. It was useless. The pain was acute, lacerating, and constant. My whole body felt like one large wound, like a poultice of burning lava. A few hours later, I became immobilized by the pain, which scared me. I imagined that my spinal cord was kaput and that I would waste away like a forgotten soldier on the battlefield.

I dozed off for half an hour. A heavy nosebleed woke me up. I wet my neck with water and managed to position my head off the edge of the bed, tilting it backwards, which stopped the nosebleed. Three additional painkillers kept my suffering under control until almost 9 in the evening. Around then, a raucous mêlée broke out at the hotel entrance. I heard the drunken voices of the half-breed landlady and her husband insulting each other. The tumult lasted a solid half-hour. It apparently ended with the woman locking him out in the street. Since the guy was still ranting and raving, the woman tossed a bucketful of urine on him from the balcony, which succeeded in quieting him down.

With the return of silence, that sad and anguished silence of the Andean plateau, the pain that had been momentarily held in check attacked me with intensity. I had never imagined that a beating could leave you so devastated, incapable of any movement. And that wasn't all; I became feverish. First came the chills and then my esophagus felt like a burning chimney. One hundred and four degrees? One hundred and five? I'll never know how high my fever was that night. I simply thought that my time was up, that the moment I'd been hoping for and fearing, that I'd seen as inevitable, had finally arrived. I decided to play my last card.

I swallowed the rest of the painkillers, more than twenty of them. I had enough time to pay my respects to the saints and the sinners, to Blanca and to Isabel, the unattainable one. It was a sinister and laughable fate to die alone in a rented room in El Alto, penniless, frustrated, and defeated. It couldn't be worse. When the half-breed lady found me cold, she would throw me to the hogs for sure. All for an American visa that in the end turned out to be fake.

"If I hadn't seen it with my own eyes, I wouldn't believe it, Alvarez," as Don Antonio would say.

When I opened my eyelids, a Kafkaesque scene slowly became frighteningly real. I could see that I was in a room painted entirely white. Through the window, the sun shone with a blinding intensity. A strong smell of disinfectant pervaded the place. Opposite me, a fully dressed man had been laid to rest on top of a cot. Beside his bloody head, I made out a motorcycle helmet. One of the guy's arms was dangling off the side of the cot. In the far corner stood a sink and a small table. Under the table, a cat, which appeared to be suffering from terrible allergies, was scratching its back with zeal.

I thought I was delirious so I pinched my cheek. It worked. I was awake, in some sort of clinic. I felt my body up and down. I was almost naked, except for the black underpants covering my family jewels. Luckily, I hadn't been operated on; there weren't any signs of scars or incisions. The pain from the beating, the memory of which abruptly returned, had ceased. The only thing I felt was a kind of pleasant drowsiness. I was obviously under the influence of a sedative.

Suddenly, I heard footsteps. Clacking heels approached through what I gathered was a hallway. They stopped in front of the door. A few seconds later, a short nurse entered and came straight toward me. Her face was small, dark, and almost completely covered by enormous sunglasses. She smiled happily and declared, "It's about time you woke up."

"Where am I?" I asked.

"In a clinic in El Alto. They brought you here the day before yesterday, in the afternoon. We thought you had poisoned yourself. We pumped your stomach. What made you sleep like that?"

"More than twenty painkillers. I was in a lot of pain."

"Painkillers? Thank goodness. Up here there are people who take rat poison. Of course, they don't just fall asleep—they die."

"And that guy on the stretcher?" I asked.

"He's dead. He was driving a motorcycle drunk when he crashed into the back of a truck. He forgot to put on his helmet; it was tied to the back of his seat."

"He's really young."

"Old people don't ride motorcycles."

"Who brought me here?"

The nurse started to delicately wash the dead man's face with a sponge after freeing him from his leather jacket. "A young woman and a half-breed who said she was the owner of the place where you had been staying."

"I feel great. What did they give me?"

"A shot of Demerol. You got the living daylights beaten out of you. I bet there were lots of them."

"Four; they stole everything."

"You were lucky. Usually, if they rob you, they kill you. How much did they take?"

"About a thousand dollars."

She stopped cleaning up the motorcyclist and looked at me incredulously. "And what were you doing with a thousand dollars in that part of El Alto?"

"I missed my plane to the United States. I got drunk because I was upset."

"You could have waited for the next flight."

"It's a long, sad story; tragic and funny at the same time. I'd be better off dead."

The nurse looked at me with a mother's tender gaze. "The young lady who brought you here doesn't think so. She cried her eyes out thinking that you were going to die. She was very happy when she heard you still have a lot of time left on earth."

"What young lady? I don't know anyone in El Alto."

"She seems to know you well. It's good to have someone like that at your side who loves you. Besides, she's very pretty. She'll be back in a few minutes. She went to the pharmacy to buy you some medicine."

"Will I be able to leave?"

"Of course."

"I don't even have money to pay for the medicine."

"It doesn't cost much. You've got two broken ribs. I think she looked in your pockets, and when she didn't find anything she said she would cover it." The nurse took the limp arm of the motorcyclist and placed it on top of his chest, forming a cross with the other. She then crossed herself and said: "Nobody has come for him since yesterday.

But a thousand dollars! Are you telling me the truth or are you pulling my leg?"

"You have my word. Those bastards won the lottery."

She smiled benevolently. "Are you going to report it?"

"Better to just forget about it. In any case, I won't get the money back."

"The important thing is that you're alive. Your life isn't worth losing over a thousand lousy dollars," she said.

At that moment Blanca arrived. Upon seeing me awake, her face lit up. I had never seen her so radiant. She greeted the nurse and approached my bed.

"Who told you?" I asked.

"The owner of the Primavera; she had written down that your previous address was the Hotel California. The manager's helper took the call and told us. Your friends say hi. Don Antonio wanted me to give you this book."

The nurse was a witness to this affectionate encounter between a sentimental whore and a survivor. Had she been a priest, she would have married us on the spot.

"The visa was fake," I said. "They beat the hell out of me. I've got nothing left."

"You have me. That's not much, of course." Blanca sat on the edge of the bed and kissed my lips as if they were part of some crystal palace. I choked up and shed a tear . . . That hadn't happened in a long time.

"You can take him with you, señorita," the nurse said. "Sign some papers for me on your way out." Turning to face me, she added, "The next time you come up to El Alto, stay away from the dump." She left the room, but not before shooting an indifferent glance at the motorcyclist.

"That guy's dead," I said.

"I know," Blanca responded.

I felt a kind of raw, unspoken love . . . the love of a poor sinner.

"You got yourself into quite a mess," Blanca said.

"All for nothing. I don't even have clothes."

"When we leave, we'll stop by a used clothing store. They have stuff from Switzerland that's good and cheap."

"I don't have plans to go back to the Hotel California," I said forcefully. "That would be too much."

"We'll travel to my hometown," she said. "I'm sick of Villa Fátima. I want to go home. You're coming with me."

"I don't need a visa?"

"Just goodwill." She laughed and stroked my hair. "The truth is that I was glad you didn't leave."

"Where were you on Friday?" I asked.

"Wandering around. I don't like goodbyes. I wasn't feeling well. I wanted to talk to you, but I knew it was hopeless. You were obsessed with that visa. Did you get over it?"

"By force," I said. "What day is today?"

"Tuesday."

"I was here for two days. How much did they charge you?"

"A hundred pesos."

"I'll pay you back once we get to . . . to . . ."

"You don't want to go down to La Paz?"

"If we're going to travel somewhere, I'd rather wait for you here at the hotel. I paid for a week."

Blanca stood quietly for a few moments, then said, "I can go to La Paz to get my things and my money from my savings account. It won't be a lot. I'm going to write a check and cash it at a bank in Riberalta.

I'll look into whether it's possible to get a flight back home today on a cargo plane. In the meantime, buy yourself some clothes. I'll come back this afternoon, whether it's to travel today or sleep and then go tomorrow."

Her idea made sense to me. I put on my pants and a shirt that she had bought me. I still didn't have shoes. We left the hospital, which was in La Ceja of El Alto. Blanca gave me fifty pesos for the clothes and then left on a bus for La Paz. Before parting ways, we kissed tenderly.

A couple of blocks ahead, in the middle of Tiwanacu Street, I stopped at a used clothing store. The place smelled like Swiss cheese, mothballs, and dirt. I bought myself a horrible, coffee-colored check-ered jacket and a beige shirt, which had belonged to some Swiss farm boy, and a pair of shoes that had been around the world but were still usable. On my way out, I looked at myself in the mirror. Charlie Chaplin couldn't have made me laugh that much. The strain hurt my broken ribs.

I walked sluggishly down Avenida Antofagasta and arrived at the Primavera. The half-breed was startled to see me. To calm her down, I told her that I would leave that afternoon or the next day at the latest.

"You stay out of trouble, sir," she warned.

The dogs recognized me and accompanied me back to my old room. I lay down and mentally recapped everything I had been through in the past week. I had gone from being a poor visa reject to a wealthy killer, only to turn into a dud from El Alto. I had survived the most humiliating beating of my life and a simple peasant girl from Beni had rescued me and saved me from a schizophrenic future. That's destiny for you: It makes us win, it makes us lose, it gives us hope, it screws us over, it makes us happy, and it makes us see life for what it is.

Someone knocked on the door and I got up. It was the half-breed lady offering me a glass.

"This *chicha* just arrived from Tarata. It's ice cold," she said, then left.

I drank the *chicha*, a cold and tasty balm. Then I took off my jacket and shoes and slept.

Around 2, Blanca returned with her luggage and two tickets to Riberalta on a cargo plane, an old DC3.

"When does it leave?" I asked.

"Tomorrow at 6:30 in the morning. It's a good time to fly. We'll have a stop-over in Trinidad. What do you think?"

"We'll get married in Riberalta. Isn't that what you want?"

"Aren't you still married to that woman who left you?"

"According to the law, I'm as free as a bird . . ."

She took off her clothes at the foot of the bed and got under the sheets. During the act of lovemaking, she called me several names, including "visa wannabe." She was happy, and I was glad about that . . .

As for myself, I didn't know what to feel. But the girl had grown on me. She was returning to me the soul of my adolescence. I no longer had dreams, only Blanca.

I peered out the window: The City of the Future, and in the distance Mount Illimani, the majestic protector of the valley and the bedroom city of El Alto. In some way, I was now part of their misery, their hopes, and their humble people.

"I'm free—will you marry me?" I asked.

She laughed the way people do in eastern Bolivia, with that happiness that doesn't disappear even in the hardest of times.

"I think I'd like that, Don Mario."

I imagined a child taking in the sun, bathing in a river, with the sincere and tender eyes of Blanca.

THE END

Afterword

Mario Alvarez may escape from La Paz a changed man, but has he exorcised his demons? Is this the end of his peripatetic existence? His restless imagination has spurred him to make hasty decisions before. *Un hombre cualquiera,* an everyman with a strong survival instinct, he now appears reconciled to his fate. But is he?

During the course of the novel, Alvarez proves to be a modern Raskolnikov. His moral dilemma pushes him to the edge. His plight is utterly Kafkaesque. Like Joseph K. in *The Castle,* he's lost in a labyrinth without exit, condemned to a miserable life. He might be a patient guy eager to uproot himself, but how many blows can he endure? Will the environment drive him mad? And is he fully aware of the extremes of his personality?

Alvarez's odyssey speaks powerfully to the global debate surrounding citizenship and immigration in our post-9/11 world of ever-hardening visa and border enforcement policies. Like millions of others, he'll stop at nothing to make it to *El Norte.* Ultimately he decides to take the game beyond mere forgery to pull off the fraud.

In Latin American letters, *American Visa* is a by-product of the '90s, a period of intense reaction to magical realism and its forgotten generals, clairvoyant prostitutes, and epidemics of insomnia. Those fashionable elements were showcased in Gabriel García Márquez's *One*

Hundred Years of Solitude, published in 1967, and were inspired in part by William Faulkner's wrenching depiction, in his fictional Yoknapatawpha, of the deep American South after the Civil War. Juan de Recacoechea, along with an entire generation, became allergic to these stories, finding them too remote, too ethereal. Instead, he prefers the dirty urban landscape of La Paz, where the only thing magical is one's talent to make ends meet.

In his style—sharp, acerbic, pungent, expressionistic—he follows another gringo: the Hemingway of "The Killers." Like the author of *Death in the Afternoon,* Recacoechea went from journalism to fiction. I would describe his style as "picaresque noir." His closest regional model is probably *realismo sucio,* the hard-boiled technique of the Mexican writer Paco Ignacio Taibo II, who is responsible for the one-eyed detective Héctor Belascoarán Shayne. Yet American crime fiction is Recacoechea's prime stimulation. His prose makes frequent references to Dashiell Hammett, Raymond Chandler, Chester Himes, and to the movies based on their oeuvre.

I came to *American Visa* circuitously in 2004, when Adrian Althoff, a student of mine at Amherst College, conducted an independent study on Bolivia. We stumbled upon the novel and were immediately enthralled. Althoff translated the first twenty pages as his final project. A year later, a film adaptation, close in spirit to Recacoechea's fast-paced plot, reached the screens, directed by Juan Carlos Valdivia, with Demián Bichir playing Mario Alvarez. It was a coproduction between Bolivia and Mexico that received an Ariel, the Mexican equivalent of an Oscar, for best adapted screenplay, as well as a nomination to Kate del Castillo for best female actress in the role of Blanca.

Althoff was involved in the movie and subsequently completed his translation, at once faithful and free-flowing, lucidly recreating

Recacoechea's voice in English. The book's publication in the United States is welcome news, not least because Bolivian fiction in translation is a rarity. The nation's three official languages are Spanish, Quechua, and Aymara. Less than a dozen Bolivian novels composed in Spanish have been rendered into Shakespeare's tongue, including Renato Prado Oropeza's *The Breach* and some of Edmundo Paz Soldán's cyber-narratives.

Yet unlike in these other works, in Recacoechea's book *la mentalidad del subdesarrollo,* the so-called "Third World frame of mind," is put to a test. It provides an extraordinary window on the tensions at the heart of Bolivian society, while entertaining at the same time. The novel's quiet yet forceful critique of the United States gives it a sense of urgency. The scene at the consulate early in the novel, in which the bureaucracy treats the native population with condescension and disrespect, helps to illuminate the ambivalence many Hispanics throughout the hemisphere nurture toward Americans. Can't live with you! Can't live without you! But I surely can live in you, says Alvarez, if only I can get across. Why not? Bolivia offers little to him. Or does it? His romance with Blanca triggers unexpected emotions, complicating his endeavors even further.

In all his ambiguities, Alvarez is one of us, *uno de los nuestros,* an immigrant—even at home—relying on the magic of his imagination to overcome adversity.

Ilan Stavans
Amherst, Massachusetts
February 2007

Words alone cannot express the thanks I owe to my mother,
Maria Angela Leal, for her invaluable editorial contributions
and her tireless love and support.
—A.A. (translator)

Also from AKASHIC BOOKS

THE UNCOMFORTABLE DEAD
a novel by Paco I. Taibo II & Subcomandante Marcos
268 pages, trade paperback original, $15.95

"Great writers by definition are outriders, raiders of a sort, sweeping down from wilderness territories to disturb the peace, overrun the status quo and throw into question everything we know to be true . . . On its face, the novel is a murder mystery, and at the book's heart, always, is a deep love of Mexico and its people."
—*Los Angeles Times Book Review*

TANGO FOR A TORTURER by Daniel Chavarría
344 pages, trade paperback original, $15.95

Whores, history, and political violence mingle in Havana in the new novel from the Edgar Award–winning author of *Adios Muchachos*.

"I recommend that we all do as Fidel likely does: light up a cigar and turn Chavarría's pages, with pleasure."
—Thomas Adcock, author of *Grief Street*

ADIOS MUCHACHOS by Daniel Chavarría
*Winner of a 2001 Edgar Award
245 pages, trade paperback original, $13.95

"Daniel Chavarría has long been recognized as one of Latin America's finest writers. Now he again proves why . . ."
—William Heffernan, author of *The Corsican*

BEULAH HILL by William Heffernan
282 pages, trade paperback, $13.95

"The whispered revelations that come spilling out of *Beulah Hill* are like ghostly voices you sometimes hear in the attic—soft, sad, and disturbingly urgent."
—*New York Times*

LIKE SON by Felicia Luna Lemus
266 pages, trade paperback original, $14.95

"*Like Son* moves on the wings of a soulful, visceral kind of androgeny. Old men, young men, hot girls—all step forward and sing from their stuttering hearts. *Like Son* is one terrific read."
—Eileen Myles, author of *Cool for You*

SUICIDE CASANOVA by Arthur Nersesian
368 pages, trade paperback original, $15.95

"Sick, depraved, and heartbreaking—in other words, a great read, a great book. *Suicide Casanova* is erotic noir and Nersesian's hard-boiled prose comes at you like a jailhouse confession."
—Jonathan Ames, author of *The Extra Man*

These books are available at local bookstores, or online through www.akashicbooks.com. To order by mail, send a check or money order to:

AKASHIC BOOKS
PO Box 1456, New York, NY 10009
www.akashicbooks.com   Akashic7@aol.com

Prices include shipping. Outside the U.S., add $8 to each book ordered.